Like an angel floating to earth, Virtue did not acknowledge her stunned audience. With her caned mask covering the upper half of her face, she looked straight ahead, her chin elevated, a small smile playing about her lips.

Roman's one uncovered eye widened in wonder. Was it a living woman who moved toward him or some sort of celestial fantasy?

Damn the eye patch! He tilted his head to the side to better focus on the approaching goddess. His eye narrowed. He had seen those full lips before, he had held that pointed little chin in the palm of his hand. . . .

Good Lord, could such loveliness have been embodied in the prim Miss Goodbody all this time without his being aware of it?

When the vision was in the middle of the staircase, he took a step forward and called up, "Miss Goodbody, is that you?"

Virtue continued her descent, but did deign to turn her gaze downward in Roman's direction. Her darkened brows rose above the satin mask. "Miss Goodbody?" she questioned, an amused lilt to her voice. "I know of none by that name. I am Lady Selena, a citizen of ancient Rome."

"But you were supposed to be a puritan!" Roman blurted out.

Her soft laugh, more beguiling than mocking, drifted down to him. She continued her descent. A few steps from the bottom of the staircase, she paused and slowly lowered her mask. With her huge gray eyes smoldering like a snuffed flame, she leaned forward and whispered for Roman's ears alone, "You forget, Sir Pirate, a lady can change her mind."

Roman felt as if he had been hit by a bolt of lightning. Miss Goodbody had somehow assumed the undeniable essence of womanhood, becoming the eternal Eve. In her gray-eyed gaze, not bold but provocative, he read an age-old challenge: Pursue me if you dare!

He definitely dared.

Books by Kathleen Beck

THE SPIRITED MISS CAROLINE
VIRTUE'S PRIZE

Published by Zebra Books

VIRTUE'S PRIZE

Kathleen Beck

Zebra Books
Kensington Publishing Corp.
http://www.zebrabooks.com

ZEBRA BOOKS are published by

Kensington Publishing Corp.
850 Third Avenue
New York, NY 10022

First Printing: October, 1999
10 9 8 7 6 5 4 3 2 1

Printed in the United States of America

*This book is dedicated to
Shary Irwin—
dearest daughter and dearest friend*

One

Virtue, in the great world, should be amenable.
—Molière

Virtue Goodbody, daughter of the late Vicar Goodbody, was not at all what she seemed, for beneath the prim exterior of her modestly cut gowns there beat the wildly throbbing heart of a true romantic.

She yearned to marry, but not merely to *any* man. She wanted a gentleman, as handsome and noble minded as the heroes in the novels she secretly read.

If Virtue had had the counsel of a loving mother as she grew to womanhood, she might have known better than to wish for a match so far above her station, but her only friend and confidante was Mrs. Ramsay, the Squire's wife, a woman of great kindness and little sense.

Virtue had been introduced to the world of novels by Mrs. Ramsay, who, after dutifully giving birth to four robust sons in as many years, had declared herself an invalid and retired to her rooms.

One of Virtue's duties as the vicar's daughter had been to read aloud to her persistently indisposed friend several afternoons a week. Early on, one romantic had recognized another. By some tacit understanding, *Fordyce's Sermons* had been replaced with the latest romances, ordered by Mrs. Ramsay directly from Hooker's in London.

The two women were sitting in her private upstairs sitting room one particularly fine afternoon in May. Virtue had just finished reading. After a long, sigh-filled silence, Mrs. Ramsay lifted a languid hand to brush away a tear. "What a lovely story that was, Virtue dear, and you read it so beautifully."

Virtue smiled dreamily. She was a young woman of seventeen, with hair the color of dandelion fluff and large expressive gray eyes. She should have been a beauty, but she was not. Her hair was pulled back too severely from her forehead, giving her a peeled-egg look, and she was thin to the point of emaciation. The late vicar had espoused a diet of weak broth and tea and toast for young women as being conducive to pure thoughts. As a result, Virtue had grown up famished, though faultless.

Still lost in a world of fantasy, she smoothed with work-reddened fingers the slender volume that lay open in her lap. "Was it not fortunate that Prince Orlando arrived in time to save Lady Estelle from marriage to the evil moneylender? If he had not, I am sure she would have killed herself as she threatened, rather than face a future married to a man she could not respect."

Mrs. Ramsay nodded in rapt agreement. She herself had married beneath her, and she often wished that someone had rescued *her* before she had wed the Squire.

The thought of marriage and of the future in general, however, raised a question in Mrs. Ramsay's mind. A delicate question to be sure, but one she felt obligated to ask. She shifted the velvet roll cushion to a more comfortable position behind her back and reached for another sweetmeat. "Your time at the vicarage grows short, Virtue, dear. Have you had word from your mother?"

The question brought a flush of shame to Virtue's pale cheeks. Her mother, Suzanna Combs Goodbody, had abandoned her when she was but an infant. For all her life, Virtue had believed—nay, had been *strongly encouraged* to believe—that her mother had died in childbirth.

Never, not in a million years, would Virtue forget the fateful night just weeks before when she had learned the awful truth. Her father, in the last throes of a putrid fever, had raised up from his rumpled sheets and rasped, "A pox upon your mother! Damn her immortal soul! She is not dead. She abandoned us to live a wanton's life in the City. If I die of this illness, you must go to her and seek a home under her roof. It is a fate I would not wish on a dog, but you have no choice. May God have mercy on you." With that weighty pronouncement, the vicar had indeed turned up his toes and died.

Virtue closed the book and placed it carefully on the Pembroke table by the side of her chair. "My mother has not answered my letter, but that does not signify she does not wish to have me come to her. Her lack of response could be for many reasons. The Season will soon commence. No doubt she is busy planning parties and entertainments—the Bow Street runner you hired to ascertain her whereabouts *did* comment on the elegance of her establishment, did he not?"

"Of course, dear, of course." Mrs. Ramsay popped the sweetmeat into her mouth and bit down hard. The Bow Street runner had had other comments to make as well. If his judgment could be trusted, Suzanna Combs Goodbody, now known as Suzanna Combs—she had dropped the Goodbody years ago—did not wish to be encumbered with "virtue" of any kind.

As if she had read Mrs. Ramsay's gloomy thoughts, Virtue slumped spiritlessly in her chair. She sighed. "I cannot continue to put a good face on my situation, especially to as dear a friend as you, Mrs. Ramsay. I have little money left. The new vicar is due shortly in the village and expects to find the vicarage vacant. I must start for my mother's house in London before he arrives, whether I have word from her or not."

Her voice quavered. "Oh, Mrs. Ramsay, what if my mother will not accept me. I have no other place to go."

Mrs. Ramsay blinked through a veil of unshed tears. After the runner's report, she had been secretly glad that Virtue had *not* heard from her mother. Accordingly, good soul that she was, she had generously made contingency plans for Virtue's future. Still, appearances must be maintained.

"Nonsense, pet," she said briskly. "Your letter most likely has been lost *en route*. I am sure your mother will be more than happy to have you. In any event, I have arranged for the hiring of a hack-chaise to take you directly to her door. As you are no doubt aware, Mrs. Snipe has—how shall I put it?—*business* to attend to in the City and has agreed to accompany you. If your mother does not want—is not at home, that is—you are to go at once to my old nurse's house. I will give you her direction. She is a good and decent woman. You can stay with her for as long as you need, and she has promised to help you find suitable employment. As for money, I shall see that you do not do without on your journey. Call it a loan, if you must, but do not fret. All will be well."

Virtue nodded and straightened in her chair. Her small pointed chin lifted. The quaver gone from her voice, she said, "Of course, how could I have doubted God's plans for me, his humble servant? I know all will be well. As dear Father often said to many a poor supplicant before turning him away, 'The Lord will provide.' "

She reached over and took Mrs. Ramsay's hand in

hers. "How can I ever repay your kindness? You have done so much and continue to do so much for me. . . ."

The arrival of the maid carrying a heavily laden tea tray stayed Virtue's words and reminded her that it was time for her to go. She rose reluctantly. "I must take my leave. Your dear little boys will soon be here for their afternoon visit."

Mrs. Ramsay shuddered delicately. She saw her sons, now aged five, four, three and two, for a scant hour each afternoon. Often, that hour was not scant enough.

"Ahhh, yes, the little dears will be coming shortly with Nurse Bludgeon. But would you not stay and help distract—I mean watch their playful antics?"

Declining what she thought was an unselfish offer on Mrs. Ramsay's part, Virtue gratefully accepted the remains of the seed cake, kissed her hostess upon the cheek and departed for the vicarage.

The small village of Oversite, bright with flowers and sunny breezes, was at its best in springtime. Virtue, however, took little notice of the purple violets dotting the roadside or the pink valerian peeking out between rocky ledges. She passed the trembling stalks of willow herb and yarrow, still a promise in the meadows, without so much as giving them a glance.

Despite her brave words to Mrs. Ramsay, she *was* apprehensive about her future. And, as was her wont, she escaped into a world of daydreams, a sleight of mind she often used to lighten her dreary life at the vicarage.

Once again she envisioned the handsome Prince Orlando, his fair hair shimmering in the sunlight, his elegant white hand reaching out to the beautiful Lady Estelle. His rescue of her had come at the very moment she was to be wed to the evil moneylender.

Virtue pictured Prince Orlando and his lady riding

away together on a white stallion to the prince's castle, a majestic edifice that gleamed golden in the distance.

A subtle smile curved Virtue's pale lips. In this rendition of her daydream, Lady Estelle's violet blue eyes had changed to gray, and her blue-black tresses had become the color of dandelion fluff.

Roman Knightley awoke from a restless sleep, opened his eyes, raised his head and winced. Gingerly, as if it might shatter, he lowered his aching brain-box back to the pillow and lay staring up at the ceiling. His temples drummed and his mouth tasted like a stableman's heel.

He was, for a moment, at a loss to account for his deplorable condition. It had been an evening of celebration, but exactly *what* he had been celebrating escaped him. He remembered drinking with his old friend and army comrade, Henry Wentworth. Sometime during the shank of the evening, Henry had challenged him to a drinking duel. He vaguely recalled a fourth bottle of port. After that, nothing.

He moaned softly, knowing that sooner, not later, he *had* to assume a vertical position. The effects of the last night's copious consumption of spirits were making themselves painfully apparent.

Gritting his teeth, he counted to three, swung his long legs out of bed and, wearing the sheet like a tippet, heaved himself upright. He staggered to the nightstand and fumbled for the chamber pot. With a long, heartfelt sigh, he relieved himself. As he replaced the pot, he caught sight of his reflection in the cheval glass on the other side of the chamber.

He paused, straightening his shoulders and pulling in his lean middle. He was vain about his looks and not without reason. The furtive coupling of a Romany fortune-teller with the then Earl of Larchmont some thirty years before had produced a strikingly handsome man. From his Gypsy mother, Roman had acquired his darkly bronzed complexion and thick ebony hair, but the eyes beneath his smudged black brows were like his father's, a vivid, English blue. He was tall, well over six feet in height, his muscled body whipcord thin and marred only by a jagged scar on his right buttock.

He frowned at his reflection. It was six months since his discharge from the army. Six months spent wenching, gaming and drinking. His jawline looked faintly blurred around the edges. Was his dissipation beginning to show? He raised his chin slightly to tighten the offending feature, then swore softly at his own vanity.

As he did so, the reason for last night's celebration suddenly hit him like a clout to the codpiece. That was it! His heartbeat quickened. He made his way to the writing desk. On its littered surface lay a file of official documents. Hurriedly, he shuffled through them. Ahhh, there it was, the final certificate of issue, sworn to and testified to by the Ordinary, the Archbishop, himself.

He drew in a deep breath. He, Roman Knightley, the Gypsy's bastard, was at last destined to be the next Earl of Larchmont. At his Uncle Simon's death, which had been imminent for years, Bentwood Manor would be his!

He stared down at the papers, noting for the first time the marked contrast between the crisp white sheets and the scarred and callused hands that held them. For a moment, time stopped, then raced backward. An image of himself as a small lad, his days spent toiling in the stables at Bentwood Manor, wormed its way up through his memory. A mixture of feelings, part revulsion, part longing, flooded through him.

Grimacing slightly, he tossed the certificate back on the pile and shrugged the bedsheet to the floor. He kicked it into a heap. As much as he had longed for this day, there was a price to be paid for the privilege of being legitimized and named his uncle's heir. Soon he would have to pay the piper. He would have to marry, and his bride would be a chaste, God-fearing woman of his uncle's choosing.

"Damn the devious old hypocrite," Roman growled aloud.

As if cued, Perkins, his valet, threw open the door and stepped into the room. He bowed gravely, ignoring the fact that his master was nude and obviously cup-shot to the extreme. Perkins had once been valet to the infamous Duke of Cumberland. Nothing flustered him. He had more subtle ways of showing his censure.

With measured paces, he made his way to the window and, in one sadistic movement, pulled the drapes aside. The entire room was immediately flooded with a merciless light. Roman moaned and shut his eyes tightly.

"Feeling poorly this morning, are we, sir?" Perkins intoned politely.

Roman responded through clenched teeth. "Not half so poorly as *we* will be feeling if I get my hands on you. Close those damned drapes, bring some coffee, then leave me to die in peace."

"I am afraid that is not possible, sir. Upon your arrival home at four o'clock this morning, you asked to be awakened in time for a three o'clock appointment this afternoon—with a lady, I believe. Your bathwater will be here shortly."

Roman inched his eyes open. More sober moments of the long and thirsty evening began to filter though his sodden brain. He remembered the best part first. Lady

Dimwitty, a truly delectable morsel with sparkling blue eyes, acres of creamy bosom and a gouty, stay-at-home husband of advancing years, had promised to drive out with him. Those sparkling blue eyes of hers had promised him other things as well.

A wicked smile lifted the corners of Roman's well-shaped mouth. He had sworn he would marry whom his uncle dictated, but until then, he would find his enjoyment where he pleased.

Forty-five minutes later, bathed and barbered and showing no signs of the excesses of the night before, the next Earl of Larchmont stepped through the front door of his elegant townhouse. He paused on the stoop to admire the pleasant view of St. James's Park, then tossed a coin to a passing ragamuffin.

Leaping deftly into his waiting curricle, Roman seized the reins from his tiger and tooled off down the street. As he went, he showed off his chiseled profile, with chin slightly elevated, to all the admiring ladies.

Meanwhile, just blocks away in an elegant townhouse in Grosvenor Square, Suzanna Combs sat cross-legged on her bed and frowned at her reflection in a looking glass. Had the lines deepened around her sea green eyes since last she looked? Had her fair hair darkened? Was there a hint of crepe beneath her chin?

She sighed. After running away from the vicarage at the tender age of eighteen, she had lived by her assets: her arresting beauty and her considerable talents in the bedchamber. The latter were undimmed; the former, she was convinced, was fading fast.

Aging was a condition that was very much on Suzanna's mind of late. Her confidence in her youth and beauty had suffered a severe jolt several months before when her comfortable year-long arrangement with a wealthy gentleman had come to an explosive end. The blighter had left her for a chit of sixteen.

She turned slightly and surveyed her latest lover, her expression akin to that of one finding an insect in one's soup. Sir William Rushmore lay asleep and naked on the rumpled sheets. Dressed or undressed, he was not a particularly arresting man. At four and forty, of medium height with sparse, glue-colored hair and squinty brown eyes, he possessed not a single outstanding feature.

As if to confirm her assessment, Suzanna's gaze dropped to the area directly below his navel. She sighed again. In spite of Sir William's shortcomings, he *could* give her the one thing she truly desired: security.

She tossed aside the looking glass. She felt old and worn-out. Her life had been dedicated to the pleasures of the flesh. At six and thirty, the flesh was beginning to rebel. She longed now for the unique comforts that only a wealthy husband could ensure.

Her eyes flitted like restless moths around the lavishly furnished chamber. It was a pretty, high-ceilinged room with long windows opening out onto a small garden area.

Suzanna had chosen her favorite color green in all its tints and shades, with accents of pale pink, for the drapes and bed-hangings. A particularly fine Aubusson carpet covered the parqueted floor, and hothouse flowers filled the tall vases. Beneath the white marble chimneypiece, a cheery fire of fragrant wood crackled on the grate, adding a touch of warmth and spice to the ambience.

From outward appearances it looked as if Suzanna were financially well fixed, but money ran through her fingers like water through a sieve. The house and furniture were rented, and aside from her clothes and jewels, she had little else to call her own. She frowned. There was also the steadily mounting sum of her gambling debts.

She glanced again at Sir William. Not only was he rich as a nabob, but he was farsighted—literally farsighted, another asset considering her fading beauty—and none too bright. Married to him, she could have her cake and share select slices of it with whomever she desired.

Her eyes narrowed in speculation. That Sir William was infatuated with her she did not doubt, but could she lead him to the parson's trap?

As if in pain, her lover suddenly stirred in his sleep. Was he awakening? Suzanna leaned over him, carefully arranged her face into a mask of adoration, then tickled his sparse chest hair.

Her silken touch was enough to fully waken Sir William from the distressing dream he was having. In it, he had been changed into a chicken and someone had been viciously plucking him clean. He blinked his eyes, once, twice; then the blurred image of his beloved Suzanna floated above him.

She smiled and spoke, her soft breath drifting over him like mist over water. "Awake now, my darling?" She giggled naughtily. "Awake or asleep, I can scarcely take my eyes off you. Or my hands." Her clever fingers trailed suggestively down his chest.

Reluctantly, Sir William stayed her hand. "No more, my sweet. I must leave you now."

Suzanna pouted prettily. "So soon? Not for long, I hope. You know how apprehensive I become when you are not here to care for me."

Sir William's heart swelled within his concave chest. A feeling of manliness pulsed through him. He loved

Suzanna and wanted to care for her forever, but first . . . He frowned slightly. "I leave you only for the nonce, my sweet. I must go to Sussex. I have a . . . favor to perform for an old friend, the Earl of Larchmont. When that bit of business is dealt with, I assure you, I shall be at your beck and call."

Two

*Men's evil manners live in brass; their virtues
we write in water.*

—Shakespeare

A hack-chaise containing two women, a varied assortment of tattered trunks and a food basket the size of Wales left the village of Oversite and headed north for the Brighton Road.

It was early morning on a muggy spring day with a sullen overcast sky hinting at rain to come. Virtue, wearing a shabby, high-necked cambric gown inexpertly dyed a rusty black, continued to wave to the villagers through the open window of the chaise until the last rooftop of Oversite had faded from her sight. Wiping tears from her eyes, she pulled her head back through the opening. As she did so, her limp-brimmed bonnet, a too-large black straw shaped like a coal bucket (a castoff from Mrs. Ramsay), caught on the rolled-up leather curtain. It tipped forward engulfing Virtue's face down to her chin.

Without embarrassment, she adjusted the offending finery and smiled mistily at her companion. "I cannot believe, Mrs. Snipe, that so many of the villagers turned out to see me off." She hastily added, "Mind you, not that I think the gathering was in *my* honor. It was, I am sure, the villagers' way of paying a final tribute to the memory of their beloved vicar."

Mrs. Snipe, a mountain of a woman with an air of dampness about her that excess flesh seems invariably to impart, did not answer. She sniffed instead. She knew, if Virtue did not, that the Vicar Goodbody, with his stern and unforgiving brand of religion, had been thoroughly disliked by his flock, and only Virtue's many—though often misguided—kindnesses to the villagers had saved her from being tarred with the same brush. The unexpected gathering this morning had been a loving farewell to Virtue, not the vicar. *Damn his ranting soul to hell!*

Mrs. Snipe had good reason to be incensed. One Sunday not long ago, after the vicar had delivered a particularly virulent harangue, taxing his parishioners to abandon the pleasures of the flesh, her own beloved Mr. Snipe had cleaned out the till and run off with the wasp-waisted barmaid from the Cock and Bull. The runaways had been spotted recently in London. Mrs. Snipe was on her way there to pound her own brand of religion into the pair of them. She could hardly wait till she got her hands 'round the barmaid's scrawny neck.

Sniffing again, she reached into the food basket and drew out a cream cake. She took an enormous bite and chewed it vigorously.

Undaunted by Mrs. Snipe's sniffs, Virtue settled back against the shabby leather squabs. The hired chaise, called a "yellow bounder" because it was painted a bright yellow, was none too clean, and the excess of straw strewn upon its floor was mildewed and smelled of the stable. Yet, to Virtue, the disreputable chaise was like a magic carpet. She felt happy this morning, almost carefree.

There was a reason for Virtue's lightheartedness. During her remaining days at the vicarage, she had prayed long and hard, asking God why He had seen fit to place her in such a dire predicament. While a definitive answer had not been forthcoming, a reasonable question had. Could God, working in mysterious ways, be tasking her with the redemption of her wayward mother?

It *could* be so. By stint of her "good works" among the villagers, Virtue considered herself highly skilled in the art of redemption. Just recently she had reformed John Walker, a toper of note. Had not John sworn never to touch another drop of gin if only she would leave off praying over him?

Undoubtably, her mother had been . . . morally unrestrained in the past, but a moral lapse or two did not signify her beyond the pale, especially for a redeemer with expert qualifications.

For a delicious moment Virtue allowed her imagination to drift along these pleasant currents. *Presently she pictured herself standing, arms outstretched, in the middle of a verdant valley. She wore a gown of flowing white, her entire figure engulfed in a golden glow.*

Her mother stood before her, eyes downcast. Her gown was off-white and not so flowing, and she had little in the way of a glow, golden or otherwise.

The drama intensified. Suddenly, from overhead, a beam of pure light sliced down from an impossibly blue sky. The beam, like an arrow plucked from a heavenly quiver, painlessly pierced Virtue's meager bosom. A deep voice—surely God's—resounded throughout the valley.

"Miss Virtue Goodbody, I know you to be a skilled practitioner in the art of redemption. Thus, I am tasking you with the salvation of your mother's eternal soul."

Another heavenly arrow was unleashed; this time its target was Suzanna. Again the same deep voice suggested

*most forcefully, "Suzanna Combs Goodbody, I say to you,
atone for your sins. Repent, repent—"*

Virtue frowned, staying the daydream and suspending
God's colloquy in midsentence. Was she being prideful,
having God recommend her by name? Pride was a sin—
almost everything was. The furrows in her forehead
deepened. Still, would it not be a *worse* sin to allow one's
God-given gifts to lie fallow?

A loud snapping noise momentarily distracted her
from this interesting dilemma and returned her reluctantly to the real world. Mrs. Snipe had finished the
cream cake and, after breaking apart a roasted chicken,
was now noisily dispatching the entire front portion of
the hapless bird. Their eyes met over the fowl carnage.

"Didn't know you had any family left at all, dearie,
much less folks in London."

Virtue flushed painfully. Mrs. Ramsay had strongly
suggested, and Virtue had agreed, that news of her
mother's "resurrection" should be kept secret from the
villagers. While most were fair and decent folk, there
remained a marked tendency among some to stone by
association.

Mrs. Snipe observed her companion's crimson cheeks
with the gloomy satisfaction of a woman who perceives
another of her sex in worse straits than herself. Poor daft
lamb, she thought, looking hard at Virtue. Seventeen
years spent with a clench-hearted, psalm-spouting father
and now shot off to some distant kin where she'd more
than likely spend her days runnin' and fetchin'.

After liberating a wad of tender breast meat from a
crumbling back molar, Mrs. Snipe fastidiously licked her
fingers, one by one, cleansing them of chicken grease.

"Can't recall their names, heh, dearie?" She chuckled.

"Never mind then, I'm sure whoever takes you in will be real happy they did."

Considering her Christian duty done, Mrs. Snipe tossed the chicken carcass out the window and reached into the basket for another cream cake. She eyed it suspiciously. The first one had tasted a bit off. Still, there were five left to go. Waste not, want not. She bit into the cake. Her eyes closed in pure bliss. The cream, though slightly bittersweet, was as soothing on her tongue as cow's balm on a sore teat.

Averting her eyes from Mrs. Snipe's unseemly enjoyment of the cream cake, Virtue attempted to return to the comforts of her daydream. A more urgent matter, however, claimed her immediate attention. It began to rain, light at first, then increasing in intensity. Large drops spattered onto Virtue's rust-hued black lap. Quickly, she let down the leather curtains. Within minutes, the darkened chaise grew as close and airless as a crypt.

With nothing else at hand, Virtue commenced fanning herself with her Bible. As if in protest to this bit of blasphemy, a muted roar of thunder reverberated in the distance. In spite of the heat, Virtue shivered. The long, rolling rumble had had an ominous sound to it, as though heralding some fast-approaching disaster.

Perkins adjusted the expertly tailored coat, an example of Weston's finest, over Roman's broad shoulders, then stepped back to survey his *tour de force*.

No wool wadding or padded calves needed for *his* master. The gilt-buttoned, dark blue coat, the discreetly striped silk waistcoat and the cream doeskin breeches fit

Roman's lean and muscular body like a second skin. He was the answer to a valet's prayers.

Perkins's chest swelled with pride. While he knew full well that his impeccably turned-out master would probably come home after a night of carousing looking like a stray cat's arse, he preferred to dwell on the perfection of the moment.

As did Roman. Lady Dimwitty had agreed to meet him at the Goose and Gander, a small, discreet inn just south of the city, to share an evening of passion. Lady Dimwitty was willing and anxious to fall from grace, and Roman was looking forward to the trip.

"Your curricle awaits you at the front entrance, sir. The rain has stopped, but the sky still threatens. Perhaps a closed carriage would offer better protection from the weather."

"Thank you, Perkins, but the curricle will do. I predict clear skies for this evening."

Roman carefully positioned his high-crowned beaver upon his hair styled à la Titus and admired the effect. "That will be all for tonight, Perkins. Don't wait up. I can see myself to bed."

Perkins hesitated. "If I may say, sir, last evening you had trouble mounting the stairs."

Roman raised an eyebrow in his valet's direction and grinned. "I assure you, Perkins, I foresee no trouble in my mounting of anything this evening. Go to bed."

Whistling, Roman went down the broad staircase and out the front doorway. He paused on the entrance steps to inhale deeply of the freshened, rain-washed air. As he did so, a muted roar of thunder reverberated in the distance.

In spite of the sultry heat, Roman felt a sudden chill. The long, rolling rumble had had an ominous sound to it, as though heralding some fast-approaching disaster.

**

The miles from Oversite to London crawled by, rain-soaked, bone-jarring miles, marked only by the measured stops to change horses at the post-houses strung along the route. Virtue's dreamy euphoria had long vanished. The City now lay but a scant hour away, but it might as well have been on the moon.

Her head ached. The atmosphere in the closed chaise was as steamy as a swamp, and the dank miasma emitting from Mrs. Snipe's person grew worse with every passing minute.

Dear Lord, thought Virtue, breathing desperately through her mouth, would this trip never end? She folded back the brim of her heat-wilted bonnet and eyed her companion with less than Christian zeal. While Mrs. Snipe appeared to be dozing, her massive limbs twitched convulsively, and at times she moaned, as if in pain.

Was she ill? Her skin had a yellow, waxy look, as though she had been dipped in tallow. Virtue leaned over to take a closer look. As she did so, Mrs. Snipe's eyes popped open. She sat bolt upright, clutched her ample middle and groaned, "Ahhh, Lordy, I've got the colly-wobbles; I got 'em bad."

Virtue drew back in dismay. The growling sounds emanating from Mrs. Snipe's nether regions signaled some coming cataclysm of a most odious kind.

Quickly, Virtue rolled up the curtain and thrust her head out the window. "Driver, driver. Pull into the next inn you come upon. My companion has taken ill."

At the shouted command, the postboy's eyes bulged in fright. Christ on a crutch! If that mound of a woman cast up her accounts in the chaise, he'd have a proper mess to clean. Remembering a small inn off the main road, he cracked the whip over the heads of the tired horses. The chaise leaped forward.

Virtue drew her head back from the opening just seconds before the sudden jolt of speed removed said appendage from her shoulders. Reaching over to the side of the chaise, she rolled up the other curtain. A breath of fresh air, laced with a subtlety of soot, blew through the chaise. At least the rain had lessened. She pushed back against the squabs, as far back as she could go. Mrs. Snipe looked ready to erupt.

"Breathe deeply, Mrs. Snipe, and trust in the Lord," Virtue instructed in a firm tone. "As my dear father used to say—"

Mrs. Snipe sent a vicious snort Virtue's way. *"That* spindle-shanked bastard. If it weren't for his stiff-arse bleatin'—" She suddenly shrieked and fell sideways on the seat. "Oh, the pain. I'm dying. It's dying I am!"

Throwing caution to the winds, Virtue again thrust her head out the window. "Faster, driver, faster!"

Snapping his leather driving gloves smartly against his thigh, Roman watched as his beloved grays were led to the stables at the back of the Goose and Gander.

Then, being careful to avoid damage to the exquisite shine on his boots, he strode across the puddle-laced courtyard. He was early. Lady Dimwitty's carriage was not due for a quarter-hour. Time enough for him to freshen up and see that the accommodations were as he had requested.

As he approached the inn's front entrance, he heard the rumbling wheels of a carriage coming on full tilt. He grinned to himself. Lady Dimwitty was in a hurry. Their rendezvous would be one to remember.

Moments later, a scruffy hack-chaise thundered into the courtyard. Though disappointed—Roman knew Lady Dimwitty would not be caught *flagrante delicto* in a hack-chaise—he was intrigued by the bizarre scene unfolding. A woman, wearing a bonnet that looked like a collapsed umbrella, hung out the window screaming at the driver to make even greater speed.

As Roman watched, the postboy yanked the horses to a stop and jumped down from the crossbar, sloshing through a lake-size puddle to open the hack's door. A woman of behemoth size instantly appeared at the opening.

At the sight of her, the postboy leaped aside and ran back to the horses' heads as if fleeing for his life.

Groaning mightily, the woman lunged forward, her rolls of flesh oozing around the doorjamb. She stopped short, a look of anguish on her face. Bloody hell, Roman thought, she was stuck fast!

At that moment, the black bonnet espied Roman. "Help us, sir, please help."

While not a gentleman born and bred, Roman had a kind and generous heart, which is the *true* essence of a gentleman. Women with a gleam in their eye were for tumbling, women in distress were for saving. Bloody hell, he thought again. He sighed, bid a reluctant *adieu* to the shine on his boots and did as requested.

Between moans, the fat woman watched his splashing approach with wary, shoe-button eyes. It was the bonnet that spoke. "My companion is very ill, sir. Please help free her."

Nodding curtly, Roman sized up the situation. To extract the obstacle, pressure would need to be applied simultaneously both from the front and the back. "You there!" he shouted to the driver. "I will need your help."

Cowering behind the steaming horses, the postboy violently shook his head.

Smothering an oath, Roman turned to the bonnet and barked, "Take a position at the obstacle's . . . rear. When I say push, push."

With a frightened nod, the bonnet disappeared from the window.

Confronted with the stated objective, Virtue hesitated, then took a deep breath. Bracing her back firmly against the squabs, she planted her sturdy half boots on Mrs. Snipe's massive *derrière*. Breathlessly, she waited for the signal.

When Roman saw the bonnet was in position, he took a firm hold of Mrs. Snipe's fleshy shoulders and began a slow, steady pull forward. Deeming the time ripe, he shouted, "Push!"

Virtue did, with all the strength she could muster. Mrs. Snipe suddenly shot from the door like a rocket. She was aimed straight at Roman.

Horrified, he threw up his hands and braced himself for the strike. She was almost upon him when he felt the heels of his boots begin to slip in the mud. She hit him with the force of a battering ram, and they went down together in a wave of dirty water, Roman on the bottom.

The breath exploded from his body. Dear God, the woman had the weight of a rhino and smelled worse. He tried to roll her off him, but Mrs. Snipe had another method in mind for gaining mobility. Using Roman's doeskin trousers for traction she literally scrambled up him on her hands and knees.

Roman's eyes widened in horror. This monstrous woman would be the ruin of him. "Your knee, Madam!" he howled. "Watch where you put your bloody knee."

Mrs. Snipe's knee missed his most vital part by a frac-

tion of an inch. She got her feet beneath her and, with
a cry like a banshee, lumbered off toward the wooded
area surrounding the inn.

For a long moment, Roman lay where discarded. He
stared up at the gray sky, saying a silent prayer of thanks
for his narrow deliverance from a fate worse than death.
Then he remembered the black bonnet.

He raised up on one elbow. The bonnet's owner stood
on the top step of the chaise staring down at the moat
surrounding her. He could not see her face.

Wearily, he got to his feet and wiped his palms dry as
best he could on the front of his discreetly patterned
waistcoat. With both hands, he reached out to lift the
bonnet and its owner to dry ground. The sacklike gown
she wore gave no hint as to where her waistline lay. He
circled where he devoutly hoped it might be. His fingers
tightened, then met in the middle.

He drew in a surprised breath. Under the ghastly bonnet dwelt a girl, not a woman, a girl as thin as a gosling,
as light as a gosling's feather. He could feel the delicate
stepping-stones of her back.

Gently, as if she might shatter, he plucked her up and,
holding her at arm's length, carried her across the puddle
and set her down. The bonnet slowly lifted. Beneath its
sodden brim, a small pale face peeped out. Roman had
a fleeting impression of large, trusting, mist-colored eyes,
a straight little nose and full lips that should have been
sensuous, but were not.

As he wondered why they were not, the lips parted.
The girl spoke. "Thank you, Prince Orlando. How can
I ever repay you?"

Prince Orlando? Who the hell was Prince Orlando?

The sound of tinkling laughter, derisive and *familiar*
laughter, momentarily distracted Roman. He swung

around. Lady Dimwitty's coach had arrived without his
being aware of it. How much of the degrading scene had
she witnessed? Had she seen him pinned beneath the
rhino woman? Obviously she had. The blue eyes peeping
over the ornate fan were bright with malicious glee.

Snapping the fan closed, Lady Dimwitty rapped it
smartly against the window frame. At the signal, the
coachman shouted to the horses, and the carriage departed, its wheels spewing a froth of muddy waters in
their wake.

There were others in the courtyard as well, unnoticed
by Roman until now: servants, hostlers, even the inn's
French chef, all smirking but afraid to laugh aloud.

He was suddenly aware of how ridiculous he must
look. Soaked and muddy, and standing like a gawk before
a wisp of a girl wearing a sorry jest of a bonnet. A sudden anger engulfed him. In spite of his arrogant demeanor, Roman was sensitive about his background and
quick to take offense. Most of all, he hated to be made
the fool. He had to vent his feelings on someone or ex-
plode. If the bonnet had not asked for his help, this would
not have happened.

He spun around, intent on giving the scrawny chit the
set-down of a lifetime. But she was gone.

Three

Who can find a virtuous woman?
for her price is far above rubies.
                    —Book of Proverbs

Virtue fled toward the woods, throwing frightened glances over her shoulder as she ran. When she was certain she could not be seen from the courtyard, she halted, leaned back against an oak tree and took a labored breath. She was trembling, shaken to the core of her being. She had met the prince of her dreams!

True, he possessed neither fair hair that shimmered in the sunlight nor elegant white hands. *Her* prince had hair the color of midnight and dark deeds, his hands being sunburnt and scarred. Strong hands that had circled her waist and lifted her. Gentle hands, their touch exciting both warmth and shivers.

In her short lifetime, Virtue had known little of gentleness. The vicar had firmly believed that the regular beating of children was good for their souls. While Virtue's soul was impeccable, it had yet to blossom. Still, the first burgeoning of love had begun and, with it, love's first pain.

Though innocent and unsophisticated, she had sensed at once the connection between Roman and the laughing, blue-eyed woman. The look of longing and regret on his

face for love lost, or at least postponed, had been like
the twist of a knife through Virtue's heart. It was painfully obvious that *her* prince preferred another.

She stifled a sob. And why should he not? Because of
her, he had been humiliated beyond words, squashed and
stepped upon and laid level in a dirty puddle. And then,
rather than remain there and allow him to vent his anger
upon her, a deserved reaction for her misdeeds, she had
fled from him in cowardly shame.

The bark of the oak tree was harsh against her slender
back, but she did not move. The laughter of the blue-eyed
woman seemed to mock her from afar. What do you have
to offer a prince? it asked. Virtue was painfully aware
that she had nothing.

For the first time in her memory, she felt the pangs
of jealousy. A livid rage roiled within her breast. Life
was unfair! Why had not *she* been born with beauty and
wealth instead of plainness and poverty—?

A crashing of the underbrush some distance to her left
distracted her. "Miss Goodbody?" Mrs. Snipe's voice,
now strangely diluted, called out. "Would you be good
enough to attend me?"

Virtue glared in the direction from which the voice
had come. She had a sudden urge not to answer, to let
Mrs. Snipe "attend" to herself. It was the first unsym-
pathetic thought Virtue had ever permitted herself. She
was shocked at how very good it felt.

Perkins was aghast! The dark blue coat and discreetly
striped waistcoat were filthy and water stained beyond
keeping. And the cream breeches! Good Lord, they
looked as if a wild animal had run amok on them. Sadly,
he shook his head over the ruined garments. And to think

this degradation of fine fabric had been accomplished in a matter of hours.

He was thoroughly miffed. He felt he "deserved" better from Roman, especially considering the disgraceful way he, once valet to the highest of the high, had been recruited into Roman's employ. To be won in a card game—moved from hand to hand like a common tart—the heart grew faint just contemplating it.

Roman, wearing a pair of baggy, white cotton trousers—an affectation from his days spent in India—shrugged into his after-bath banyan and tied it loosely at the waist. His chest and feet were bare, his expression circumspect. He could sense his valet's profound censure. It would have been difficult to miss.

Forcing a comrades-in-arms-type of smile to his lips, he asked in a jocular tone, "So, what think you, Perkins? Can anything be done with the clothing?"

Perkins raised a condemning brow. "Aside from burying them, sir? I think not."

"Surely the poor box at church would welcome them."

"If I may venture, sir, the poor have enough problems." Stiff-lipped and with obvious reluctance, Perkins draped the soiled garments over the arm of his impeccable livery jacket. "Will that be all, sir?"

Roman nodded. "Yes, Perkins, of course, and ummm, thank you."

As the door closed behind the indignant valet, Roman thumbed the stopper from a crystal decanter and poured a generous snifter of brandy. Why was it, he asked himself, that he could confront a corps of French cavalry without blinking, but faced with Perkins's ire, he cowered like a schoolgirl?

Roman knew the answer, and as if to drive the truth of it home, he muttered the damning words aloud. "No man—especially an uncouth ex-soldier whose youth was spent mucking out stables and dealing cards in a Gypsy caravan—is, or could ever be, a hero to his valet."

And yet, Roman was a bona fide hero. He had been a respected and highly skilled rifleman in His Royal Majesty's Rifle Brigade, formerly the 95th Foot. During the brilliant but bloody fighting at Salamanca, Corporal Knightley had saved his unit commander from becoming French mince. For his bravery, he had been promoted from corporal to Sergeant Major, a leap in rank rare in the annals of the brigade.

Reflecting back, Roman shook his head. There were times when he missed the harsh army life, especially his comrades. A braver bunch of bastards never existed than those in the 95th.

His mouth twisted in a wry grin. And, thank the Lord, those same brave bastards had not witnessed his tail-between-the-legs return home after what was to have been an *extended* assignation with a lady. He would have been hooted out of the corps.

All his carefully laid plans had gone awry. He had not so much as set foot in the Goose and Gander. After the gray-eyed mouse had vanished, he had vented his anger on the hostler. Never before had a hostler moved with such speed! Within minutes the grays had been hitched, and Roman had been on his way home, a dismal, chilly way home, made worse by the brisk breeze blowing through his wet clothing.

Grabbing the brandy decanter in a stranglehold, he stalked to the shabby settee in front of the fire. His still-damp feet left a string of moist footprints in his wake. Something else with which Perkins could silently reproach him.

He flung his lean body amid the deep cushions and

groaned aloud. Even after a hot soak, his ribs were as sore as a housemaid's knee. He glowered into the snapping flames, hearing again the mocking laughter of Lady Dimwitty.

The whole of the humiliating episode, in all its demeaning detail, replayed itself in his mind. Lord! He had looked—and felt—a fool. Damn that rhino woman! And damn the gray-eyed mouse, *especially* damn the gray-eyed mouse, with her bones as fragile as fine porcelain.

He took a large gulp of his drink, swallowed it down, then took another. The bolted brandy burned his throat and brought tears to his eyes. As he blinked to clear his gaze, a bittersweet memory returned for review. He was suddenly a tyke again, toiling in his uncle's stables. While cleaning the stalls one morning, he had come upon a dove with a damaged wing cowering in the corner, seeking warmth in the straw.

He had cradled the dove against his ragged shirt, feeling its delicate bones beneath his fingers, the pulsing beat of its frightened heart an odd echo of his own. The gray-eyed mouse had reminded him of that dove, fragile and helpless. And she, too, had flown away.

A futile anger rose within him. Damn all fragile and helpless women to perdition! They were capable of causing a slew of unsuspected troubles for a man. And, a slew of unanswered questions. The mouse had called him "Prince Orlando." What would a chit like that know of a Prince? It was a conundrum that continued to bedevil him.

Like a troll rising from a cave, Gaffe, Suzanna's personal maid, came up from the basement kitchen of the Grosvenor Street town house, holding a wicker bed tray on which rested a crystal bowl filled to the brim with syllabub. A linen napkin carefully washed, starched and tied with a narrow green ribbon sat beside a Sèvres plate and silver spoon. Gaffe had made the syllabub herself from the freshest cream and eggs available in the markets. And she had used her own money for the purchases. Nothing was too good, or too much trouble for *her* Miss Suzanna.

Rounding the newel post in the black-and-white tiled foyer on her way up the stairs, Gaffe heard the soft sounds of furtive footsteps directly behind her. "Miss Charlotte has been eating paper again," a sepulchral voice whispered ominously close to her ear. "And this time, the footman saw proof of it!"

Startled, Gaffe whirled around, sending the crystal bowl on a merry slide. As she righted the tray, she snapped, "Do not sneak up behind me like that, Rhett. I have told you time and time again, it's enough to give a body apoplexy."

Gaffe glared at the butler as she spoke. He was tall and stooped, with dark, ringed eyes and skin the color of soiled snow. She could barely tolerate the man. She felt he was not as respectful of *her* Miss Suzanna as he should be. Not that he had ever *said* anything, it was just a feeling Gaffe had.

Gaffe was correct in her assumption. In his baser ruminations, which were his usual ruminations, Rhett thought of Suzanna as "The Slut," and Gaffe as "The Maggot." He did not, however, dare risk a face-off with Gaffe. The Slut considered The Maggot indispensable, and Rhett had a gambling problem which kept him financially bereft. Since The Slut paid top wages, he was forced to swallow his pride.

Arranging his face in a mask of obsequiousness, he

bowed low. "Beg pardon for startling you, Gaffe, but I thought the mistress would want to know about Miss Charlotte."

"I shall tell her, do not doubt it. And I shall tell her about your startling me again, do not doubt that either."

Gaffe sped up the stairs, her chin raised to a lofty tilt. She was a small, sparrow of a woman with beady, bird-like eyes. At the top landing she paused and leaned over the banister as if she were about to peck it to pieces.

"And, Rhett, Madam is expecting her modiste, Mademoiselle Madeleine. Do not bother to announce her, but show her to Madam's *boudoir* at once—not when you feel like it."

Boudoir! Rhett scoffed to himself. *More like a School of Venus.*

Once more his face betrayed nothing of his thoughts. "Very good, Gaffe. And again, I humbly beg your pardon for startling you."

Cursing "The Maggot" under his breath, he went down to the kitchen to cuff the potboy for traces of grease found that morning on one of the kettles. As he trudged down the stone steps, his mind churned with the usual array of get-rich schemes. Getting rich was all Rhett thought about.

He was too nervous to steal, but soon, very soon, he knew he would have to think up a clever endeavor that would make him a lot of money. Then he would pay off his creditors and tell The Slut and The Maggot what he really thought of them.

After a perfunctory knock, Gaffe bustled into Suzanna's bedchamber. "Look here, pet, I have made a little something to tempt your appetite."

Suzanna was recuperating from a head cold. She sat in her elaborately carved four-poster bed propped up by a phalanx of lace-trimmed pillows. At her feet lay a portly pug dog.

She glanced up from the latest copy of *La Belle Assemblée,* which she was listlessly thumbing through.

"Thank you, Gaffe. What would I do without you?"

"Tut, tut, pet, what a question. As if you will ever have to do without me."

Gaffe had been Suzanna's abigail when Suzanna was the spoiled, only child of a doting, well-to-do father. In spite of a lifetime spent with a mistress whose itinerary frequently included dodging irate suitors and moneylenders alike, Gaffe was convinced *her* Suzanna could do no wrong.

She set the bedtray before her "pet" and fussed about with the napkin. "You know I do not like to complain, love"—she gave an injured sniff—"but that Rhett. He sneaked up behind me again. Likes to startle me, he does. And that voice of his, straight from the crypt it is."

Suzanna sighed. "What was it about this time?"

"It was about Miss Charlotte. Rhett says she has been eating paper again. Says the footman saw 'proof' of it."

Suzanna gave the porcine pug a lazy nudge with her foot. "Well, Miss Charlotte, what do you have to say for yourself? Are you the cause of my 'lost' invitations?"

Miss Charlotte opened rheumy eyes and turned them on her mistress. The dog subsisted on a diet of heavily creamed dishes and sweetmeats. The rich delicacies caused havoc with Miss Charlotte's select but somewhat sluggish digestive system. She ate paper, not out of pique, but out of necessity. She preferred letters to cards of invitation as they were easier to chew and digest.

Several weeks ago, a particularly tasty letter had come

in the mail. The paper had been of cheap quality but had produced some very fulfilling results.

"Saw proof indeed! If you ask me," Gaffe said importantly, "Rhett does not like Miss Charlotte, and he told the footman to make up the story. No doubt Rhett lost the invitations and seeks to place the blame on poor Miss Charlotte. From now on, I shall take her for her morning walk myself. It will be an added chore, but as you know, pet, I am not one to shirk my duty like certain others in this household."

Suzanna sighed again and declared as if by rote, "I shall tell Rhett he is not to startle you again, Gaffe, and I shall have Rhett tell the footman to stop bearing tales about Miss Charlotte. It would be best if you did walk her for a few days; then perhaps we will solve the riddle of our lost invitations. Although, this week I have been too out of curl to care whether I received any or not."

Sensing a reprieve, Miss Charlotte wheezed once, then settled down to pleasant dreams of more letters to come.

Placated, Gaffe slid the bowl of syllabub closer to Suzanna. "It is one of my best efforts, pet. Smell the delicate aroma. I added just a hint of lemon zest."

Suzanna stared listlessly down at the syllabub.

Gaffe cocked her head. "What is it, pet? Troubles with Sir William?"

Suzanna nodded. "He was so preoccupied when last he was here. I had trouble keeping his . . . attention up."

"Tut, tut, do not fret so, love. Sir William is besotted with you. He told me so himself. 'Your mistress is an angel sent from heaven, Gaffe,' is what he said to me. And I said, 'You have the right of it there, Sir William.' And he said—"

Suzanna groaned. "Enough, Gaffe!" She tossed aside the fashion magazine. "I have been cooped up for days.

If that dressmaker does not arrive the soonest, I shall scream!"

As she said the words, a muted roar of thunder reverberated in the distance. In spite of the crackling fire, Suzanna shivered. The rolling rumble had had an ominous sound to it, as though heralding some fast-approaching disaster.

Four

Virtue is bold, and goodness never fearful.
—Shakespeare

Mrs. Snipe had been left at the inn to recover from the worst case of intestinal knots the hastily summoned doctor declared he had ever encountered. After writing the note that the innkeeper would send on to Mrs. Snipe's sister, informing her of the reason for the delay, Virtue had been free to go.

Now, a scant few minutes from her mother's house, she sat rigidly upright in the chaise, staring out the window. The streets and sounds of the vast city surrounded the slow-moving vehicle.

London was a study of contraries: the soot-laden buildings rescued from uniformity by their lighted shop fronts of extraordinary brightness and beauty; the dull, dark clothing of those lesser blessed in life meanly bracketed by the colorful attire of the *ton;* the spicy scent of gingerbread and apples countering the steamy aroma of horses and smoke, and the fusty smell of too many people. Hawkers hawked, street sweepers swept, strollers strolled.

Virtue, considerably lessened in personage and diminished in spirit since the devastating experience at the

Goose and Gander, found the city more terrifying than titillating. She was sick with apprehension.

As the minutes ticked by, all the fleeting fears and doubts of the past weeks had come roaring back, coalescing into one great ball of trepidation. She clutched her Bible with trembling fingers. How would her mother react to the daughter she had abandoned so many years before? If Virtue's letter had been lost *en route,* would her mother be angry at her unexpected arrival? Or would there, could there, be just a touch of love remembered?

Virtue began imagining the most pleasant of the scenarios. *Her mother would be anxiously waiting at the window for her long-lost daughter to appear. When at last they were together, face-to-face, for the first time in eighteen years, Virtue would pause shyly for the slightest fraction of a moment. Then, in unrestrained joy, she would rush into her mother's loving, welcoming embrace—*

The chaise lurched to a stop.

"Here we be, miss," the postboy called out.

Virtue peered expectantly at the facade of an impressive town house. No one waited in the window.

The postboy leaped from his perch and tossed a penny to a street urchin to hold the horses' heads. He helped Virtue alight, then unstrapped her trunk from the rear platform and hoisted it to his shoulder. "I'll sets it on the front step, miss."

From the funds supplied by Mrs. Ramsay, Virtue gave him his expected gratuity of five shillings. He tipped his white beaver hat and was off with a speed born of evident and heartfelt relief.

As if on her way to the gallows, Virtue ventured up the gray stone steps leading to an impressive, white-painted door. She was engulfed by a nagging feeling that perhaps redemptions were not so easily performed in London as in Oversite. The grandeur of the neighborhood bespoke wealth and consequence. Redemption did not offer an increase in worldly rewards, usually, quite the opposite.

The highly polished brass knocker, the face of a gargoyle, looked uncomfortably like the suffering Mrs. Snipe. It seemed to eye Virtue with licentious intent. Gingerly, she took its protruding lower lip and rapped it timidly against its brass chin. She had not long to wait.

A scowling butler dressed in black livery opened the door. "I am—" Virtue began.

"I know who you are," he rasped. "You are expected." He looked down his nose at her tattered trunk. "I'll have the footman take up your samples."

Virtue did not hear a word of what the butler said, beyond, "You are expected." Her heart turned cartwheels within her breast. She was *expected!* Her mother was *expecting* her!

Eagerly she followed the butler's tall stooped figure into the two-storied entrance hall, its black-and-white floor tiles gleaming like a spill of water in the candlelight. Wax candles, not tallow. Woodwork painted a glossy white. Oil paintings on the walls, fragrant hothouse flowers in a tall vase on an entry table. Virtue felt close to tears. It was all too elegant, too beautiful. . . .

"Dear God!" the butler blasphemed. He had turned and gotten a good look at her. "If you ain't an apeleader!"

Virtue had not the faintest idea she had just been insulted and labeled a homely old maid. The poor man, while no doubt a valued retainer, was obviously deranged, she thought. Floundering for, and finding, a polite reply, she delivered it with a small polite smile.

"While I have never met an ape and so have never led one, I have always been fond of animals."

Nonplussed by Virtue's response, Rhett sneered at her and gestured to the stairs. "Go on up. Second door on the right. And be quick about it. It don't do to keep the mistress waiting."

He watched her climb the stairs, her sturdy boots clumping up the steps. If that's a French dressmaker, he thought, God save the Frenchies. His brow creased into a speculative frown. There was something havey-cavey about that chit, and he intended to find out what it was.

Virtue paused outside the door to her mother's bedchamber, knocked softly and entered. An impression of warmth, light and lavish furnishings struck her; then her eyes focused on the dainty, fair-haired woman sitting up in bed. Could it be *her* mother? Surely the startled expression on the woman's face was one of maternal fullness.

Tearfully, Virtue held out her arms. "Mother, it is I, Virtue, your daughter."

As she rushed forward for the imagined embrace, a compact fury of fur suddenly launched itself off the coverlet and latched onto the sleeve of her dress. Momentarily driven back, Virtue flailed her arms wildly. She was successful in detaching the furred fury and sending it, "it" being unmistakably a small dog, in a winging arc across the room where it landed in the corner with a resounding thud. Still clutched in its jaws was a portion of her sleeve.

After staring in horror at the dazed dog, Virtue returned her stricken, wide-eyed gaze to her mother's face. Suzanna's rosebud mouth was agape. She screamed hysterically, then fainted. She fell forward, her face cozily cushioned by the syllabub in the crystal bowl.

Frozen in place, Virtue watched in dismay as an elderly female servant frantically extracted Suzanna's liberally besmeared face from the bowl and attempted to revive her.

Virtue trembled with dread. As far as redemptions went, this one was off to a poor start. Had she killed both her mother *and* her mother's little dog? Twisting her thin fingers together, she prayed for a miracle, one that entailed the floor opening up and swallowing her whole.

When the old woman had wiped the worst of the stickiness from her mistress's face, she turned an angry, accusing eye on Virtue. "Look what you've done, you great gawk of a girl."

Suzanna moaned.

Distraught, she took a step forward. "Oh, please, do let me—" A warning growl, thready but still threatening, emanated from the heap of fur in the corner. Prudently, Virtue stayed her footsteps.

Suzanna struggled to sit up, globs of syllabub clinging to her front curls. "Gaffe, oh, Gaffe, tell me I was dreaming. Tell me that there is no dreadful girl in a black sack pretending to be my—"

Espying Virtue, Suzanna cried out as if stabbed and sank back amid the pillows. "It is true!" she wailed, tossing her head from side to side. "It is all horribly true."

"There, there, love," Gaffe crooned, "I will fetch a basin and some cloths and have you tidy in no time; then we shall see about—"

Recovering somewhat more, Suzanna impatiently waved the woman away. Focusing her arresting green eyes, as bright and hard as emeralds, on Virtue, she snapped, *"You* there, if you *are* my daughter, why have you come here?"

Virtue swallowed a painful lump in her throat. "I *am*

your daughter, Virtue Goodbody. Before my dear father, the vicar, died—"

"Dead, huh?" Gaffe tossed over her shoulder as she knelt and commenced rummaging through the lower shelves of a press cupboard. "Good riddance, I say, to that pinch-penny old wigsby—"

"Gaffe, please! Go on, *you.*"

"Well then, just moments before dear Father was taken into the Lord's Kingdom, he told me that you were not dead as I was led to believe, but living in London. He directed, should the putrid fever carry him off, that I seek you out."

"So," Suzanna scoffed, "you presumed, after all these years, that you could descend into my life without warning?"

"I did not know what to do. I had no money and no other place to go. I wrote a letter to you, asking permission to come, but did not receive a reply."

At Virtue's words, a muted growl issued from the dog as it moved cautiously across the rug on its way back to its mistress. Both Suzanna and Gaffe eyed the dog suspiciously, then exchanged shrewd glances between themselves.

"How did you find me?" Suzanna inquired coldly,

Keeping a cautious eye on the moving fur ball, Virtue, her voice dipping and faltering, told all. From the Bow Street runner, to Mrs. Ramsay, to the unfortunate incident with Mrs. Snipe and their subsequent rescue by a strange gentleman—a gentleman Virtue contrarily described as of middle height and fair haired. For some perverse reason, she did not wish to share *her* dark prince with anyone, not even her mother.

Unaware that she had taken her first step into the shallow depths of romantic subterfuge, Virtue went on to describe the laughing, blue-eyed woman. Hearing this, Suzanna clutched at her syllabub-bedecked breast.

"Oh, no! That would be Lady Dimwitty. It has been rumored that she has started a new *affaire d'amour*. She is one of my bosom bows; we cannot stand each other. If she finds out that I have a daughter, especially of your age and appearance, I shall become the laughingstock of London."

Balancing a basin of water and a stack of linen cloths, Gaffe bustled up to the bed. "There, there, pet. It is not so bad. Lady Dimwitty could not possibly know of Virtue."

Suzanna harrumphed. "Lady Dimwitty would not know 'virtue' if she fell over it."

Again she shooed Gaffe away. Her eyes narrowed in speculation. "Let me think."

The glittering green gaze once more pinned Virtue where she stood. "What do you want from me?"

What Virtue wanted was her mother's love and acceptance, things that could not, should not, have to be put into words. She blinked back tears. "I thought you might want me . . . might allow me to remain with you, but if you do not, my friend, Mrs. Ramsay, has given me direction to the home of her childhood nurse. I can go to her. She will help me find employment."

"Employment!" Suzanna echoed the word. On her lips, it sounded like a deviant doing.

A rare resentment welled up within Virtue's slight frame. She straightened her thin shoulders and lifted her chin. "I am quite well educated. I could serve as governess to the children of a Christian family. Dear Father had an extensive library. . . ."

With a *soupçon* of guilt, Virtue remembered her clandestine forays into her father's library in search of crudition. If he had learned of her dupery, he would have beaten her blue. "I have taught myself to read French and Latin, I can use globes and am adept at watercolors and embroidery and—"

"Enough!" Suzanna shuddered, causing a blob of pudding to detach itself from a front curl and slide down her nose. She swiped at it with the back of her hand, said a few words that had never been used at the vicarage, then wailed like a spoiled child, "Gaffe, clean me off, at once!"

During the lengthy cleansing process, Virtue stood—no one had offered her a seat—silently by, growing more aware with each passing moment how far removed her daydreams were from her real life.

It was quite obvious that her mother was in dire need of redemption, but for a proper redemption to be effected, Virtue required time and access to her subject. Redemptions were rarely spontaneous; they were more a gradual wearing away of the subject's defenses. Since it was Virtue's God-given task to redeem her mother, she knew she must somehow overcome this latest obstacle placed in her path.

Saying a short prayer for guidance, she ventured, "Would it be acceptable, Mother, if I spend tonight only with you? My journey with Mrs. Snipe was most fatiguing."

"I find *your* arrival most fatiguing!" Suzanna shot back. "And do not call me Mother!"

When the ablutions were finished, the restored Suzanna sat silent and circumspect. During the lengthy quietude, Miss Charlotte, now recovered from her flight across the room, heaved herself up on the bed. Gathering the small dog to her damp bosom, Suzanna regarded Virtue with resentment. "I have come to a decision. You will stay here, where I can keep my eye on you, until *I* find you suitable employment, preferably in Scotland. Until then, you are my 'cousin,' much removed. Under no circumstances are you to call me 'Mother.' Forget that I am your mother. Do I make myself clear?"

Virtue nodded. In spite of the hurtful sentiments expressed, her heart lifted. She could stay! Her prayer had been answered. The redemption could commence first thing in the morning!

Suzanna eyed her suspiciously. "Very well, then. Gaffe, take 'my cousin,' Miss Goodbody, to the guest chamber."

Gaffe went to the door at once, opened it and gestured for Virtue to precede her. As Virtue did so, head bowed, she heard her mother whisper in a loving voice. "Poor Miss Charlotte. Is Mama's precious baby all right?"

Strange to be envious of a dog named Miss Charlotte, but Virtue found that she was.

Rhett smacked his lips over a succulent bit of roasted quail and washed it down with a swig of wine. The second bottle of the evening was almost empty. He belched loudly and smirked, reveling in his own uncouthness.

Leaning back in his chair, he crossed his stockinged legs at the ankle. So, he thought, the ape-leader in black was The Slut's long-lost daughter, was she? Not lost long enough, to hear The Slut tell it. Fancy that!

Bleary-eyed, he looked around the basement kitchen, confident that soon he'd be out of it for good. He had never tried his hand at blackmail before, but then, he had never been handed such a juicy tidbit to work with. He wondered what Sir William would say if he found out The Slut had a daughter a scant ten years younger than she herself professed to be. And what a daughter! A fiddle-faced frump!

As he reached for the bottle to refill his glass for yet another toast to his good fortune, his face folded in a drunken frown. What was holding him back? Why not march upstairs and confront The Slut with what he knew? There had to be a reason.

He gave the question great deliberation before coming up with the answer. Cunning! That's what was holding him back. Some sixth sense had told him to wait a bit, that there would be more to be learned of this brouhaha.

Belatedly, he tipped the bottle over his glass, sloshing a goodly portion of the wine across the tabletop. He smiled to himself. It was all a matter of timing.

Five

Repentance is the virtue of weak minds.
— Dryden

Roman took a sip of brandy and savored it, rolling it around on his tongue. He swallowed and beamed beatifically at the room's other occupant. "Well, what think you, *Captain* Wentworth? Does the brandy pass muster?"

Henry Wentworth, now Lord Dunsby, to whom the inquiry was addressed, lay sprawled, or as sprawled as a former brigade commander in His Majesty's Army could sprawl, on the leather sofa in Roman's cozy library.

He grinned lazily and lifted his brandy snifter in a toast. "I would say, *Sergeant Major,* that your talent in choosing a French brandy is almost, but not quite, superior to my talent in choosing a French beauty for my wife-to-be."

"I say we should drink to our remarkable talents," Roman proposed.

"Excellent decision, *Sergeant Major.*"

After their synchronous swallows, Roman sighed lustily.

"I envy you, Henry. Your Marie is all that any man could desire in a wife, and more."

Henry reached for the brandy decanter. He was a thin

young man, not overly tall, with a head of pale, wheat-colored hair that resembled a flyaway haystack.

"She is that, indeed. I am a fortunate man."

Henry spoke from the heart. He was amazed, as were his friends, that he had secured the hand of the lovely and lively Marie de Chalfant.

Though decent and kind, Henry was not overly bright. He was, nevertheless, bright enough to realize that if a certain Corporal Knightley had not taken the then downy Ensign Wentworth under his wing several years back, said ensign would not have lived to drink the corporal under the table on numerous occasions thereafter.

Despite the differences in background and rank, the two men had become friends, the link between them more firmly forged when Roman had saved Henry from losing his head to a grenadier's hatchet. For his heroism, along with his promotion to sergeant major, Roman had acquired a jagged wound to his right buttock—a manly blemish of much interest to the ladies—and Henry's undying gratitude. They had promised to serve as bridesmen, one to the other, on the occasion of their upcoming marriages.

Henry continued to sip from his freshened drink, his gray-eyed gaze fastened pensively on his friend. Roman was the brunt of the latest scandal broth being brought to the bubble by the voracious *ton,* and it was up to Henry, as Roman's best friend, to inform him. But, he was demmed if he knew how to go about it.

Oblivious to Henry's dilemma on his behalf, Roman mused ruefully, "Speaking of wives-to-be, I received a note from Sir William in this morning's post. It seems my dear uncle has turned down yet another prospective candidate for my marriage bed. The unfortunate girl had the audacity to have used a dusting of rice powder to hide what Sir William delicately termed 'a deplorable complexion.' My uncle accused the girl of employing artifice and banished her from Bentwood."

Roman stretched his stockinged feet closer to the fire—although it was the month of June, the weather in London was unseasonably cool—and took a reflective swallow of his drink.

"My uncle has hated me since the day my father first brought me to Bentwood Manor to be raised on an equal footing with my cousin Elroy. Despite my uncle and aunt's disdain, and cousin Elroy's feeble attempts at bullying, my early years were happy ones—until my father died.

"On the day of his funeral, my uncle, aided and abetted by his psalm-spouting wife, beat me to within an inch of my life and then escorted me to the stables to assume what he called my 'true calling' in life. I was eight years old at the time."

After a small but significant pause, Roman continued. "Now that my benevolent kinsman is being forced by circumstance to recognize me as his heir, he hates me more than ever. This is his revenge, you see, his turn of the screw. I will be saddled for life with a woman who will consider it her duty to make me miserable. I tell you, Henry, if not for the thought of being master of Bentwood Manor, I would have never considered the agreement."

Roman's chuckle had a sardonic twist to it. "From lowly stableboy to master of the Manor, an advance in rank unequaled even in the British army, and one that I could not resist. My uncle may be a queer card, but he is cunning. He knew the Manor to be my weakness, and he acted on it. So you see, my friend, I have much to rejoice about and much to despair of."

He sighed, his shoulders lifting in a wry shrug. "Damn, there are times I miss the army life. I had the

King's shilling in my pocket, pipe clay under my nails and little else, but I was sure of who I was." He sent an oblique glance at his former commander. "And you, Henry, do you miss the army?"

Henry chuckled derisively. "You should know better than to ask. I loathed the army and was no demmed good at it. I purchased a commission because I thought I would look good in the uniform. Frankly, I was relieved when Papa unexpectedly bought the farm. He went too young, of course, but after a bottle or two, he *would* insist upon showing off his jumping skills."

Roman cradled his brandy snifter in the palm of his hand, sending the amber liquid in spiraling swirls around its crystal cage. "At least you knew what to expect from your destined situation in life when it came. I am a Gypsy's bastard. When my uncle sticks his spoon in the wall, will I be accepted as the next Earl of Larchmont, or will my elevation be a source of raillery among my 'betters'?"

With the impenetrable perception of one to the manner born, Henry artlessly observed, "You forget, Roman, your natural father was the Earl of Larchmont before your uncle took over the title. That connection goes far in excusing the circumstances of your birth. Already you have been most eagerly embraced by the *ton*."

Henry spoke the truth. Since his legitimacy, Roman Knightley, the Gypsy's bastard and erstwhile common soldier, had been vigorously sought after by society. A lot could be forgiven an heir to an Earldom—especially if he possessed Roman's dark good looks—no matter on what side of the sheets he had made his entrance into the world.

As Henry pondered his own profundity, it suddenly dawned on him that he had just created the perfect opening to introduce the bad news to Roman. His mind moving with the speed of a bent wheel, he chuckled wryly, "I have just thought of a clever play on words: Roman Knightley has not only been embraced by the upper class, but he has been most eagerly embraced, or should I say flattened, by a squab of the lower class."

Roman frowned his displeasure. "I shared that debasing episode at the Goose and Gander with you, Henry, and no one else. No offense, old man, but I would prefer to hear no more of it. I only hope to bloody hell that Lady Dimwitty will keep her mouth shut.

"Damn that gray-eyed mouse for having involved me in such a humiliating situation. I swear if I could get my hands on her this minute, I would shake her senseless."

Henry took a large gulp of brandy and swallowed hard. Obviously, this was not the time to tell Roman that Lady Dimwitty had already told the story to everyone who would listen. What the devil should he do now?

Employing an optimism spawned by a weak intellect, Henry endeavored to look on the bright side. With luck, he cogitated, the story would make the rounds and be quickly forgotten. He perked up immediately. If that proved the case, there was no need to tell Roman anything about it.

Still benumbed with sleep, Virtue woke, as was her wont, at first light. Her hands rested outside the covers. What was beneath her fingers? It felt like silk, silk as soft and fine as thistledown.

She opened her eyes. Her gaze lowered. It *was* silk beneath her fingers, quilted silk. Slowly, she turned her head from side to side. She was surrounded with silk, bed-hangings of soft blue washed to a pearly gray by the morning light.

It had been too dark last evening, and Virtue had been too exhausted to fully appreciate her lavish surroundings. Now she could, and did.

She drew in a deep breath and sat up. It was so beautiful, like waking in a fairy bower. She reached out and touched the bed-hangings, running her fingers down their cool length.

Suddenly, she realized what she was doing. She was coveting! A sin when it came to one's neighbor's wife and probably silk bed-hangings as well.

Quickly she swung her feet onto the floor and knelt to ask forgiveness. She opened her prayer book at random and read, "A bundle of myrrh is my well beloved unto me; he shall lie all night betwixt my breasts."

A disturbingly vivid vision of *her* prince lying betwixt *her* breasts flashed through Virtue's mind. She could see the smooth bronze of his skin, the dark silhouette of his well-shaped head as it rested in sharp relief against the whiteness of her bosom. She could almost feel his warm breath sighing against her breast tips.

What would it be like to lie with a man, she wondered, with a prince, *her* prince? She felt a sudden wave of heat rise in her cheeks. Good heavens! What was happening to her? This place with its silken temptations was another Sodom and Gomorrah! She was not exactly certain what had taken place in those cities of the damned, but whatever it was, it had not been acceptable.

Hastily she rose, forgetting her usual morning prayers for the first time since she could speak, and went to the washstand. No wonder her mother was morally lax, living in such surroundings! Virtue could only hope it was not too late for the redemption to take hold.

Quickly, she washed herself and donned a bedraggled black gown, a virtual twin to the one Miss Charlotte had torn, making sure she was not completely naked at any time during the process. Nakedness was another sin she wanted nothing to do with.

As she brushed and dressed her hair, her stomach rumbled its need for sustenance. She ignored it. There would be time later for tea and bread. Now she had work to do. A redemption to perform.

Armed with her Bible, she peeked out into the hallway. Strange, she thought. The sun was almost up, but no one was stirring. She was about to step into the hallway when the door to her mother's chamber opened. Gaffe, dressed in cloak and bonnet and holding Miss Charlotte in her arms, tiptoed out.

How fortuitous, Virtue thought. She had forgotten about Miss Charlotte, whose protective proclivities would be a definite hindrance during a redemption. Wisely, Virtue waited until she heard the front door open and close, signaling that Gaffe and Miss Charlotte were safely out of the way.

Hurrying down the hallway, Virtue knocked softly at her mother's bedchamber. No sound or voice issued forth. She knocked again, eased open the door and entered. The window drapes were drawn, but the bed-hangings were not. She could see the spill of her mother's fair hair against the pillow, the smooth curve of her pale cheek supported by a slender hand. She was fast asleep.

This presented a problem. For Virtue's particular brand of redemption to work, the one being redeemed must be fully conscious. Ergo, her mother had to be awakened, even jolted, from her present insensible state of imperfection into a state of blessed awareness.

Of their own volition, certain lines from the Bible

sprang forth loud and clear from Virtue's lips, " 'Silly women laden with sins, led away with divers lusts. ' "

The lines worked like a miracle. Suzanna sat up in bed, her eyes wide with fright. Seeing the gaunt black figure silhouetted against the glossy white of the woodwork, she opened her mouth and shrieked.

It was a reaction that Virtue was familiar with from past redemptions. Gratified, she rolled her eyes heavenward and launched into a verse from Revelations: " 'And I heard a voice from heaven, as the voice of many waters, and as the voice of great thunder—' "

Something exploded with a thunderlike crash on the wall beside her head. Could it be a sign from above?

With increased volume and relish, Virtue trumpeted, " 'And I heard the voice of harpers harping with their harps.' "

"I will give *you* harps!" Suzanna screeched. There was another explosion behind Virtue's head, this one a shade closer than the other had been.

"Get out, ninnyhammer!" The order was punctuated with another explosion of porcelain, then another. It suddenly dawned on Virtue that her mother was *throwing* bibelots at her, and she seemed to have an endless supply to throw. One of which was sure to find its mark.

Sagely abandoning the redemption, Virtue turned on her heel, jerked open the door and dashed into the hallway. As she did so, yet another bibelot shattered above her head, christening her with a shower of shards.

She made it to her room and locked the door behind her.

It was a gloomy, overcast morning. The gloom within Sir William's traveling coach, however, far exceeded the gloom without. The trip from Bentwood Manor to London would take four hours. To the coach's three occupants, it stretched before them like eternity.

Sir William was frustrated. The Earl of Larchmont had rejected, for the second time in a little over a week, yet another bridal candidate for his nephew, Roman Knightley.

The disgraced young lady sat sniveling across from Sir William, her reddened eyes matching the overall hue of her unfortunate complexion.

Since the girl's banishment, her mother, a hatchet-faced matriarch, had not stopped berating her daughter, employing as she did so the same accusation over and over again. *"Why* did you dust your face with rice powder when I distinctly told you the Earl did not like artifice? You are a willful, disobedient girl. You have had two failed Seasons. *What* will become of you?"

A practiced pause. "I shall tell you what will become of you. You will be shipped to India. *That* is what will become of you."

The young girl shuddered at each recital and cried all the harder. Sir William did not blame her. Even in India, considering the chit's lack of looks and address, she would be lucky to attract a hard-drinking, pox-infested John Company clerk. Damn. He had thought her the perfect choice!

Although Sir William liked to think of himself as a charitable man, he was not. He closed his eyes and his mind to the blue-deviled girl and her brutish mother, and thought instead of his Suzanna. He still could not believe his great good luck. That he had won the love and devotion of the beautiful Suzanna Combs astonished him.

His newfound sexual prowess also astonished him. He was able to bring Suzanna to fulfillment time after noisy time. That had never happened with the shopgirls he had paid to warm his bed. Their reviews of his lovemaking had been both direct and damning.

He chuckled to himself as he recalled his first time with Suzanna. Her spirited response had likewise astounded her. It had never happened with the only other gentleman she had known, she shyly confessed.

Poor, brave, dear little Suzanna. She had cried so piteously when she'd confided how, at seventeen, she had been driven from her home by a drunken and abusive father and into the arms of a rake who had taken her innocence by brute force.

But all that was over now, and he would see his beloved before the day was ended. He frowned. He hoped he would not be troubled by another embarrassing lapse in . . . readiness. Damn! This "favor" for the Earl was taking its toll on his strength.

Actually, it was not a "favor" per se. The Earl had somehow obtained documents pertaining to several shady business dealings from which Sir William had profited, and the old bastard now hinted at disclosure.

If only the Earl would die, Sir William thought callously, or, better still, be packed off to Bedlam. Lord knows, he was short a sheet. Fox, the Earl's longtime butler, had whispered that his master had frequent "lapses," times when he was convinced he was the Duke of Wellington.

The Earl was a devotee of the Duke's life and career, and during his lapses, became uncannily like the Duke in both disposition and bearing.

Still, Sir William concluded glumly, neither death nor Bedlam would claim the Earl soon enough to do anybody any good. The old devil had a vulturelike ability to thrive off the misery of others. He would retain his physical health and mental acumen long enough to see his bastard nephew unhappily married, and he would enjoy every moment of it.

Six

Virtue is like a rich stone, best plain set.
—Francis Bacon

In a swirl of Forester's green silk, Suzanna paced Virtue's bedchamber. To and fro she went, delivering a jaw-me-down *par excellence* with every step she took.

"Redemption, was it? Did you hear that, Gaffe?" For dramatic effect, Suzanna raised her voice to a sharp pitch. "That racket this morning was my presumptuous cousin's attempt to redeem me!"

Gaffe, who stood as close as Suzanna's elbow, winced at her pet's penetrating tone, and tsk-tsked with feeling. "Dreadful girl!" she proclaimed dutifully for the twentieth time.

Whirling around, Suzanna glared at Virtue. "How dare you presume to redeem me?"

Virtue, cheeks flushed, head bowed, whispered miserably, "I am so very sorry, Cousin."

Seven hours had passed since the disastrous redemption attempt. During the long hours, Virtue had remained crouched in a chair in her bedchamber awaiting her fate.

Meanwhile, Suzanna had gone back to sleep. She had been awakened at ten by Gaffe with her morning cup of chocolate. At eleven, lulled by a warm bath, Suzanna had decided on the gown she would wear to confront the morning. At twelve, she was dressed and becurled and ready to attend to the first order of the day, the first order being the berating of Virtue.

The berating had already been going on for some minutes.

"I shall never do so again, Cousin."

"Silence! For your brashness, you will be locked in your room for the remainder of the day. Is that understood?"

Virtue nodded.

"And tomorrow, something will have to be done with your appearance and wardrobe, just in case someone should see you. More expenses that I cannot afford."

"It is kind of you to offer, Cousin, but not necessary. I am inured to my plainness. As dear Father often quoted, 'Vanity of vanities, saith the Preacher, vanity of vanities; all is vanity.' "

Suzanna muttered a word that sounded like "balderdash," but was not quite as long.

"Enough of your father!" she snapped. "You will do exactly as *I* tell you to do. You are unacceptable for any employment as you are. A governess. Hah! A kitchen maid is more like it."

She resumed her pacing, "I may be entertaining an important gentleman this afternoon. Under no circumstances is so much as a whisper to emanate from this room. You are to be quiet and think about your transgressions."

Virtue nodded again. Her pale lips trembled. "Will my punishment include deprivation of food *and* drink? Since I had ample sustenance at the inn yesterday afternoon I am not *exceptionally* hungry, but a pot of hot tea would be most comforting."

At Virtue's beseeching words, Gaffe emitted a soft,

involuntary sound of sympathy. Even the aloof Suzanna seemed affected. She froze in midstep, turned slightly and, like a hunting dog coming to a point, gave Virtue a long, considering look. "The vicar, did he punish you that way, depriving you of food?"

Virtue nodded. "Gluttony was a sin dear Father especially deplored."

"A sin only in others, I presume?"

The question caused a moment's hesitation on Virtue's part. A memory mocked her. She could almost smell the succulent roasts of beef, the flaky crusts of sizzling meat pies that had graced the vicar's table. None of which she had been allowed to partake of. Her mouth watered; she felt faint with hunger.

Suzanna's harsh swallow was audible in the stillness of the room. "I see," she said.

It was all she said. She turned on her silken heel and left with the faithful Gaffe trailing behind.

For what seemed a long while, alone and miserable, Virtue wandered aimlessly about the room. Pausing at the dressing table, she picked up an ornate silver-backed hand mirror and studied her reflection. Sad gray eyes, fatigue tinting the heavy lids, hollowed cheeks, pale lips, a face that not even a mother could love.

A knock sounded on the door. Guiltily, Virtue replaced the mirror and called, "Enter."

A footman carrying a heavily-laden tray walked sedately into the room. He set the tray on the baize-covered card table near the fire and, with a flourish, removed the hot covers for Virtue's inspection.

She stared hungrily at the food. Accompanying the requested pot of tea were buttered eggs, thick slices of ham and poppy-seed muffins warm from the oven.

"There must be a some mistake. I did not request this."

"No mistake, Miss," the footman replied haughtily. "Orders from the Mistress."

Sir William sighed. "I am afraid your gallant steed is not responding to the bit, my dear."

Suzanna stifled a yawn. She had hoped Sir William's "business" in Sussex would have kept him from the City for another day at least. Virtue's descent on her from out of the blue had been trying enough without having to cater to Sir William's faltering conceits as well.

Managing to look both adoring and askance, she chucked Sir William under his nonexistent chin. "Nonsense, my darling. You are preoccupied, is all. I do not doubt your agile mind is busy with complex moneymaking dealings that this silly little woman could not even imagine."

Suzanna hoped that this was so, as she intended to touch her inert lover for a substantial sum once their tenuous lovemaking was over. Her current streak of bad luck at the gaming tables had taken on a seemingly unending dimension.

Nibbling absentmindedly on Suzanna's fingertips, Sir William sighed again. "No, my love, I am afraid that my distress stems from a more deeply embedded thorn than that. It is the . . . favor I have undertaken for the Earl of Larchmont that has me in a quandary. You see, the Earl has sought my help with—what he terms—an *affaire de coeur.*"

Suzanna was shocked into a rare verbal *faux pas.* "The Earl has sought *your* help for an *affaire de coeur?* He must be mad!" Before she could rectify her blunder, Sir

William looked at her thoughtfully. "Ahhh, then you have heard of the Earl's unfortunate malady—his mental lapses."

Suzanna breathed a sigh of relief. "One hears talk," she replied airily. "But do tell me more. Perhaps I can be of assistance."

"It has to do with the Earl's bastard nephew, Roman Knightley? Have you heard talk of *him?*

Who had not? Suzanna thought. Her green eyes took on a prehensile gleam. She smiled. "More than talk, Sir William. Actually, I have seen the gentleman from afar. At a rout several weeks ago. It was a ghastly crush, so we were not introduced."

"That is all to the good, my sweet. Knightley is not the type with whom you would wish to associate."

"He looked quite presentable." Suzanna replied, thinking she would not be opposed to a ride around the mattress with the disreputable Roman.

"Outward appearances can be deceiving."

Not always, Suzanna thought, irreverently eyeing Sir William's sunken chest. She willed an expression of loving regard to her face. "And how is Knightley the cause of your concern, my darling?"

"The Earl has tasked me with finding him a bride."

Suzanna's winglike brows arched in amazement. Was Sir William even more fat-skulled than she had first thought? Any woman with blood in her veins would gladly part with her eye teeth to have Roman in her bed.

Giving her nodcock lover an oblique glance, she asked, "And *you,* my love, are finding this difficult to do?"

Ruefully, Sir William shook his head. "There are unfortunate circumstances connected to the task. The Earl's only son, Elroy, a saintly lad, died two years ago whilst performing the Lord's work among the soiled doves of

Fleet Street. Lady Larchmont died shortly thereafter of a broken heart. There were no other offspring."

Sir William heaved a sanctimonious sigh. "His lordship is not a well man. Under great personal duress, he had Knightley legitimized and named as his heir. He did so, distasteful as it was to him, to save the Larchmont estates from reverting to the Crown upon his demise.

"The Earl is a deeply religious man; the sordid circumstances of Knightley's birth and licentious lifestyle are a source of continuing pain to him. In order to ensure—as best he can—that the title remains free of future besmirching, he has directed Knightley to marry, and his bride must be a plain, chaste woman of the Earl's choosing."

"And Knightley has agreed to this?"

"He has sworn in writing to do so."

Sir William breathed a weary sigh. "His lordship's criteria are extremely high. He has turned down two excellent prospects already; one because she did not recognize a quote from the Bible, and the other because she had used a dusting of rice powder to enhance her looks.

"The Earl is not a well man, he has these odd . . . spells, lapses in awareness, imagines himself to be the Duke of Wellington; although his mental keenness was not in question when last we met. At that time he . . . entreated me most firmly and at the very soonest to find a bride for his nephew. The woman so favored must be chaste and possess an abundance of virtue.

"I admit, I am stymied. Where can I find such a paradigm of moral excellence?"

Suzanna raised up on one elbow, her eyes narrowed in intense speculation. What a fortuitous coincidence! she marveled. The Earl of Larchmont was looking for an abundance of "virtue," and she had an abundance of "Virtue" of which she was anxious to rid herself.

Why not attempt to kill two birds with one stone? If successful, she would get Virtue off her hands and in the bargain could gain higher consequence for herself. As the bride's devoted cousin and only female connection, she would be constantly at Virtue's side. She would travel in more rarefied circles and, given the right setting, was sure to snag a gentleman with more *panache* than the tiring Sir William. Perhaps even the bird-witted Earl himself.

Her sudden laugh tinkled like the contents of a moneylender's pouch. In a fleeting butterfly kiss, she touched her pert nose to Sir William's beetlelike proboscis. "My darling," she trilled, "trust your Suzanna to find the perfect solution to your problem. My dear cousin Virtue, daughter of the late Vicar Goodbody, has lately come to stay with me. I am looking for a husband for her. If you will meet with her, I think you will find her exactly what the Earl desires."

Her voice took on a husky sensuous quality. "It would please me so much to have my cousin's future assured; I think that I would do just about . . . anything to thank you."

Sir William took the bait with indecent haste. "I would like to meet your cousin above all things. And at once!"

Suzanna giggled naughtily. "Should you not dress for your meeting with my little cousin?" She ran a suggestive hand down his thin shanks. "I would not want her to be jealous of *my* good fortune."

With fingers made awkward by haste and apprehension, Virtue retied the laces of her boots and smoothed down her skirts.

Things were moving too swiftly for her to comprehend. One moment "cousin" Suzanna was vexed beyond words and wishing her to perdition, the next . . . Virtue paused. Perhaps she had not heard correctly.

She glanced warily at Suzanna who, with wineglass in hand, was nervously pacing the floor. "You did say, did you not, Cousin Suzanna, that you have found me a potential husband?"

"Yes, I did, you tiresome girl, and an heir to an earldom, at that. Will you please hurry?"

"Should I brush my hair for my meeting with Sir William?"

"No! Let me look at you." Suzanna paused in her pacing and took a step back. With a pragmatic eye, she noted Virtue's pale cheeks and lips and her shadow-rimmed eyes, features that bespoke an ascetic lifestyle, bordering on sainthood. Repressing a shudder over the ill-fitting black gown—if the girl possessed a bosom, it was certainly not noticeable—and the clumsy boots, she pronounced, "You are fine as you are."

She resumed her pacing. "Now, remember, your meeting with Sir William is of the greatest importance. It is imperative that he approve of you if matters are to proceed to a successful conclusion."

She sipped at her wine, squinting her eyes as if peering into the future. "If Sir William should inquire as to your parents, your father remains the same; your mother, however, was the late ummm, Sarah Cotswell will do, a gentlewoman who died giving birth to you."

"Sarah Cotswell?" Virtue questioned. "I have never heard of the woman."

Suzanna gave an exasperated sigh. "It is a fictitious name, you goose. If all goes well with your meeting with Sir William, I shall have to obtain a counterfeit birth certificate for you—more expense—but you cannot be married without one."

Virtue gasped. "But that is a lie. I cannot tell an untruth."

"I am your mother," Suzanna shot back, "and you will do as I say." Ignoring the incongruity of her statements, she continued. "It is a small lie, and the fictitious Miss Cotswell and I do share the same initials. That should count for something."

Virtue's mind reeled. Counterfeiting and falsehoods. Could such misdeeds be condoned by the fifth commandment? Perhaps "honoring one's father and one's mother" could accommodate a dram of deception, but surely this was going too far.

"Stop daydreaming," Suzanna snapped. "Sir William is waiting." She put down her empty glass, turned and swept toward the door.

With every step she took, she flung further instructions over her shoulder. "Be mindful of all that I have said. You are to be yourself—within reason. Sir William has little regard for flighty young girls. And remember above all else, we are cousins only. Oh yes, do not forget your Bible."

As Suzanna and Virtue made their way downstairs, their trains of thought traveled diverse, yet disturbingly similar tracks. Suzanna was not burdened with maternal feelings. The fact that she planned, if at all possible, to deliver her innocent daughter into the hands of a recognized hellrake—heir to an earldom notwithstanding—did not discommode her. *Au contraire.* If all went well, she reasoned, Virtue would be in her debt for life.

Virtue was of the same mind. Marriage was the only "advancement" for women. An unmarried woman was pitied by many; an unmarried woman without beauty or

consequence was despised by all. Any husband was better than none! Her heart beating like a recruiter's drum,
Virtue willingly followed Suzanna into the drawing
room.

They stepped over the threshold. Suzanna executed an
elegant curtsy, stepped to one side and indicated Virtue
with a graceful wave of her hand. "Sir William, may I
present my cousin Virtue."

Trembling like an aspen, Virtue curtsied, her eyes
downcast.

Sir William gasped. He was delighted with what he
saw. The girl was a perfect fright!

Excitement flushed his veined cheeks. He forced a
smile to his lips and bowed. "How do you do, Miss
Goodbody. I am sure your cousin has told you of the
great honor that may be yours. Tell me, does the prospect
frighten you?"

Virtue raised her head, her clear gray eyes shining with
conviction. "While I am apprehensive over my *worthi-
ness* for such a great honor, Sir William, I am not frightened. My Bible tells me: 'Be strong and of good courage;
be not afraid, neither be thou dismayed: for the Lord thy
God is with thee, whithersoever thou goest.' "

Sir William let out a strangled sob. "Miss Goodbody,
with your cousin's permission, I shall write to the Earl
at once."

It was past midnight. Rhett sat in his room before a
smoldering fire, the second of two bottles of wine pil-
fered from Suzanna's cellars by his side. For the ump-
teenth time he was congratulating himself on his
shrewdness. How wise he was to have delayed confront-

ing The Slut about her "cousin." It had been difficult to contain himself, but the waiting was paying off.

By concealing himself in the closet adjoining The Slut's bedchamber, he had been able to overhear all of what had transpired between her and Sir William. He snickered coarsely. Not that much had transpired in the rogering department. The poor blighter had had yet another blank day.

Still, Rhett thought, better days were coming, at least for himself. If "Cousin Virtue" was successful in snagging the Earl's by-blow nephew, The Slut would have a much deeper money pot to plumb than that of the mutton-headed Sir William, and he, Rhett, would be right beside her to demand his fair share.

That happy thought called for another drink. He reached for the bottle and found that it was empty. Groggily, he debated whether it was worth his while to sneak back to the cellars for another bottle? Better not, he decided. He was tipsy as it was, and he had a great deal of planning to do before he showed his cards.

Seven

Prosperity doth best discover vice,
But adversity doth best discover virtue.
                              —Shakespeare

Sir William's elegant traveling coach, leather lined, mahogany trimmed and accented with brass, bespoke a rampant masculinity. A pity the same could not be said for its owner, Suzanna thought indifferently. Sir William's mewling lovemaking was getting on her nerves.

For the past week she had used the trials of packing for the visit to Bentwood Manor as a buffer to his advances. The ruse had not been an all-out canard. It *had* been a difficult time.

The securing of a forged birth certificate for Virtue had necessitated a leveling visit on Suzanna's part to a particularly unsavory part of town. It had also been an expensive visit. The forger, who called himself The Constable, was the best to be had. Suzanna had used him several times before to make subtle changes to her birthdate. As The Constable often jested—to Suzanna's chagrin—he was her fountain of youth.

The squabbles in the household had been equally fatiguing. Early on, Gaffe had accused Rhett in the disappearance of several bottles of vintage wine. Rhett, in turn, had incriminated a recently hired footman and immediately dispatched him, leaving the household staff short by one.

The two had continued at sword's point, their animosity reaching new heights this morning. Gaffe had loudly insisted that she and Miss Charlotte accompany Rhett in the hack hired to convey the luggage to Bentwood Manor so that he could not steal from their belongings.

Sighing like a martyr, Suzanna glanced over to where Virtue sat primly in a corner. Another burden to be borne! Little had Suzanna realized how taxing her role as devoted cousin would be. She had had to be fitted for several new gowns more subdued in color and cut than she usually wore, and Mademoiselle Madeleine, insolent émigré that she was, had been less than cordial about the outstanding balance of her accounts.

At least, Suzanna thought peevishly, she had been spared the expense and bother of supplying her "cousin" with a new wardrobe. The Earl wanted a woman without vanity for his nephew, and Sir William felt Virtue, as she was, was more than distinguished in that regard.

Suzanna shuddered fastidiously. Who could have dreamed such an absurd scenario? A disinterest in fashion actually being deemed an asset! Idly, she wondered what Virtue would say when she learned *all* the circumstances peculiar to her good fortune.

In a harmony of understanding, Suzanna and Sir William had agreed not to acquaint Virtue with the details of Knightley's unfortunate birth, his unsavory reputation and the fact that he was being forced to the altar by obligation and not by desire. There would be time enough for the sordid disclosures when the betrothal was on solid ground.

Suzanna lightly shrugged her shoulders, discreetly clad

in the finest of rep silk. No matter what Virtue thought, she would do exactly as she was told.

Duly noting Suzanna's lingering interest in her, Virtue's heart swelled with love and gratitude. Surely, "cousin" Suzanna was kindness personified to have arranged such a wonderful future for such an undeserving girl, and surely, a *soupçon* of maternal concern was involved in the arrangements.

Settling back against the squabs, Virtue closed her eyes, intent on occupying her mind with prayers of thanksgiving. Time and time again, however, her wayward thoughts strayed to her possible future, now rosy beyond her wildest dreams.

If the Earl approved of her, she would be married to his nephew, Mr. Knightley, a noble gentleman unconcerned with outward beauty and trappings, but seeking instead a chaste and devoutly religious woman to be his wife.

Surely it was the will of God that she should marry this pious, God-fearing gentleman. She envisioned Mr. Knightley as a man of character, well bred and temperate in his actions. He would not be handsome, but kindly-looking, with an unassuming manner that was much admired by his peers.

Virtue's slender sternum lifted in a deep sigh of contentment. Her gray eyes took on a burnished look as she began to imagine her life paired with such a paradigm of righteousness.

It was winter without. A chill wind rattled the mullioned windowpanes of Bentwood Manor, and soft snowflakes drifted together to huddle in heaps against the deep stone sills. But inside the Manor it was snug and warm.

Virtue and Mr. Knightley sat in matching wing chairs

before a roaring fire in their cosy sitting room, she within a circle of candlelight, reading aloud from the Bible; he listening in rapt attention, his face and figure lost in shadows.

Virtue wore a modestly fashioned, but very attractive gown of fine lavender wool. Her face was flushed, and her bosom—more ample in her daydreams than in reality—rising and falling with the passion of her reading.

Suddenly, there came a curious accompaniment to her reading, a steady creaking sound. She tried to ignore it, but could not. Her eyes strayed from the printed page. She turned her head to discover the source of the sound.

It came from the movement of a worn wooden cradle that stood by the hearth. Mr. Knightley had stretched his leg out from the shadows and was rhythmically rocking the cradle with his foot. His foot was bare. Odd, to be sure.

She endeavored to return her eyes to the page, but found herself mesmerized instead by the size and movement of her husband's appendage. It was large and well shaped, with an arrogant arch and long straight toes. Back and forth the cradle rocked, its ancient creaking rhythm ruled by the press and release of toes. Bare toes, bare ankles, bare—

The rocking abruptly ceased. Virtue held her breath as her dream husband rose from his chair and stepped forward into the firelight. For the first time she saw his face, the bold features, their sharp planes softened with shadows; the thick hair, glowing with the lustrous blue-black of a raven's wing.

Startled, she gasped, exhaling a rush of suspended breath. It was her dark prince who stood before her! He smiled down at her, his intense blue eyes smoldering with subtle needs, the deep red brocade of his loosely tied banyan shimmering like flame in the flickering light. Extending his hand, he whispered, "Come, my love, it is time we filled the cradle."

Breathless, Virtue reached out and slipped her fingers, willing captives, into the shelter and warmth of her husband's hand. As she did so, her Bible slipped unheeded from her lap and fell to the floor with a thud.

"Miss Goodbody!" Once more, Sir William rapped his walking stick against the floor of the carriage. "I say again, Miss Goodbody. Are you quite all right?"

Regarding Sir William as if he had grown another head, Virtue stammered, "I am . . . quite all right, Sir William."

He thrust his pinched face forward. "Are you sure? Your cheeks are flushed and you appear to be trembling. Not taken a chill, I hope? We cannot have that."

Virtue shook her head, wishing that the earth would open and she could sink into eternal damnation. It was what she deserved. She had sinned grievously. In her fantasies, she had been unfaithful to the good and kindly husband she had yet to meet. Her dark prince had stolen into her thoughts and captured her senses. It must never happen again.

Suzanna's nerve-edged laugh interrupted Virtue's frenzy of self-flagellation. "Sir William, you see illness where there is none. I assure you, it is not unusual for gently bred young ladies to flush when their thoughts dwell on their possible entrance into the married state. Innocent dreams, to be sure. Is that not so, Cousin Virtue?"

The look on Suzanna's face told Virtue it had better be so. She managed a weak smile. "It is as you say, Cousin Suzanna. I pray always for God's guidance."

It was the proper reply. Suzanna beamed at her, arching one carefully darkened brow to an extraordinary height. "And is not Sir William the very soul of kindness and concern?"

"Indeed he is, Cousin Suzanna."

The darkened brow rose even higher. "And are we not lucky to have such a gallant protector?"

"Indeed we are, Cousin Suzanna," Virtue dutifully mouthed.

Again Suzanna smiled. She placed one gloved hand lightly on the arm of Sir William's worsted jacket.

"La, Sir William, I do not know how I shall ever be able to thank you for all you have done for my dear cousin and me." Her fingers tightened on his arm. "But I shall try, again and again."

With an effort, Sir William refrained from pawing the floor of the carriage and emitting a lusty snort. Suzanna had given him a small taste of her gratitude, and he was looking forward to a full plate.

She returned her hand to her silken lap, hoping the French leather of her expensive glove had not absorbed any of the musky scent Sir William so obviously applied to his person with a ladle. Really, the man was getting more annoying by the moment.

And Virtue—she had noted Virtue's flushed face with a surprised and jealous eye. *Praying for guidance, my arse,* she thought inelegantly. She had been gravely mistaken as to "cousin Virtue's" true nature. Beneath that abominable black trap of a gown, a sensuous nature lay ensnared just waiting to be sprung. She was sure of it.

She twisted her gloved hands. Envy and resentment gnawed at her innards. Why should Virtue get a man the likes of Roman Knightley in her bed, while she, Suzanna, certainly deserving more, had to make do with the likes of Sir William?

She gazed out at the passing scenery. They would soon be entering Larchmont lands. She had made it a point to find out more about the present Earl and his holdings. He was a sanctimonious old sod with one foot in the grave, pots of money and a bent toward lunacy. Certainly fertile ground for furrowing if one had the proper tools.

With a mind trained in trickery and made quick by the constant battle to outwit moneylenders, Suzanna explored the pros and cons of securing the most propitious future for herself. If she were to cast her wiles for the Earl and could lure him to the marriage bed, then she, not Virtue, would be the Countess of Larchmont.

After all, Suzanna mused, rationalizing her unsavory intentions, Virtue would have her turn at being Countess when the Earl popped off, which, considering how poor his health was purported to be, should not be too long in the future. Suzanna smiled to herself. *That* happy occurrence would make her a dowager countess, the perquisites of which were not inconsiderable.

A frown marred her smooth forehead. Living with a candidate for Bedlam even for a short while would be trying—the frown faded—but even that situation could have a bright side. If the Earl lapsed into one of his "Duke of Wellington" stages, she could have great fun playing a camp follower. It was a role she was familiar with.

Pensively, she nibbled her lower lip. Attempting to entrap the Earl would be a gamble, but worth the effort. Of course, Sir William would be a fly in the ointment, but one of little consequence. When no longer needed, he could be swatted and discreetly discarded. Suzanna smiled. She could barely wait to tell Gaffe of her new plan.

As if sensing his beloved's distracted thoughts, Sir

William frowned, his squinty eyes almost disappearing from view. This past week, he and Suzanna had not had enough opportunities to enjoy each other. Obviously the abstention was as trying for her as it was for him. Often she told him how her love for him was all-consuming.

His eyes touched on Virtue. The girl's flush had faded, leaving her deathly pale. Lord, she was a fright! While he considered her a godsend, her presence was a distraction, and he could not wait to get her off his hands. Still, there was little doubt that the Earl would find her suitable.

Sir William prayed this would be so. Only when the marriage arrangements were complete, would the Earl relinquish the incriminating documents. And only when the documents were destroyed could Sir William relax and—he was certain—regain his slipping sexual powers. Not that his Suzanna had not been more than "accommodating" on that score.

A wicked thought, one more potent than port, brought a sudden unhealthy flush to Sir William's sallow cheeks. In keeping with the Earl's endless spouting of self-righteous platitudes, the old blighter lived little better than his tenant farmers. The Manor was neglected and poorly staffed, but did boast a separate wing of bedchambers. Discretion would be called for, but surely tonight, after dark, love would find a way.

Eight

Ambition, in a private man a vice,
Is, in a prince, the virtue.
—Philip Massinger

Rhett sat like a sahib in the hired hack, sublimely savoring every moment of the journey. Buttressed by bonnet boxes and portmanteaus, he was scarcely aware that the worn leather seat he sat upon was spewing forth its stuffing, or that the hired hack itself reeked with the noxious vapors of old vomit and sour straw. It was, after all, a *milieu* he was accustomed to from his wretched childhood spent in Tothill Fields.

Instead, his mind was filled with blissful anticipation. He took great pleasure in imagining the upcoming face-to-face with Suzanna. He would pick the tunes to be played and The Slut would dance to them. She would have no other choice.

Reflectively, Rhett stroked his bristled chin. He would continue to bide his time. Some atavistic craftiness still cautioned him to stay his plans, making him aware that there would later be more to be gleaned from this piece of work and, subsequently, greater profit in it for him.

He glanced over to where Gaffe sat glowering down at her knitting, her gnarled fingers painfully crisscrossing strands of skeined wool into a stocking.

Accusing him of thievery! The nerve of the Friday-faced bitch. Vintage wine, my arse. The stuff had been no better than horse piss. When the time came, he would take The Maggot down a peg or two along with her mistress, tell her to stubble it if she knew what was good for her.

Gaffe glanced up and caught him looking at her. Staying his vengeful thoughts for the moment, Rhett smiled broadly, displaying a set of yellowed teeth a Welsh cob might covet.

"We shall soon be at our destination, Gaffe. Imagine, an heir to an Earldom for *our* Miss Virtue. What a fortuitous match!"

Gaffe gave off knitting for a moment. "Mind what you say, you thieving oaf. Miss Virtue is no kin to the likes of you!"

Rhett, who thought of Virtue as The Stick, managed to look injured. "I did not mean to presume beyond my station, Gaffe. Since I have heard you refer to Miss Goodbody as *our* Miss Virtue, I assumed I might do the same."

"Well, *you* might not," Gaffe blazed back. "And do not think you will be much longer in the household. The only reason you are accompanying the mistress to the Manor is to make sure your light fingers are kept out of the wine cellar while we are gone."

Rhett assumed an air of sanctity. "You do me a grave injustice, Gaffe; however, I will not take umbrage. There is something about an impending love match that makes a heart sing."

Love match, he scoffed to himself. Wait until The Stick learns of Knightley's blighted background. That should be good for a chuckle or two.

Muttering something fulsome-sounding, Gaffe resumed her knitting, manipulating the needles with savage thrusts.

As Suzanna's erstwhile abigail and present companion, Gaffe had been through many adventures with her mistress, and, if truth be told, had enjoyed them all. It was always a treat to watch her pet finesse and outwit their opponents.

Still, she had misgivings about Suzanna's present plan to wed Virtue to the Earl's bastard nephew. True, it was an advantageous match, and Gaffe did not overly object to Knightley's disreputable reputation. In an age where all men were dissolute and young misses did what they were told, such matches were a sought-after and accepted occurrence.

Nevertheless, Gaffe continued to have misgivings. Virtue had been part of the household for little over a week, and Gaffe had already grown quite fond of her.

Sighing, Gaffe wiggled her toes contentedly. An infusion of sweet basil and rosemary in rainwater, recommended by Virtue as a foot soak, had done wonders for her troublesome corns.

She sighed again. While it was a pity that Virtue had inherited none of her mother's beauty or lively nature, there was a "quality" about the girl that set her above mere beauty, an inborn gentility.

Of their own volition, Gaffe's thoughts raced back in time to the night Suzanna had come to her and told her that she was breeding. How her pet had cried, piteous tears; how they both had cried.

Dismissing the memories with a pragmatic shrug, Gaffe checked on Miss Charlotte. The small dog lay in her basket in a daze of dyspepsia. For a moment, Gaffe envied the dog, but just for a moment. What was done so many years ago was done, and nothing good ever came from dwelling on the past. As if to prove the point, she saw that she had dropped three stitches in her last row of knitting.

"Sir William, are we not approaching Larchmont lands?"

As Suzanna made the inquiry, she leaned against him to peer out the carriage window, making sure her rounded bosom was pressed tightly to his arm.

A vein pulsed in Sir William's forehead. "Indeed we are, my dear. The lodge lies just ahead. The fourth Earl of Larchmont had it built as a banqueting hall. An ornate piece of foolishness if you ask me, and as neglected as the rest of the estate."

The carriage slowed and turned, rolling grandly through the entrance gates. Virtue peered anxiously out her window. She had been expecting something along the lines of an unassuming gatehouse. What she saw stunned her. The two-storied, turret-bedecked lodge greatly resembled a small castle. Built of ancient, moss-covered stones and surrounded by walled gardens, the lodge covered more ground than the whole of the village of Oversite.

An absolute and stunning realization of her imminent situation suddenly hit Virtue like a bolt from beyond. She might one day be a countess, mistress of an enormous estate and wife to its heir, a good and godly gentleman for whom her imaginary transgressions had already proved her unworthy.

At the thought of the eminence that might be hers, her heart swelled with resolve. From this moment forth, she would strive to be worthy. She would be a dutiful, attentive wife. She would become the patroness of the tenant families under her husband's authority. She would do good works among them, sponsor fetes and tableaux to amuse and instruct them and their families. The entire countryside would come to love and respect her.

She began to daydream, picturing herself strolling in the well-kept gardens of Bentwood Manor where a fete for the tenants was already in progress. She wore a modestly cut gown of lavender muslin that subtly emphasized her bosom, a bosom again more ample in fantasy than in reality. In one soft white hand, she held a basket brimming with sweets and small toys, which she lovingly disbursed to the clusters of well-scrubbed, rosy-cheeked little ones surrounding her skirts.

The tenant farmers and their wives kept a respectable distance from her, yet followed wherever she went as if they could not get enough of their benevolent mistress.

The scene changed with chimeric ease. Virtue was now standing on the village green, about to be crowned with a circlet of flowers by her adoring entourage. . . .

"Miss Goodbody? Miss Goodbody?"

She started. Sir William was leaning toward her, his face uncomfortably close. She could smell his fusty, port-fumed breath.

Sir William, having correctly deciphered the expression on Virtue's face, decided to use it to his advantage. He leaned closer still and whispered, "If you are impressed with the splendor of the lodge, you will be overwhelmed with the magnificence of the Manor. In spite of current neglect, it remains a splendiferous dwelling."

He paused meaningfully "As its potential mistress, it behooves you, does it not, to be on your best behavior when you meet with his lordship?"

Not discerning enough to decipher the unctuous overtones of Sir William's words, Virtue smiled gratefully.

"Thank you for your apt and kind counsel, Sir William. I shall try to be worthy of your trust."

Momentarily quashed by Virtue's guileless response, Sir William slumped back against the squabs. Suzanna, having overheard their conversation, set her agile mind to work on a question that had plagued her from the start of this imbroglio.

Sir William was not a good-hearted man by any stretch of the imagination. It stood to reason that he must have some dividend to gain by his "favor" to the Earl. Her green eyes narrowed. What was Sir William's Achilles' heel? she wondered. Fraud? Larceny? Lord knows, the little weasel was capable of anything. But, whatever it was, it would behoove her to keep her eyes and ears open.

Innocent of the conspiracies swirling around her, Virtue turned her full attention to the passing scenery. The parklands surrounding Bentwood Manor were famous for the vastness and beauty of their dense woods and stream-threaded meadowlands. With every herd of deer sighted and remarked on, with every new and splendid vista encountered, Virtue's chin raised a notch. If approved by the Earl, she would begin immediately to deserve her good fortune. She would behave toward the old gentleman as a loving daughter. She would read to him, fashion nosegays to brighten his chambers and attempt to tempt his flagging appetite with special treats she would make with her own hands.

Then, if someday granted the eminence of Countess, mistress of Bentwood Manor—Virtue's eyes clouded with tears at the very thought of the dear Earl's passing—she vowed she would be everything good, everything that was commendable.

Gradually, the terrain ascended until the carriage

reached the peak of a prominence. The view of Bentwood Manor across a small valley was breathtaking. Built in the late 1600s, the Manor was of handsome dark gray stone, three-storied and rectangular in shape, its middle portion nobly crowned with an imposing octagonal cupola. On either side of the main structure, two turreted wings jutted back toward an impressive array of outbuildings. The neglect of the formal gardens fronting the Manor was evident even at a distance, yet their overall scope and majesty remained undisputed. The Manor was, Virtue thought, much like the castle where she had imagined Prince Orlando happily ensconced with Lady Estelle.

She sighed dreamily and stared into space. When her ladyship was in residence, bright silken banners would be flown from the turrets by order of the Prince. She could almost see them now, unfurling in the breeze like the wings of exotic birds. . . .

The carriage lurched forward, abruptly dispelling Virtue's fantasies, and descended a steep wooded road, crossed over a crumbling stone bridge and drove straight up to the imposing doors of the Manor.

Fox, the Earl's aged butler, awaited them on the broad stone steps. He had a face like a withered apple. His pate was bald, but for a halo of wispy white hair that appeared supported by a pair of enormous, long-lobed ears.

He tottered forward, laboriously opened the carriage door and bowed. "I am so glad you are here, Sir William. The Earl asks that you and Miss Combs and Miss Goodbody attend him in his chambers *immediately* upon your arrival."

Sir William quickly stepped down from the coach and

pulled Fox off to one side. He lowered his voice. "How does the Earl go on? Any mental . . . lapses?"

"There have been signs, Sir William, but for the nonce, the Earl is himself." The tone of Fox's voice intimated that the Earl being himself did not bode well for anyone concerned. "His lordship is most anxious to make the acquaintance of Miss Goodbody."

Sir William grimaced. "We shall make haste then. It does not do to keep the old . . . his lordship waiting."

He hesitated. "One bit of instruction, however. A hack containing Miss Combs's servants and her luggage travels behind us and should be arriving shortly." He threw a furtive glance over his shoulder. Noting that Suzanna's attention was elsewhere, he surreptitiously slipped a coin to Fox. "See that Miss Combs and her cousin, Miss Goodbody, are given separate chambers. My chamber should be convenient to Miss Combs's as I will serve as her . . . representative in this matter with the Earl."

Fox had not catered to the prurient proclivities of his betters for nigh on to forty years without acquiring a certain aplomb in such matters. Discreetly palming Sir William's coin, he inclined his head in a nod of respectful benightedness. "Very good, Sir William. I shall attend to the luggage when it arrives and will personally see to the chamber allocation."

Suzanna rapped her fan sharply against the window frame. "Is something wrong, Sir William?"

"Not at all, my dear. Allow me to assist you and Miss Goodbody from the carriage. The Earl wishes to see us at once."

Fox bowed majestically to the ladies, turned on his heel and led the party up the front steps and through the massive oak doors.

The soaring entrance hall was bathed in pale celestial-like rays from the cupola high above. Dust motes danced and drifted in the directed light, giving the hall a hushed churchlike air.

Disregarding the palpably run-down condition of her new surroundings, Virtue planted her sturdy boots firmly on a rare oriental rug that was dirty beyond description and gazed upward and around. With bated breath, she took in the double staircase of delicately veined marble, the heavily carved cornices and doorcases, the lifesize statues peering from dim niches.

"This way, if you please." Fox's voice echoed eerily in the stillness. Picking up a single tallow candle from a grimy, ormolu-trimmed table, he indicated the left branch of the staircase. "His lordship's poor health forces him to receive you in his bedchamber."

Like ducklings, the three followed Fox's slow inflexible figure up the stairs to a large balcony room overlooking the entrance hall, then turned down a long dark hallway. Evidence of neglect was rampant, from the cobweb-festooned corners of the hallway to its dusty portraits and shabby carpets. Pausing before a door at the very end of the corridor, Fox rapped sharply upon it.

As a pettish voice cried "Enter!" Fox ushered his charges into the Earl of Larchmont's bedchamber. One candle flickered on a table that stood next to an enormous four-poster bed. A gaunt figure, propped up against the mahogany headboard by a cadre of tattered pillows, glared at his incoming guests.

With a discerning eye, Suzanna sized up her potential prey with hawklike directness. The Earl lacked a prepossessing cast—advancing age, a dour disposition, and an excess of religious fervor had imposed upon him a face like a fist—still, he was not without possibilities. Within the crabbed features and skeletal form, there lurked the shadow of the tall, handsome young man he had been.

Fox drew himself up as stiff as a cockade and intoned grandly, "Sir William Rushmore, Miss Suzanna Combs—"

"I know who they are, you imbecile," rasped his master. "Leave us!"

As the door closed behind Fox, the Earl commanded curtly, "Miss Goodbody, come forward into the light. At once!"

Aided by a sharp nudge from Suzanna, Virtue advanced into the feeble circle of candlelight pooling out from the side of the Earl's bed. She dipped into an awkward curtsy.

"Enough of that. You are not here to do the pretty. Stand up straight, then turn around slowly. Let me have a look at you."

Trembling, Virtue did as she was told.

When at last the Earl spoke, his words were as brutal as a blow. "Sir William had the truth of it so far as your looks go, girl. You have none."

Virtue cringed as if lashed.

Uncaring, the Earl consulted a sheet of paper crisscrossed with Sir William's crabbed handwriting. "Your father was Vicar Stanton Goodbody, and your mother was Sarah Cotswell, a gentlewoman who died giving birth to you."

He raised his eyes in a challenging gaze. "Tell me, girl, how did you occupy your days at the vicarage?"

"I kept my father's house, helped—"

"Speak up!"

"I kept my father's house, helped him with his sermons, read to the sick and did good works among the villagers. A goodly portion of each day was spent in prayer and Bible reading."

"Bible reading, heh? Let us see how much reading of your Bible you actually did." The Earl drew himself up and bellowed, " 'For the lips of a strange woman drop as an honeycomb, and her mouth is smoother than oil. . . .' "

Without missing a beat, Virtue finished the quotation: " 'But her end is bitter as wormwood, sharp as a two-edged sword. Her feet go down to death; her steps take hold on hell.' "

The Earl exhaled, his pent-up breath the only sound in the room. When he spoke, his voice was quiet, yet resonant with bitter satisfaction. "You will do, girl. You will do." With a curt nod, he indicated the writing table in the corner of the room. "On that table you will find an agreement to marry, with my nephew's signature already affixed. Add your signature to it at once."

As Virtue scurried to do as she was told, the Earl directed his attention to the shadowy figure of Sir William. In a loud voice, he commanded, "Sir William, come forward!"

Sir William oozed obsequiously into the circle of candlelight and bowed. "May I say how pleased I am to have been of service to you, your lordship?"

"No, you may not, as your *service* to me is not yet completed. You are to return to London and meet with my nephew. You are to inform him that his bride-to-be has been chosen. My carriage will follow yours to convey him and his belongings to the Manor. Tell him I shall expect him within two days. Is that clear?"

Sir William flinched as if stabbed. "But I have just arrived, your lordship. I still have the stain of travel upon me. When you say 'immediately,' surely you mean for me to leave on the morrow."

"At once!" the Earl roared. "And directly after your meeting with my nephew, you are to go to Doctor's Common and obtain a Special License. Then to the newspaper offices—the *Morning Post,* the *Gazette,* and *The Times*—and notify them of the engagement."

"Of course, my lord."

"See that all is done and done properly. Now, the lot of you, take yourselves from my chamber and do not return until you are summoned."

Nine

Good my mouse of Virtue, answer me.
—Shakespeare

Sir William hastened to Suzanna's bedchamber to bid her adieu. He hoped to find her alone and in the mood to expeditiously assuage his love-starved loins.

It was not to be. Gaffe was with her mistress. Like an unsightly wart, the old termagant sat planted in front of a smoking fire with the rheumy-eyed Miss Charlotte ensconced upon her lap.

Suzanna, dressed in charming dishabille, rushed to embrace him. "Oh, my darling, you must leave me so soon! I can scarce contain my disappointment."

Sir William had his own disappointment he could scarce contain. Glowering at Gaffe and Miss Charlotte—the mongrel had the audacity to glower back—he allowed Suzanna to lead him to a rump-sprung sofa. She did not join him there. Instead, she pressed the back of one white hand against her forehead and proceeded to pace aimlessly about the gloomy chamber.

"I had no idea the Earl was so disagreeable!" She sighed and shook her golden curls in dismay. "It quite galled me to witness you, my sweet, so good-hearted and so accommodating, being treated with such contempt. Several times I had to still myself from ringing a peal over his lordship's head and then hying back to London with my dear little cousin in tow."

With a furtive glance, she peered from beneath her fingertips to gauge the effect her words had had on Sir William. He had turned an unhealthy shade of puce and was staring at her, his squinty eyes bulging out to the best of their ability.

"Do not . . . do not ever say or do anything of the like, my love," he stammered. "The Earl, though a bit testy at times because of his illness, is a dear friend. It is an . . . honor to oblige him."

Suzanna concealed a self-satisfied smile. Sir William's reaction confirmed what she had suspected. The Earl had him by the short hairs.

She paused in her pacing, enveloping her lover in a look of sudden and enlightened adoration. "How noble you are, Sir William! You have quite put me and my selfish thoughts to shame." She nodded sagely, as if with newfound wisdom. "Of course, the old gentleman does not *mean* to be unkind; he is besieged by his illness!"

Like an errant child, she hastened to the sofa, knelt before Sir William and gazed up at him, her green eyes as guileless as a child's. When she spoke, it was with an intensity that seemed to spring from the depths of her heart. "From this moment forward, I shall follow your sterling example of selfless friendship. I intend to spend all my spare moments with the Earl. I shall be kindness itself to him. Surely a woman's tender touch will elevate his mood and temperament for the better. Soon, I am certain, he will mellow and begin to treat you, his dearest friend, in the way you so richly deserve."

A lump rose beneath the creped skin of Sir William's throat. His mouth trembled. "You would do that for me?

You would make yourself agreeable to the Earl, in spite of his bad humor?"

With a smile so saintly it bordered on blasphemy, Suzanna gripped Sir William's liver-spotted hand. "Of course, my darling."

Gently, she drew her lover to his feet and relentlessly led him to the door. A quick, chaste embrace and Sir William found himself out in the hallway.

Sighing with relief, Suzanna closed and locked the door behind him. Thank goodness, he was out of the way, if only for a short time. While randy as a stoat, Sir William lacked the requisite qualities of stature and staying power. Catering to his inadequacies had stretched her nerves to the breaking point.

She resumed her pacing, her strides not aimless now but quick and determined. She had set the stage with her usual finesse. Forthwith, she could seduce the Earl directly under Sir William's nose, and her dim-witted lover would thank her for it. The next step would be to deal with Fox.

Well pleased with herself and always ready for plaudits, Suzanna spun on her heel and curtsied to Gaffe. "What think you, good lady, of my plan to entice the Earl into marriage?" She grinned saucily.

Gaffe absentmindedly stroked Miss Charlotte's heaving sides. "I am concerned, pet."

"Concerned?" Suzanna's green eyes widened. "What is the matter with you, Gaffe? Do you not think I can not lure a Bedlamite into my bed?" She chuckled at her little *bon mot*. "After Sir William, I assure you, the excitement will be most welcome."

Loyally, Gaffe blundered to make amends. "Silly pet! You know I would never doubt your abilities in that regard." She paused. "It was Virtue of whom I was thinking."

"Virtue?" Suzanna looked blank for a moment. In her scheming to feather her own nest, she had quite forgotten Virtue. "Whatever do you mean?"

With a guarded glance at Suzanna, Gaffe ventured, "I think she should be told the truth about her betrothed."

Still perplexed, Suzanna questioned, "But why?"

Before Suzanna's astounded eyes, Gaffe's mouth suddenly set in a straight, stubborn line. "Because Knightley is a dissolute rake and Virtue is a gentle, sensitive girl, that is why," she declared stoutly. "She will need time to grow accustomed to her . . . future."

The audacious assertion, so uncharacteristic of Gaffe, sent a quick surge of jealousy coursing through Suzanna. Through flared nostrils, she drew in a deep breath. "Your concern is unwarranted and unwanted, Gaffe. Say no more of it. Virtue's alliance with Knightley is a *fait accompli*. When the time comes, she will do as she is told."

Ignoring Gaffe's rare look of anger, Suzanna spun on her heel and exited the room, slamming the door behind her.

Rhett regained the safety of the dim alcove and concealed himself behind its resident statue just moments before Suzanna's slim figure whirled past his hiding place. His brows raised in reluctant admiration. The Slut let nothing stand in her way. With nary a qualm, she planned to seduce the Earl and snatch the title of Countess out from under The Stick's nose. He would bet she was on her way to set the wheels in motion for the old blighter's seduction straightaway.

He stifled a sneeze. The alcove was dusty and its floor

littered with rodent droppings. Still, it was convenient to Suzanna's bedchamber. With a bit of fast footwork, he had been able to eavesdrop on her conversations with Sir William and Gaffe without being discovered.

Stepping cautiously out into the hallway, Rhett checked for signs of movement. He longed to follow Suzanna and see where she was off to, but—he consulted his pocket watch—time was growing short. Country hours were kept at the Manor, which meant dinner was served at six. An ungodly hour, but one that assured him an early release from his evening duties.

He hurried toward the service stairs. The extra hours would be a godsend. What he had overheard said in Suzanna's bedchamber would require a great deal of cogitation on his part. It looked like a three-bottle night. At the thought, his steps quickened.

The Earl of Larchmont was well pleased. His nephew's intended was both devout and malleable. His nephew was neither—the old man smiled—but would soon become both.

He sat up straighter in his bed, slurped up the last of his gruel and wiped his chin on the collar of his nightshirt. How he had longed for this moment! To have his brother's bastard once more in his power . . .

A polite cough distracted the Earl from his pleasant thoughts. He glared up at Fox. "Well, what is it?"

Fox bowed slightly. "If you are finished with your supper, m'lord, I will fetch your medicine."

"See that you do. And make sure it is mixed properly. The last batch was overly bitter."

Accepting the unwarranted blame with a penitential nod, Fox took up the dinner tray and made his way to the door. After carefully closing it behind him, he muttered, "Nasty old wigsby!"

He sighed deeply. Things had indeed changed since the old days when Richard Knightley, the present Earl's older brother, had held the title. Now there was a man worthy of an earldom! Wild and impetuous to be sure, but always kind and honorable, even seeing to the care of his bastard son.

Master Roman had been but a lad of twelve when he'd run off to join his mother's people. How long had he traveled with the Gypsies before taking the King's shilling? He had done a good job at soldiering from all accounts, served under the Duke of Wellington himself.

As a boy, Master Roman had been like his father. What was he like now? Had the years of abuse and humiliation at the hands of the Earl and Lady Larchmont taken a toll? Had the man Roman become as mean and embittered as his uncle? Fox shuddered slightly. If so, he pitied Miss Goodbody. A shame it would be. She seemed a pleasant little lady.

Fox heard a light tread behind him and glanced over his shoulder. Suzanna bore down on him, her steps swift and certain. He blinked. In the dim light, Suzanna's bright hair and gauzy gown gave the discomforting illusion of an archangel looking for something to avenge. A shiver ran down Fox's spine. He managed to croak, "Madam?"

"A word with you, Fox," she said crisply, "about your master."

Virtue sat on the edge of her bed clasping her Bible to her breast, her thoughts as dank and as hoary as the bed-hangings. Once again, her daydreams had led her on a merry chase. She had imagined the Earl as a kindly old gentleman, one who would treat her with the loving regard of a fond father.

That faulty perception had been cruelly dashed by the reality of their meeting. She had come away from the encounter filled with a terrible foreboding. The cantankerous Earl's approval of her had had a malevolent intent to it, an almost gleeful spitefulness.

She crossed her ankles and stared reflectively at her shabby boots. While she was not a mistrustful person, a week in the company of Suzanna had taught her that things were not necessarily the way they were presented. Doubts plagued her. She longed to ask Suzanna for reassurance. Were there circumstances associated with her betrothal, or with her betrothed, of which she was unaware?

Suzanna tucked a vial of French brandy between her breasts and carefully arranged a lace-trimmed fichu to cover any telltale evidence of its existence.

Tilting her head to one side, she studied her reflection in the age-speckled looking glass. A dusting of rice powder and a touch of rouge high on her cheekbones had given her delicately boned face the sincere, hollowed-out look she had striven for.

She felt confident of success. Her questioning of Fox had provided her the avenue she needed to approach the Earl. By feigning a nurturing concern for her host's health, she had learned that there had been several recent instances of what Fox delicately called "lapses," when the Earl would assume the Duke of Wellington's persona. The lapses were longed-for occurrences among the staff, as the Duke's personality was vastly superior to the Earl's.

If, Suzanna reasoned, she could induce a lapse, she would have both the Earl and his household dancing to her tune. Picking up the medicinal tray Fox had delivered earlier, she hurried from her bedchamber.

She tapped lightly on the Earl's door.

To his roared "Enter," she sailed blithely into the lion's den.

The Earl stared at her with unconcealed ire. "What are you doing in my bedchamber, Madam? Where is Fox?"

Suzanna affected a timorous smile. "Fox is indisposed, your lordship, a stomach ailment, but do not be concerned. He will soon be well."

"Concerned? Balderdash! Fox does not need a settled stomach to perform his duties. Ring for him immediately and get yourself from my sight."

As if to obey the Earl's command, Suzanna moved to a table some distance from the bed and set down the tray. With her back to his lordship, she removed the vial from its warm nest and poured the brandy into the glass of foxglove tea. Only then did she allow her shoulders to slump as if with dejection. "Forgive my forward behavior, your lordship. I am here because I am a very selfish woman."

As she spoke, she turned to face him, rivulets of silvery tears streaming down her pale cheeks.

She saw she had engaged the Earl's attention. His eyes narrowed, his brows knit with curiosity. "Explain yourself, woman."

Taking the glass of medicine with her, Suzanna moved closer to the bed.

"I have had much experience in nursing, my lord."

Smiling bravely, she continued to weave her fanciful tale. "My husband-to-be was sorely wounded at the battle of Vitoria. He returned to his devoted family a mere shell of his former robust self. For months I remained at his bedside with his mother and sisters, using all my skills to cure him, but his injuries were too severe." She bit her trembling lips. "I cannot help but blame myself for his demise. I wanted us to marry before he went to war. I wanted to be with him, to be his comfort in times of despair and to tend his wounds, should that sad duty become necessary.

"Alas"—a tortured sob seemed torn from her slender throat—"my papa would not give his consent. He remained adamant that the battlefield was no place for a delicately reared young lady."

She extended the glass.

Caught up in her story, the Earl took it and gulped down its contents, his eyes never leaving her face. She sighed again. "I know now that I should have defied my father. I should have followed my beloved to the battlefield."

She allowed one white hand to rest upon her rounded bosom. "I am a nurturing female, your lordship. I *need* to serve, to give of myself." She hung her head. "That is why, when I learned of Fox's disposition, I offered my skills. I can not help myself."

Eyes still downcast, she relieved the Earl of his empty glass. "I prepared your medicine with my own hands. I trust it was to your liking."

The Earl glanced at the empty glass in amazement. The medicine had tasted like ambrosia, and never had it affected him in such a positive way. He felt suffused with a warm glow, unlike anything that he had ever felt before.

"I will go now, my lord," Suzanna said softly. Her

gaze lifted to skim across the wide width of the Earl's bony shoulders. "If I may venture to say, my lord, you have the look of a leader about you. Have you ever led men into battle?"

Two ounces of French brandy mixed with six ounces of foxglove tea was enough to cause acute confusion in any man. The earl, unused to spirits and subject to mental disarray in the best of times, had to think hard on the question. Had he ever led men into battle? Try as he would, he could not remember.

Sensing it was time to leave, Suzanna dipped into a deep curtsy. "I shall go now, my lord."

In a daze, the Earl watched her go. Did she—this ministering angel—walk or float from the room? He was not sure. His lids felt heavy. He was suddenly very tired. Closing his eyes, he slept and dreamt—of smoldering campfires and rows of sun-bleached tents.

Ten

Virtue is the font whence honor springs.
—Marlowe

While Virtue entertained suspicions of Suzanna, Sir William did not. He had taken leave of his beloved, still certain that she was devoted to him and that her offer to cater to the crotchety Earl was yet another example of her steadfastness.

Although his precipitous return to London had drained Sir William in all areas save the one most in need of draining, he had garnered his strength upon arrival and penned a note to Roman, requesting they meet at the soonest.

The next morning, an affirmative reply awaited Sir William. And so it was that at the ungodly hour of ten, he found himself in Knightley's private sitting room, being subjected to the withering eye of Perkins, Knightley's valet.

Having categorized Sir William's jacket as the work of a second-rate tailor, Perkins served its unfortunate owner a glass of second-rate wine and, sniffing disdainfully, withdrew.

Left to his own devices, Sir William glanced contemptuously about the spartan chamber. The furnishings were solid with a penchant toward comfort, and—it was Sir

William's turn to sniff disdainfully—the stacks of dog-eared books piled on a Pembroke table showed obvious signs of having been read, not once, but many times. Certainly not the *milieu* of a gentleman!

This affirmation of Roman's lowborn station did much to bolster Sir William's lagging spirits. Still seething from the Earl's treatment of him in the presence of Suzanna, Sir William was looking for someone to browbeat in return. Knightley would be his target. He would make the bastard squirm.

Straightening his padded shoulders, he raised his non-existent chin to the realm of more rarefied air. He may be on a lackey's errand, but as a gentleman, he knew how to deal with his social inferiors.

Moments later, Knightley entered. He moved with an easy confidence, his lean, broad-shouldered form appearing to diminish the room and everything in it.

Not to be outdone, Sir William rose hastily and stood tall. It was a mistake. His eyes were level with the top button on Knightley's waistcoat.

They exchanged bows.

"Sir William."

"Mr. Knightley."

Sir William resumed his seat while Knightley strolled to the fireplace, a faint smile on his face.

Arrogant pup! Sir William thought. Perhaps a recital of the projected misery that would be his for the foreseeable future might take the bastard down a peg or two.

Extracting a folded sheet of paper from the recesses of his jacket, Sir William sat for a long moment, staring at Knightley and tapping the still-folded paper against his thumbnail. During the premeditated pause, Knightley said not a word, showed not a shred of impatience.

Frowning, Sir William unfolded the paper and made

it a point to scan the whole of it before condescending to read it aloud. He cleared his throat.

"I bring good tidings, Mr. Knightley. Your uncle has chosen your bride and solicits your attendance at Bentwood Manor at the very soonest. As befitting your new station, the Earl has sent his personal carriage to convey you to the Manor."

Clearing his throat once more, Sir William continued. "In return for your marrying Miss Goodbody, you will receive a yearly allowance of five thousand pounds—a generous amount—advanced quarterly. The marriage will take place within four weeks, immediately following Miss Goodbody's mourning period for her father.

"During the remainder of the Earl's lifetime, you will reside yearlong at the Manor and will be held wholly responsible for all matters pertaining to the estate.

"But, *of course,*" he emphasized the words, "any decisions you make regarding the estate will be subject to the Earl's judgment and final approval."

Knightley's indifferent nod of agreement annoyed Sir William beyond measure. Refolding the paper with great care, he placed it on a small table beside his chair.

Then, with an overbearing smile, he ventured, "As a young man I am sure you are curious about your bride's ahhh . . . physical attributes. It pains me greatly to tell you that she is not at all comely. Quite the opposite." Here Sir William leaned forward and leered. "But, if I may say—speaking man to man, of course—'in the dark, all cats are black.' "

Knightley's subsequent movements were a blur to Sir William, save for the large hand which suddenly grasped his jacket lapels, lifted him from his chair and held him suspended in the air.

Thrusting his hard-boned face but an inch from Sir

William's own, Knightley spoke. His steely blue eyes glowed like gas flames, his words were like weapons. "No, Sir William, you may *not* say. And if you dare to utter another personal comment concerning my future wife, be assured, I will call you out."

Sir William's eyes crossed as they stared down at the callused hand directly beneath his nose. This was not the hand of a man who had moved through life on someone else's money. This was the hand of one who had had to fight and scratch for the very rudiments of existence. It was a hand that could kill with one blow.

His bowels turned to water. "I meant no offense," he sputtered.

Knightley nodded grimly. "Nor do I. Tell my uncle that I will abide by his stipulations. I, and my bridesman, Lord Dunsby, will be at the Manor within seventy-two hours."

With that said, Knightley lowered Sir William's feet to the floor, turned him astern and frog-marched him out of the sitting room and down the staircase.

Perkins, stationed by the front door, watched their descent with an approving eye. His master might be a trifle uncouth, but he, too, recognized a second-rate jacket when he saw one.

Had it been but a day since Gaffe's anarchy, subtle as it was, had begun? To Suzanna, steeped in self-indulgence, the scant twenty-four hours seemed like an eternity. She began to view herself as a martyr, misunderstood and unappreciated. Was it not enough that she had to make do with dirty, drafty chambers, food not fit for pig swill, and an Earl who refused to lapse? Did Gaffe have to turn against her as well?

Simmering with resentment, Suzanna glanced across at the sewing table at her erstwhile abigail. Not once had Gaffe asked how the seducing of the Earl progressed. Did the inconsiderate goose think debauching a Bedlamite was effortless?

Suzanna plunged her needle into her tapestry and set a careless stitch. Although it galled her to admit it, she needed and wanted Gaffe's constant and unquestioning adulation. To regain that comfortable footing, she knew she would have to acquiesce to Gaffe's demands.

Putting aside her tambour frame, she observed in a teasing tone, "I see you have resumed your knitting, Gaffe. Which tells me that you have finished the embroidery on the Earl's new nightshirt." She released an appeasing sigh. "So often I tell myself how fortunate I am to have such an efficacious and clever woman as you to share the burdens of my life."

Gaffe harrumphed over her knitting needles. "I have given Virtue the nightshirt to embroider in my stead. She is an excellent needlewoman, more so than I will ever be."

Ignoring Gaffe's harrumph, Suzanna winged on. "Now do not affect false modesty, Gaffe," she chided with mock sternness. "You are a *very* clever woman, and you know how I rely upon your excellent judgment."

Pausing for effect, she tilted her head to one side as if considering the stitch she had just set. "In fact, Gaffe, it might please you to know that I agree with you about informing Virtue of Knightley's unsavory past in advance of his arrival. She *is* a sensitive girl, and one must always respect the sensitivity of others."

Ignoring Gaffe's skeptical look, Suzanna added airily, "Actually, I intended to tell Virtue the truth from the very start. I was merely biding my time until I deemed the moment most appropriate."

She smiled lovingly at Gaffe, expecting from her trusted companion an immediate return to allegiance.

Instead, Gaffe nailed her with a trenchant look. "Since Knightley is due to arrive a few days hence," she pointed out tartly, "when *exactly* do you plan to tell her?"

Barely controlling her ire at this blatant challenge to her benevolence, Suzanna rose to her feet in one swift and graceful motion. "I shall tell her at once."

"And gently?" Gaffe demanded.

Suzanna smiled through clenched teeth. "As gently as I know how, dear Gaffe."

While Virtue diligently stitched a delicate border of embroidery around the cuffs of the Earl's linen nightshirt, her mind revolved in conforming circles. One restless question persisted above the rest. Dare she ask Suzanna about Mr. Knightley?

It had been weeks since Virtue's attempted redemption of Suzanna had taken place, yet there had been recent signs that a belated atonement was occurring. To Virtue's innocent mind, Suzanna's newfound devotion to the Earl could only signal a burgeoning sanctity, a phenomenon that rendered Suzanna much more approachable than in her less sanctified days.

Setting the last stitch in the border, Virtue put the completed nightshirt aside and rose to her feet. Her mind was made up. She would go to Suzanna at once and seek answers and reassurance regarding Mr. Knightley.

With a rare but steadfast conviction, she hastened to the door and flung open the portal. She gasped. Suzanna stood before her, her hand raised to knock.

"Cousin Suzanna! Do come in."

Suzanna brushed past her. "I have come to tell you about your Mr. Knightley."

Virtue gasped again. She had gone to seek Suzanna, and Suzanna had come to her! Surely this was another indication of God's hand at work.

Commandeering the only upholstered chair in the meagerly furnished chamber, Suzanna arranged her silk skirts, tapped her foot impatiently, and waited for Virtue to be seated.

Then, Suzanna began to speak, her words like hammer blows shattering to shards the smooth surface of Virtue's innocent daydreams.

Stunned, Virtue stared into space. She could scarce believe what she was hearing. A bastard, the product of an illicit union between a lust-crazed gentleman and a Gypsy woman? A rough and common soldier steeped in worldly vices? Such a man would be her husband? And the most shattering blow of all: Mr. Knightley did not want a plain and pious bride. He was being forced by the Earl to accept one.

As Virtue struggled to absorb these shameful facts, her future life of humiliation was coolly condensed by Suzanna. "So you see, my dear cousin, you will have dual obligations: You are to be the Earl's revenge and Mr. Knightley's redemption. 'Redeeming' is a talent, I believe, in which you profess to excel."

Wounded to the quick, Virtue raised her dulled and lifeless eyes to Suzanna. "How could you, of all the persons on this earth, do this dreadful thing to me?"

Suzanna snorted disdainfully. "Dreadful? You silly, ungrateful girl! Because of my diligence on your behalf, you will one day be a countess. That alone negates any negative aspects of your alliance with Knightley."

She picked up the completed nightshirt and held it up to inspect the stitching. "You will learn, dear cousin, as all women must, to take a man's weight on your hips and be grateful for a roof over your head. You fare better than most. Knightley is a handsome rogue, and his begetting of an heir or two should not be unpleasant."

She rose, signaling that the conversation was over. Taking the nightshirt with her, she went to the door. At the threshold, she turned. "And remember, when you meet with Mr. Knightly for the first time—no matter what his reaction to your person—you will behave with the utmost civility and decorum." She shrugged slightly. "After all, you have no alternative."

Sir William had concluded his business for the Earl in less than three days' time and had hied back to the Manor in indecent haste to be with his beloved. Unfortunately, due to Suzanna's ministrations to the Earl, they had had little time alone.

Not that Sir William was faulting his darling. *Au contraire.* He knew that everything Suzanna did for the Earl, she did on his behalf. What man could fault such a treasure? She was selfless, even going so far as to embroider a nightshirt for the crotchety Earl with her own dainty little hands.

Sir William was enjoying a rare moment with his darling, taking tea in her chamber. Unfortunately Gaffe was present and showed no signs of leaving.

Undaunted, Sir William allowed his eyes to feast longingly on his beloved. Suzanna wore a gown of diaphanous green silk, with a tucker of fine lace peeping out from the low-cut neckline. His mouth watered at the sight.

Unrequited passion, however, was not Sir William's only problem. He had done all the menial tasks that the Earl had demanded of him, had been insulted and set upon by a common soldier; and still the old blighter refused to release the incriminating papers.

Sir William knew he had to find a way to get his hands on those papers. He could not propose marital bliss to Suzanna with such a dire threat hanging over his head.

Suzanna was well aware of Sir William's lascivious attention. To divert it elsewhere, she enthused, "La, Sir William, how I wish I could have been there when you gave Mr. Knightley his comeuppance."

Sir William preened. "It was nothing, my dear. Just took the fellow by the scruff of his neck and taught him some manners."

Knowing that Sir William lacked the strength it took to pinch a flea, Suzanna nodded wisely. "Let us hope that Mr. Knightley is prudent enough not to incur your wrath again."

Sir William nonchalantly shrugged his padded shoulders. "A man in my position, my dear, learns early on how to deal with his underlings." His brow suddenly furrowed in consternation. "Although why Lord Dunsby would consent to be bridesman to a plaguey soldier is beyond me."

At the mention of the Dunsby name, Gaffe gasped and Suzanna turned pale. "Did you say 'Lord Dunsby'?" she questioned.

Sir William finished off his tea and got to his feet. He smiled down on Suzanna, a smile laced in lechery. "Yes, I did, my dear. I do not think you would know of him, though. He is a young pup still, and has not been much in Society. Off fighting the war, and such.

"He was Captain Henry Wentworth until old Lord

Dunsby's fatal riding accident. Too bad about that. I knew old Dunsby. Good sort. Drank to excess and had an eye for the ladies. Much before your time, of course."

"Of course," Suzanna said faintly.

She rose and walked Sir William to the door. He gave her a chaste kiss on the brow and left.

The moment the door closed behind him, Suzanna sagged against it. She and Gaffe exchanged horror-stricken looks.

Eleven

Virtue shuns ease as a companion.
It demands a rough and thorny path.
                              —Montaigne

Suzanna and Gaffe sat on the edge of the bed. They clung to each other as if for dear life, their thoughts mired in a time long ago—nineteen years to be exact. Suzanna had been sixteen then, the spoiled, only child of Mr. Harley Combs, a prosperous landowner.

One dark and stormy night, a coach belonging to a Lord Dunsby had broken down at the entrance to Combs Hall. Mr. Combs, always anxious to curry favor with his betters, had offered his hospitality to Lord Dunsby for the night.

Not to be outdone, the precocious Suzanna had offered her own brand of hospitality to his lordship. It had been accepted, to the mutual delight of both.

When Lord Dunsby departed Combs Hall the following morning, never to be seen again, he left behind him a miniscule portion of himself. Suzanna was *enceinte!*

Even at that tender age, she was resourceful. A visiting vicar, Vicar Goodbody by name, had paid several calls at Combs Hall. Suzanna knew Vicar Goodbody to be mean spirited and none too bright, but he had two saving graces: He was interested in her, and he was available.

With indecent haste she had drawn him into her web, and within six weeks they were married.

Virtue had been late in coming and small enough to pass as an "early" baby. The vicar had never suspected he was not Virtue's father.

Dragging her thoughts from the past, Suzanna was forced to face the future. Her senses reeled with the aftermath of that night so long ago.

Suppressing a sob, she whispered, "Lord Dunsby is Virtue's half brother, and he is coming *here* tomorrow as Mr. Knightley's bridesman.

"Oh, Gaffe, what shall we do?"

Gaffe patted Suzanna's hand. "There, there, pet, you are making too much of this. Virtue is not marrying Lord Dunsby, so what harm can come of his being here?"

Suzanna sighed. "But do you not see, Gaffe? Virtue is the image of her father. If Lord Dunsby also favors his father, surely the similarities will be noticed. Knightley is not a fool."

"You are borrowing trouble," said the ever-practical Gaffe. "Lord Dunsby might very well take after his mother's side of the family. And even if there is a slight resemblance between him and Virtue, no one could possibly suspect that he is her half brother."

Rhett removed his ear from the door of Suzanna's bedchamber. His jaw hung slack and his eyes shone with salacious glee. What a *coup!* The Slut had cuckolded the vicar even *before* they were married, and The Stick was old Lord Dunsby's by-blow!

His lips curved in a loathsome smile. The time to act was almost upon him. Once Knightley arrived and the marriage arrangements were completed, he would confront The Slut with what he knew and demand a substantial stipend for his silence.

Late afternoon of the following day found Roman just minutes from the Manor. Amid the shabby splendor of his uncle's ancient Berline, he felt like a potential potentate with Henry Wentworth as his only subject.

The carriage was a mute testament to the Earl's cheeseparing practices and dubious taste. The Venetian blinds—in lieu of shutters—were coated with dust, the silk curtains in tatters, and the morocco sleeping cushions poxed with the nibblings of mice.

Suddenly feeling less like a potentate and more like a lamb being led to the slaughter, Roman stared unseeing at the passing landscape. His meeting with Sir William continued to rankle. The odious little toad had badgered him until he had lost his temper, a lack of self-control Roman strongly regretted. As a common soldier, he had learned to hold his tongue and his temper or suffer the consequences. The lesson had long proved a useful one.

Still, he rationalized, Sir William had overstepped the boundaries of acceptable masculine behavior. A man, whether born and bred a gentleman *or* a common soldier, did not discuss in intimate terms another man's betrothed.

He sighed heavily. Regrets notwithstanding, the die was cast. He, Roman Knightley, would meet his bride within the hour.

Cognizant now of his surroundings, Roman leaned out the carriage window, his eyes searching across the valley for the first glimpse of his boyhood home. As the Berline struggled to the very peak of a steep prominence, the Manor hove into view. Roman took a deep, resurrecting breath. The Manor had not changed. He had, but it had not.

His English blood crested in his veins as he gazed out longingly upon his heritage. Someday he would be master of Bentwood Manor, as his father had been before him; and no matter what manner or mode of humiliation awaited him this day, that reality would sustain him.

The carriage jolted suddenly over a progression of deep ruts. Henry moaned piteously with each tooth-rattling impact.

Roman cast an apprehensive glance in his friend's direction. Aside from moans, Henry had had little to offer in the way of conversation during the tedious trip from London. He had looked peaked early on, now he looked downright ill. His forehead was bedewed with perspiration, and his skin was the color of boiled beef.

This was odd indeed. While it was true they had lamented Roman's impending marital fate with countless snifters of brandy, Henry was the one person in the world usually unaffected by a night's worth of excessive drinking.

Was his friend in queer stirrups from overindulgence and needing a hair of the dog, or was something else troubling him? Perhaps a bit of badinage would take his mind off whatever it was.

"It is very good of you to accompany me to Bentwood, Henry, and to stand by me for the weeks before the wedding," Roman offered heartily. "I appreciate your support."

Henry *was* ill from both overindulgence *and* apprehension. There was something he should have told Roman days ago, but he had foolishly put it off. Time was running short. He made a try for levity, his forced chuckle sounding like a death rattle. "I believe those were the same sentiments you expressed to me when I removed the grenadier's hatchet from your buttock."

A return to raillery, Roman thought. That was encouraging. He grinned. "I presume you refer to the same hatchet that was meant for *your* head?"

"I knew you would bring *that* up." Henry's guffaw was not his best effort. "Not good form, old man, bragging about your brave exploits."

With a muted groan Henry gave up the pretense. Running trembling fingers through his haystack hair, he muttered, "Know I ain't been the best of company this morning, Roman. Sorry for it."

"Nonsense," Roman lied. "You have been excellent company and, I would say, very chipper indeed for a man who drank me under the table last evening."

Henry shuddered. "Where, I vaguely recall, I shortly joined you."

"Yes, you did, and as always, I was glad of your company."

It was Roman's turn for a sudden surrender to truth. He glared at his friend. "What in bloody hell is the matter with you, Henry? Is it because you leave Marie in London? Damn it, man, it will be but days until she joins you at the Manor, but if that is what has you in the gapes, say the word and I shall order the coach to return you to the City the moment it arrives at Bentwood."

Henry looked injured. "You know I would never leave you to face the bait in the parson's trap without me," he sputtered indignantly. "Besides, leaving Marie ain't the cause of my fit of the dismals. Although I do miss her already." This last was said with the wistfulness of a man who had been lately allowed certain connubial pleasures in advance of the marriage vows.

"Will you get on with it then, Henry? We are almost to our destination. What is bedeviling you?"

Henry sighed for pleasures postponed and bad news that could no longer be. Convoking his courage, he plunged into troubled waters. "Probably a good thing you're leaving town to rusticate for eternity, Roman. Lady Dimwitty's spilled the soup about your puddle-diving at the Goose and Gander. It's been the *on-dit* for the past week or more."

Roman's dark brows knit in a ferocious frown. "Damn that woman! I should have known she would talk."

"More than just talk," Henry muttered. He shifted uneasily, the cushion beneath him emitting a mournful cloud of dust, and removed an oblong sheet of paper from his jacket pocket. "Copies of this were in the windows of all the print shops this morning."

Cautiously, he handed it over. He had carefully folded the offending paper to conceal the worst of it and could only hope to Jehovah that his clever subterfuge would go unnoticed by Roman.

Roman took the proffered paper. "What the devil is it?"

Horrified, he stared at a caricature, one of Gillray's finest, depicting the humiliating episode at the Goose and Gander in all its ludicrous detail.

As he stared, fresh waves of humiliation crashed against his fragile ego. There could be no mistaking the identity of the unfortunate gentleman floundering in a puddle and about to be flattened by the flying fat woman. Gillray had put the Larchmont crest on Roman's jacket and given him a soldier's high hat.

"Knew I had to show it to you," Henry croaked. "What with your engagement being announced in the papers this morning, I wouldn't put it past Lady Dimwitty and her friends to flood you and your . . . intended with copies of the blasted thing."

Roman scarcely heard Henry, so intent was he upon the caricature. It had been folded in such a way, he noted, that a section of it was hidden from view. Carefully smoothing it out upon his knee, he saw what his dear friend had so obviously sought to conceal.

There was another skillfully drawn character in the drawing, a girl. Dressed in a shabby black gown and wearing a scuttle-shaped black bonnet, she stood in the doorway of the carriage strewing improbably-sized rose petals over the debasing scene.

It was the gray-eyed mouse!

The humiliating incident at the Goose and Gander now fresh upon him, Roman crammed the offending paper into the recesses of his jacket. Leaning back against the squabs, he squeezed his eyes shut. Bloody hell! At a time when he needed every ounce of self-confidence—even effrontery—to face the situation ahead of him, the gray-eyed mouse had once again succeeded in cutting him down to size.

The infuriating little chit! After wreaking her own brand of havoc that wretched day, she had disappeared without a trace, only to return, albeit in paper form, at the most inopportune time. How he longed to get his hands on her!

The afternoon had gone sultry, the air close. Not a breath of breeze stirred. Somewhere, far beyond the Manor's gates, a storm brewed.

The Earl had summoned Sir William, Suzanna and Virtue to his darkened bedchamber but an hour before. Conversation among them was not forthcoming.

The Earl, resplendent in the nightshirt which Virtue had embroidered, sat upright in his bed, staring at the door, as if by the sheer strength of his will he could command his nephew's immediate entrance through it.

He was consumed with hatred and feverish for revenge, his thoughts stagnating upon the day his brother, the then Earl of Larchmont, had brought his bastard son to Bentwood Manor.

What heresy! To subject dear Elroy—that sainted child—to such corruption. To rear a Gypsy's cur as Elroy's equal—nay, as Elroy's superior. Remembering the gross profanation as if it were yesterday, the Earl uttered a strangled cry of rage.

Suzanna leaped forward at once to pat his hand and soothe him. "There, there, your lordship. This distressful meeting will soon be over."

The Earl jerked his hand away and glared at her. "Have we met, madam?"

Suzanna's smile was as strained as a corset string. "It is my privilege, your lordship, to mix your evening medicine and bring it to you."

The Earl nodded vaguely. Yes, there *was* something familiar, something comforting, about this woman. He suffered her to plump his pillows, then waved her away and resumed staring at the door.

Sir William, in turn, stared at the Earl. How he would like to get the better of the old bastard! A deft idea suddenly pierced the dense gray matter of Sir William's brain. The incriminating papers must be hidden here, somewhere in the Earl's chambers. Suzanna was often in attendance, she could search for them while the old devil dozed!

It did not bother Sir William one whit that, if found, the papers would reveal his larcenous dealings to

Suzanna. The dear little thing, like all women, had no head for business. She would not understand a word of what was written. He would approach her with the idea at a more opportune time.

He only hoped the strain of all this would not prove too much for his darling. The last few days she had been exceptionally nervous and on edge.

Suzanna was nervous. Her thoughts were a quagmire of apprehension. What if Lord Dunsby resembled Virtue to an extent that the similarity was remarked upon? While Sir William would not notice, Knightley might. He was not a flat by any means.

She returned to her chair by the Earl's bedside and directed her gaze at Virtue. Or rather, at Virtue's back. The vexing girl had stationed herself at the window, where, for the past hour, she had stood motionless, gazing out upon the drive.

While her positioning could be perceived as maidenly anticipation, her stance revealed her true feelings. Dressed in the ubiquitous black gown, head bowed, shoulders slumped, she resembled a collapsed umbrella, set aside and forgotten, ignored until needed.

For some obscure reason, Suzanna felt an odd unease. An air of reproach seemed to be directed toward her from the silent black figure, and the subtle censure, whether real or imagined, was unsettling.

Since guilt and culpability were quite foreign to her nature, Suzanna attempted to remove her gaze from Virtue's offending back, but found that she could not.

Annoyed, she chided, "Do be seated, Cousin Virtue. While I know you are impatient to view your intended, it is not seemly for you to dangle out the window like a veritable gape-seed."

Virtue quit the window at once and slunk to a straight-backed chair at the outer reaches of the room. All but invisible in her black gown, she retreated into the shadows.

In spite of Virtue's ready acquiescence, Suzanna's vexation remained. Although she no longer felt compelled to look at Virtue, she still could not get her out of her thoughts. A question that had been lurking around the edges of her mind, persisted in coming to the fore: What was Virtue thinking?

Virtue was not thinking. She could not. The truth about Mr. Knightley had crushed her gentle spirit and drained her of emotion. Only an unthinking shell remained.

Wounded to the quick, she had retreated to the one sanctuary left open to her: her innocent daydreams.

Lady Estelle had been rescued from the evil moneylender by Prince Orlando just moments before her wedding. Was it not possible that Virtue's dark prince would come and rescue *her* from a lifetime of shame with the infamous Mr. Knightley?

Twelve

*There are some faults so nearly allied to excellence
that we can scarce weed out the fault without eradicating the virtue.*

—Oliver Goldsmith

Roman's homecoming was bereft of ceremony. Only
an elderly servant dressed in tired livery stood waiting
before the entrance door, and he appeared to be sleeping
on his feet.

The noise of the Berline's wheels rattling down the
drive obviously alerted him to their arrival. As Roman
watched, the old man raised his head, straightened his
slumped shoulders and, with the studied movements of
an automaton, made his way down the broad steps.

The old man's lack of speed was obviously tempered
by an uncanny sense of precision. When the Berline
braked to a halt, he was perfectly positioned to open its
door. He bowed as Roman stepped down from the carriage.

"Welcome home, Master Roman."

Roman's heart took a curious leap within his breast.
Could it be Fox—after all these years? He peered into
the servant's creased face. "Fox, is it not?"

The old man beamed. "Indeed it is, Master Roman."

Roman clapped him gently on the shoulder. "Good to see you again, my good fellow."

Henry struggled down the carriage steps in Roman's wake. Listing slightly to port, he eyed the lone butler with an observant air. "They ain't exactly rolled out the red carpet for you, Roman, now have they?"

Roman threw a steadying arm around Henry. "Fox, this is Lord Dunsby, my friend and bridesman."

For a long moment, the word "bridesman" hung upon the air like a foul smell, an almost palpable reminder of what was to come.

There was an awkward pause. Then, with a heartiness so feigned it made his teeth ache, Roman demanded, "Let us get on with it then, shall we, Fox?"

"At once, sir. Lord Larchmont awaits you in his chamber. Miss Goodbody, Sir William and Miss Combs— Miss Goodbody's cousin—are also in attendance. If you will follow me . . ."

As the three ascended the Manor's broad steps, a supple switch of lightning suddenly chastised the sullen clouds that hung directly above their heads. An acrid smell of sulfur followed them to the entrance hall.

Once they were in the gloomy foyer, Henry was dispatched to his chamber under the dubious guidance of a slovenly footman, and Roman followed the shepherding Fox up the left branch of the divided staircase and down a long dim hallway.

The Manor's dank ambience made a good match for Roman's sudden, almost overwhelming feeling of despair. His pulse pounded in his throat. After so long a wait, after months of apprehension, the moment was now upon him. What wretched, ill-tempered fright had his uncle found for him?

With each step forward, he steeled himself for the inevitable, vowing that he would not give his uncle the satisfaction of seeing his despair.

"We are here, sir," Fox intoned. As the two men paused before the massive, time-darkened door, a subtle change occurred between them. Their respective roles of master-servant were momentarily suspended. They exchanged a long, conspiratorial look. "Have heart, Master Roman," Fox whispered. He turned and rapped once upon the portal.

A raspy voice called, "Enter."

Fox flung open the door, crossed the threshold and bowed low. "Your lordship, may I present—"

"I know who he is, you blasted fool," the Earl roared. "Usher him in and get yourself from my sight."

As Fox made his scurrying exit, Roman stepped into the Earl's bedchamber. Like a doomed gladiator looking for potential perils, he allowed his eyes to rake the darkened arena.

The Earl sat upright in his bed, his eyes burning like hot coals. Sir William and a beautiful blond woman— Miss Combs by all reckoning—stood off to one side. Roman's eyes narrowed. But where was Miss Goodbody?

Miss Goodbody was where Fate had left her, hidden amongst the shadows. Agog, she stared at Roman, not daring to believe her eyes. By some heavenly sleight of hand, the infamous Mr. Knightley had been changed into her dark prince! And, miracle of miracles, neither the Earl and Sir William nor Suzanna seemed to notice the substitution.

The Earl, however, had noticed Roman's surreptitious survey of his surroundings. "Looking for your in-

tended?" he inquired shrewdly. He cackled in evil anticipation. "Then let us not wait a moment more. Miss
Goodbody, come forward!"

Virtue heard her name called. In a daze, she rose from
her chair, convinced now that she had been touched by
divine intervention. Her heart overflowed. She longed to
acknowledge the marvel of it. An appropriate quotation
obligingly sprang to mind. Arms outstretched, she walked
toward her dark prince, her voice rising to the heavens.
" 'Hope deferred maketh the heart sick; but when desire
cometh, it is a tree of life.' "

Roman gaped in astonishment as Virtue materialized
from the gloom. What sorcery was this? Had he taken
leave of his senses, or did the psalm-spouting Miss
Goodbody greatly resemble the ubiquitous gray-eyed
mouse?

As the question reverberated through his thoughts, the
icy hand of reason gave his heart a swift and savage
squeeze. There could be no mistaking that small pale
face with its pointed little chin, those large, mist-colored
eyes. By some monstrous twist of Fate, Miss Goodbody
and the gray-eyed mouse were one and the same.

Interpreting Roman's horrified expression as an early
manifestation of love's benightedness, Virtue kept true to
her course.

As she advanced, Roman retreated. When he felt his
back against the wall, he instinctively braced himself as
if to ward off a blow.

His defensive gesture stopped Virtue cold in her tracks.
In the face of so tangible a rejection, even she could not
sustain a belief in miracles. Her outstretched arms
dropped to her sides. Suddenly it was all painfully clear.
There had been no celestial twisting of Fate, merely a

malicious one. Mr. Knightley *was* her dark prince—they were one and the same—and they both despised her.

As she stood in mute despair, she heard the Earl cry out, "Bravo, Sir William. Just see how my nephew cringes from his intended. You could not have made a better choice than Miss Goodbody."

Virtue's face flamed. The injustice of it all rose like bile in her throat. Seventeen years of humiliation and deprivation had culminated in this, this cruelest of blows. She could endure no more. She turned, flung open the door and ran from her tormentors.

As she pelted down the dark hallway, she heard sounds of pursuit: a muster of footfalls, Suzanna's shrill shrieks, Sir William's shout of, "You little ingrate."

Not daring to glance back, she increased her speed. The hallway opened onto the balcony room that overlooked the entrance hall. The bedroom wing was just beyond. If she could make it to her chamber and lock the door . . .

Her pulse pounding in her temples, Virtue took a ragged breath and attempted the final sprint to freedom. Her heavy black gown proved her downfall. Just yards short of her goal, her skirts became tangled around her ankles. As she struggled to disentangle them, she pitched forward and landed in a sprawled heap upon the rug.

Winded, but still game, she rolled to one side and attempted to rise. She was too late. Sir William stood over her, his fist raised. Defeated, Virtue squeezed shut her eyes and, with tears trickling down her cheeks, braced herself for the blow. It never landed.

Cautiously, she opened her eyes. Sir William was no longer a threat. He sat in a tidy heap against the far railing. Mr. Knightley stood over him. He was obviously conveying to Sir William a few words of wisdom.

Virtue could not hear what Mr. Knightley said, but whatever it was, it was enough to turn Sir William's face an unsightly shade of green.

She now became the object of Mr. Knightley's attention. He strode over to her, his expression grim. Without a word, he gathered her off the floor and carried her toward the hallway beyond, the sound of his boots echoing like distant drumbeats.

Virtue went limp with fear. Unused to any physical proximity with a man, she found the sheer strength of the arms that held her, the intimate curl of male fingers on her flesh, the masculine heat emanating from the rock solid body overwhelming. Where was Mr. Knightley taking her, and what did he plan to do with her when he got her there?

With Gillray's caricature burning like a brand within the pocket of his jacket, and the gray-eyed mouse firmly within his grasp, Roman had not the faintest notion of what he would do next.

He had sworn to shake the daylights out of the mouse, if and when he ever got his hands on her, but now that he held her, the delicate bones and flesh almost weightless in his arms—

Damn!

He strode on, hardening his heart. The gray-eyed mouse had a question or two to answer. And answer she would!

At that auspicious moment, Suzanna caught up with the pack. Sir William, whose tight corseting prevented mobility, was on his hands and knees attempting to rise. When he spotted Suzanna, he stretched out a supplicant's hand. She ignored it. Undaunted, Sir William began to crawl after her.

All flying curls and outraged dignity, Suzanna came

We'd Like to Invite You to Subscribe to Zebra's Regency Romance Book Club an Give You a Gift of 4 Free Books as Your Introduction! (Worth $19.96!)

If you're a Regency lover, imagine the joy of getting **4 FRE** **Zebra Regency Romances** and then the chance to have th lovely stories delivered to your home each month at the lowest prices available! Well, that's our offer to you and here's how you benefit by becoming a Zebra Home Subscription Service subscriber:

- **4 FREE Introductory Regency Romances are delivered to your doors**

- **4 BRAND NEW Regencies are then delivered each month (usually befo they're available in bookstores)**

- **Subscribers save almost $4.00 every month**

- **Home delivery is always FREE**

- **You also receive a FREE monthly newsletter, *Zebra/ Pinnacle Roma News* which features author profiles, contests, subscriber benefits, b previews and more**

- **No risks or obligations...in other words you can cancel whenever yo wish with no questions asked**

Join the thousands of readers who enjoy the savings and convenience offered to Regency Romance subscribers. After your initial introductory shipment, you receive 4 brand-new Zebra Regency Romances each month to examine for 10 day Then, if you decide to keep the books, you'll pay the preferre subscriber's price of just $4.00 per title. That's only $16.00 fo all 4 books and there's never an extra charge for shipping and handling.

It's a no-lose proposition, so return the FREE BOOK CERTIFICATE today!

Say Yes to 4 Free Books!
Complete and return the order card to receive this $19.96 value, ABSOLUTELY FREE!

(If the certificate is missing below, write to:)
Zebra Home Subscription Service, Inc.,
120 Brighton Road, P.O. Box 5214, Clifton, New Jersey 07015-5214
or call TOLL-FREE 1-888-345-BOOK

FREE BOOK CERTIFICATE

YES! Please rush me 4 Zebra Regency Romances without cost or obligation. I understand that each month thereafter I will be able to preview 4 brand-new Regency Romances FREE for 10 days. Then, if I should decide to keep them, I will pay the money-saving preferred subscriber's price of just $16.00 for all 4...that's a savings of almost $4 off the publisher's price with no additional charge for shipping and handling. I may return any shipment within 10 days and owe nothing, and I may cancel this subscription at any time. My 4 FREE books will be mine to keep in any case.

Name _____

Address _____ Apt. _____

City _____ State _____ Zip _____

Telephone ( ) _____

Signature _____

(If under 18, parent or guardian must sign.)   RG10A9

Terms and prices subject to change. Orders subject to acceptance by Zebra Home Subscription Service, Inc.

AFFIX
STAMP
HERE

ZEBRA HOME SUBSCRIPTION SERVICE, INC.

120 BRIGHTON ROAD

P.O. BOX 5214

CLIFTON, NEW JERSEY 07015-5214

abreast of Roman. Struggling to keep up, she shrieked, "Sirrah! Where are you taking my cousin?"

Without breaking stride, Roman answered, "I am taking Miss Goodbody to her chamber. Once there, I intend to have a *private* conversation with her."

He lowered his head a notch and demanded of Virtue, "Which *is* your chamber, Miss Goodbody?" Following her trembling finger, he approached the door she had indicated and applied the sole of his boot to it.

Suzanna scurried after him, Sir William in her wake. "Sirrah! You overstep your bounds. As my cousin's chaperon, I insist on accompanying you into her chamber. It would not be proper otherwise."

Roman grunted contemptuously. "If there is anything at all 'proper' about this marital arrangement, Miss Combs, I fail to see it."

He stepped over the threshold, being careful not to bang Virtue's boots against the jamb, then turned and faced Suzanna. "May I suggest, madame, that you give your concern where needed. Look behind you. Sir William is wearing out the knees of his pantaloons in an attempt to keep up with you."

Spinning on her heel, Suzanna spotted Sir William several yards behind her. Upon her feigned cry of solicitude, Roman promptly slammed the door shut.

Virtue's breath caught in her throat as Roman carried her across the darkened room and deposited her on the bed. She tried to sit up, but was immediately imprisoned within his outstretched arms. He leaned over her and brought his face just inches from hers. She took in a deep breath, her lungs filling with the heady male scent of him.

"You seem to be everywhere I look," he said softly. "I want to know how you manage that, but first, just who in the hell is Prince Orlando?"

A deep crimson flush stained Virtue's pale cheeks. She would have to share with this stanger her secret vice. She lowered her head. "I read romantic novels," she confessed in an agonized whisper. "Prince Orlando is a character in one of them."

Roman's dark brows shot upward. "A vicar's daughter reads romantic novels?"

Virtue swallowed hard. "It is a sin, I know. But," she hastened to assure him, "Prince Orlando is all that is noble. He rescued Lady Estelle from an unwanted marriage to the evil moneylender."

"At the Goose and Gander you called *me* Prince Orlando. Why?"

"Because you rescued me—Mrs. Snipe, I mean— when she was trapped in the door of the chaise. I was on my way to my . . . cousin's house in London. Mrs. Snipe was acting as my chaperon. She had eaten a whole chicken, you see, and cream cakes, quite a lot of cream cakes and became ill."

The growing look of aversion on Roman's face stopped Virtue's stammering soliloquy. As he slowly straightened, she cringed, expecting him to strike her. He did not. For a long moment he merely stood staring down at her. Then he turned and walked to the far window.

Virtue immediately sat up and pulled her skirts down to a more modest level. All the while she kept her eyes trained upon Roman's broad back, now but a darkened silhouette against the gloomy skies without. What was he thinking?

Lord, thought Roman, what a travesty! At this very moment, Gillray's uncanny likeness of Miss Goodbody was being displayed in every print shop in London. If Lady Dimwitty and her ilk got wind of his engagement to this selfsame Miss Goodbody, he would be the laughingstock of the *ton,* not only for the nonce, but for as long as he lived. Damn his rotten luck!

Feeling as if he were in the midst of a bad dream, he rubbed the back of his neck. Gradually, his resentment faded. In his heart of hearts, he knew the gray-eyed mouse was not the cause of his humiliation, past or present. She was, in a most poignant way, more victim to his uncle's madness than he. His brow furrowed in concentration. What could be done to lessen the onerous sentence passed upon them both? Slowly, a solution surfaced.

The longer Roman stood before the window, the more fidgety Virtue became. The incongruity of her situation pressed in upon her. She was alone in her bedchamber with a man, a stranger, with whom she had been forced to share a shameful secret. She had no means of escape. She was, for all intents and purposes, his captive.

At the thought, a peculiar tingling sensation invaded her entire body, a sensation so pleasant that Virtue feared it must be the workings of the devil. Prayer was her only defense. Trembling, she slid off the bed and fell to her knees. " 'Give sentence with me, O God, and defend my cause against the ungodly people. O, deliver me from the deceitful and wicked man.' "

Upon hearing Virtue's lament, Roman's resentment returned with a vengeance. He turned and glared at her. "Dear God, woman, cease that god-awful caterwauling and get up."

Virtue struggled to her feet. "Sir," she said, summoning up all her courage, "you have blasphemed."

"I have done far worse, I assure you," he muttered.

He began to pace the floor, his hands clasped behind his back. "Look, Miss Goodbody. I—we—the both of us—have no choice. We must marry—each other."

He gave her a whetted look in passing. "I have been thinking. I propose we make a bargain. I will need sons—two at least—to inherit the title. After you have performed your . . . duties, I will make no further demands on you. You—and I—will then be free to pursue whatever . . . diversions we desire. I will demand discretion, of course."

He paused. "You do understand what I am proposing?"

Virtue nodded.

Anxious to get the awkward moment over with, Roman quickly queried, "Then you agree?"

Again Virtue nodded.

"Good," he exclaimed heartily. "Let us shake hands on it."

He strode over to her, his hand extended.

She offered hers.

He claimed it, a small, work-roughened hand. His fingers gently tightened, bringing his own scarred knuckles into view. Appalled, he stared down at their joining. Dear God, he thought, in a strange way Miss Goodbody and he were two of a kind.

As the door closed behind her dark prince, Virtue willed the strength back to her legs. Slowly she walked to the far window, the very window at which he had stood before.

It suddenly seemed important that she see what he had seen, on the odd notion that the shared observation could somehow accord her a greater understanding of him. She inhaled deeply of the rain-washed air and waited for enlightenment.

When none was forthcoming, she turned from the window and sought refuge in the arms of a tattered wing chair. Reluctantly, she faced reality as she knew it. Her dark prince did not love her, but would marry her. Her middle would swell with his children, once, twice or however long it took to beget the obligatory two sons. And that would be the end of it.

She sighed. The problem was, she was in love with her dark prince and half in love with Mr. Knightley. She glanced down at her hands, a glance that renewed the memory of his touch, the gentle possessive pressure of his fingers. His hands had betrayed him, as did hers. Her roughened skin had not come from plying silk threads, as his callused palms and scarred knuckles had not been gotten in a drawing room.

Virtue's gray eyes took on a sudden, speculative look. In a strange way, she thought, she and Mr. Knightley were two of a kind.

Thirteen

Is it a world to hide virtues in?
—Shakespeare

"Well, I'll be blasted. Miss Goodbody and the gray-eyed mouse are one and the same, you say?"

"I do say," Roman muttered.

The two were in Henry's chamber, to which Roman had retreated after sealing his agreement with Virtue. Henry was reclining on a moth-eaten settee and sipping a medicinal brandy, while Roman sat at the writing table finishing the last of three hastily written notes.

Folding them over, he applied a daub of wax to each, then reached for the bellpull. "There, it is done. A statement written in my own hand, advising my uncle, Sir William and Miss Combs that Miss Goodbody and I are to be married as planned."

He grunted ruefully. "After the brouhaha following her flight from my uncle's chamber, I am sure some questions exist as to the terms on which Miss Goodbody and I now stand. These missives should end the speculation once and for all."

With the benign complacency of a man engaged to marry a beauty, Henry nodded sagely. "Might be a good thing after all, Roman. Your marriage to the mouse, I mean. When Fox brought me the brandy, he stayed to have a word. Said Miss Goodbody seemed a pleasant girl."

He nodded again. "Good recommendation that, coming from a servant. Helps immensely if the underlings like their mistress. Remember my mama saying, 'Make sure the servants like you, or you'll find rodent droppings in your biscuits.' "

Ignoring Henry's household homily, Roman extracted Gillray's caricature from his jacket pocket. He studied it for a long while. Then he heaved a heavy sigh. "What a bloody day this has been. I can only hope Lady Dimwitty never finds out the girl Gillray portrayed in this drawing is my intended, Miss Goodbody. I do not think I could stand the further humiliation."

As usual, Henry chose to focus on the brighter side of the situation. "Do not let it trouble you, Roman. What is the *on-dit* of the *ton* this week is forgotten the next. Lady Dimwitty, I am sure, has other fish to fry."

"Perhaps you have the right of it, Henry."

"I know I do, old man."

Reaching behind to the drinks table, Henry snagged the brandy decanter. "I say we drink a toast to"—there was an awkward pause—"oh, hell, to anything."

Roman was more than happy to oblige.

Suzanna sat at her dressing table while Gaffe arranged her golden tresses à la Venus. As was evident by her tone, Suzanna was in a pronounced pique with her companion. "Why do you fret on about Virtue? The marriage will take place as planned. We have Mr. Knightley's word in writing. It is a *fait accompli.*"

Pouting, she pushed aside her Chinese box of colors. "I do think you would give some consideration to *me.*

My nerves are raw with worry over the prospect of my meeting with Lord Dunsby at dinner tonight."

Addressing Suzanna's reflection in the looking glass, Gaffe persisted, "But, pet, Virtue has been sequestered in her chamber for the last three hours. Why have you not spoken to her since receiving the note from Mr. Knightley?"

Suzanna's carefully darkened brows rose at the implied censure. "I saw no need of it," she replied tartly. "Mark my words, I shall have plenty to say to the brazen chit when I send for her later on."

Gaffe tried again. "But, pet, are you not anxious to know what transpired between Mr. Knightley and Virtue when they were alone in her bedchamber?"

Suzanna frowned. "I demanded to be present, and would have been had not Sir William insisted on my accompanying him back to his chamber. By the time I finished . . . administering to his imagined . . . injuries, Mr. Knightley's note was delivered."

"Do you think Mr. Knightley . . . had his way with her?"

"Nonsense!" Suzanna snapped. "Virtue's virtue remains intact. I am sure of it. Mr. Knightley's initial repulsion upon meeting her was excessive, even considering her lack of appearance. He will bed her when needed and not before. And I want no more speculation on the matter from you."

She added perversely, "Perhaps Mr. Knightley is subject to spells of madness, like the Earl. *That* might explain his excessive reaction, might it not?"

As Gaffe's eyes widened with ever-growing concern, Suzanna gave a brittle laugh. "I tease you, Gaffe. All men are a dash mad. It is the nature of the beast."

Ignoring Gaffe's dark look, Suzanna picked up the

looking glass to admire her companion's handiwork and her own slim white throat.

Virtue sat in the middle of the bed, hugging her knees to her chest. A delicious shiver ran down her spine. She was in love with Mr. Knightley!

It had been three hours since he had proposed his marital agreement, and three hours since she had accepted. In those three hours she had undergone a profound change. For the first time in her life, she had looked deep within herself and acknowledged her own "wants." She wanted to be admired. She wanted to be happy. And, above all, she wanted Mr. Knightley to love her.

That presented a problem. New as she was to the art of allurement, she had not the faintest idea of how to entice a man. Ordinarily, she would pray for guidance, but lately, she felt the answers to her prayers had taken on an oddly malicious twist.

As she pondered what path to take, a knock sounded on the door. With pounding heart, she scampered off the bed. Was it the irate Sir William? Or Suzanna? Which would be worse, a physical beating or a verbal one?

Cautiously, she opened the door. It was neither Sir William nor Suzanna. It was Rhett. He loomed over her and smiled, his teeth resembling enormous slabs of yellowed ivory. "Ahhh, Miss Virtue. Miss Combs desires your presence in her chamber immediately."

Virtue nodded, resigned to her fate. "Thank you, Rhett. I shall be there directly."

Moments later, she stood before Suzanna's bedchamber, tapping timidly upon the door.

Gaffe opened it a crack. With a furtive glance behind

her, she whispered, "Virtue, dear, are you still . . . intact?"

Misunderstanding entirely, Virtue responded in a like whisper. "Mr. Knightley was able to restrain Sir William, so you see, I am quite intact." Attributing the startled expression on Gaffe's face to a sudden attack of wind, Virtue stepped past her into the room.

Suzanna sat on the edge of a ragged wing chair, sipping wine. In a gown of brightly striped silk, she had the look of a resting butterfly. There the comparison ended.

As the baffled Gaffe resumed her seat and picked up her knitting, Suzanna proceeded to ring a peal *par excellence* over Virtue's head. Her vitriolic review of Virtue's faults came in sparsely spaced bursts that fortunately required no answers.

"You made a thorough cake of yourself this afternoon, young lady. I was mortified. You can be thankful that Knightley *has* to marry you. Any man not so obliged would have run from such a blatant show of emotion."

There was a pause while Suzanna took a refreshing sip of wine. Then: "How many times must I tell you that gentlemen admire passivity in an unmarried girl? A well-bred maiden is to show little emotion before marriage and only a little more afterward. The only sentiment truly acceptable is boredom."

Another sip of wine. Then: "Sir William was shocked by your bold actions, after all he has done to ensure your future. I can tell you, he is *most* disappointed."

The image of the "disappointed" Sir William, his fist raised to strike her, invaded Virtue's thoughts. She wondered what Mr. Knightley had said to Sir William to have caused his complexion to turn such an odd shade of green.

Someone banged upon the door, interrupting Virtue's mental meanderings. As Gaffe left her knitting to answer the summons, Sir William stormed in. His squinty eyes bulged with suppressed rage, his complexion now an odd shade of puce.

Sir William felt as tapped out as a wedding keg. First Miss Goodbody's missish behavior, then Knightley's threatening to relieve him of his manhood if he so much as touched the chit, and finally—

"La, Sir William," Suzanna trilled. "How went your meeting with the Earl? Was he pleased to receive Mr. Knightley's written reassurance?"

Sir William nodded, but said not a word. His actions spoke louder than trumpets. He headed straight for the drinks table. A pox on the Earl, he thought. The old bastard had again refused to release the incriminating papers.

A sudden supposition chilled Sir William to the very marrow of his bones. What if the Earl intended *never* to release the papers? His hand shook as he poured himself a glass of wine. He gulped it down and poured another. He had shilly-shallied long enough. It was time to enlist Suzanna's aid in the matter.

Feigning a calm air, he turned and addressed her. "I should like to discuss my meeting with the Earl *in private,* my dear."

Suzanna's answering smile was syrup smooth. "Of course, Sir William." Drat, she thought, as if she did not have enough to worry over. What did the despicable little worm want now?

"Cousin Virtue, Gaffe, would you excuse Sir William and me?"

Virtue was only too happy to be excused. As she scurried past Sir William, he caught her by the arm and snarled, "Whilst in the company of your betters, you would do well to study your cousin's behavior and learn from it, Miss Goodbody. Your shocking display of bad manners this afternoon was a disgrace to us all."

The cavernous dining room was dark and dank. The only light came from a row of flickering tallow candles that marched forlornly down the center of the long narrow table. The air smelt of ancient dust and moldering silk.

There had been no champagne toasts to the newly betrothed couple during their first dinner *en famille* and very little conversation. The metallic scrape of silver against china had the sound of clashing cymbals in the self-conscious stillness of the room.

Roman presided over the head of the table, Virtue at the other end with Lord Dunsby on her right. Suzanna, on Roman's right, faced Sir William across from her. Her positioning afforded her only an oblique view of Lord Dunsby. But it was enough.

She could scarcely take her eyes off him. While he and Virtue were remarkably similar, the same slight build, the same pale hair and gray eyes, there were enough dissimilarities afforded by gender to sidetrack the casual observer. Gaffe was right. Her secret was safe.

Everyone, it seemed, had secrets, including Sir William. It was as she had expected. The Earl had incriminating papers dealing with Sir William's shady business practices, and Sir William wanted her to search for them.

She suppressed a smile. If blackmail was good enough for an Earl, it was certainly good enough for her. If she found the papers, she would make Sir William squirm.

Henry's reflections were more benign, and rose-colored

with wine. He speared a forkful of mutton. He was pleasantly surprised. Miss Goodbody was a taking little thing, shy, but well spoken. She might even be fairly pretty if she would dress in something other than that black shroud. His Marie would not be caught dead in a getup like that, he thought proudly. The clever play on words amused him, while the thought of his Marie titillated his senses. She would arrive at the Manor in two days' time. He could hardly wait.

While Henry ruminated, Sir William fumed. Here he was, a gentleman of wealth and breeding, being forced to share a table with a crude by-blow and his bridesman. It seemed a fitting ending to a bloody awful day.

Glancing contemptuously across the table at Lord Dunsby, Sir William could scarce constrain his outrage. The man was a disgrace to his heritage! His lordship actually regarded Knightley as some sort of hero—treated him as an equal or better. How an officer and a gentleman could voluntarily associate with one who so obviously belonged to the lower classes was beyond Sir William's ken. Of course, what could one expect from a man engaged to marry a "Frenchie" slut.

Furtively, Sir William assessed the cut of Dunsby's jacket. Weston's work, by the look of it. Envy twisted within his innards. If not for his darling Suzanna and her never-ending love and support, he would go mad. He picked up his wineglass and gulped down its contents. He was drunk and getting drunker.

Roman ate and drank sparingly, his mind preoccupied with the estate. He had spent part of the afternoon on a tour of the Manor with Fox. After years of neglect by the penny-pinching Earl, the amount of repairs and refurbishing that needed doing immediately was staggering.

If the Manor was this neglected, Roman speculated, what was the condition of the land? Tomorrow he would ride out on an inspection of the farms and see to the housing conditions of the tenants.

He took a sip of wine, his eyes and attention absentmindedly straying to his intended. He would have little time for her in the next weeks, a state of affairs she would no doubt welcome, and one that he was not particularly averse to.

In a way, he felt sorry for her. She seemed scared witless of everyone at the table except Henry. As Roman watched, Henry leaned forward and whispered something to her. Whatever it was, it was amusing.

Her soft answering laugh seemed oddly familiar to Roman. His mind drifted back to his days in India. The black velvet nights, stars like a spill of diamonds, exotic noise subdued by darkness. That was it. Miss Goodbody's laugh had reminded him of temple bells stirred by a warm breeze.

From beneath her lashes, Virtue observed her husband-to-be observing her across the expanse of smudged mahogany. He had the look of a pirate about him: bronzed skin, gleaming black hair, a saturnine slant to his mouth. Yet, oddly enough she did not fear him. He was in every way but birth a gentleman.

As he glanced away, she could sense his indifference. Rather than discouraging her, his disinterest only served to strengthen her resolve. Somehow she would find a way to make him love her.

While the occupants of the house were at dinner and Gaffe walked Miss Charlotte, Rhett sneaked into Suzanna's bedchamber and secreted himself in her dressing room.

Cradling a bottle of wine in his arms, he hid behind her bathing screen and waited. As he waited, he fortified himself with frequent swigs from the bottle. Dutch courage was what was needed when dealing with the likes of The Slut. Too bad he hadn't brought along a spare.

The evening ended early. The gentlemen decided to forgo their port and join the ladies in the drawing room. A cup of weak tea was drunk, strained bits of conversation exchanged, and that was the end of it.

Suzanna was in her bedchamber at nine, fatigued from a day filled with tension and turmoil. She sat at her toilet table while Gaffe brushed her hair, and smiled at Gaffe's reflection. "As always, dear Gaffe, you were right in your assumptions. Although Lord Dunsby and Virtue are similar in stature and coloring, they are not *that* alike. We have nothing to fear. Our little secret is safe."

"How did you find Lord Dunsby?"

"Dull as dishwater. He seemed to find Virtue amusing, so you can imagine the level of his sophistication. All in all, however, the evening was not as distressing as I had feared. Though the food was atrocious, the wine was superb. Knightley was preoccupied, and Lord William got disgustingly drunk."

Gaffe waited. When nothing more was forthcoming, she prompted, "And Virtue?"

Suzanna made a moue. "She did well enough. After her atrocious behavior this afternoon, it was the least the silly chit could do."

Suzanna turned slightly and perked up her ears. "What

was that noise, Gaffe? I think it came from the dressing room."

"Sounds to me like the bathing screen has been tipped over. Rats, I should imagine. I shall have it right in no time."

Suiting action to words, Gaffe hurried to the dressing-room door. Before she could reach it, it was flung open by an unseen hand. As she reared back in fright, Rhett made a dramatic entrance.

Suzanna came out of her chair, green eyes blazing. "What were you doing in my dressing room? I command you to leave at once, or I shall scream for help."

Rhett sneered and strolled over to a wing chair. He sat down and nonchalantly crossed his legs. "You"—he snapped his fingers at Gaffe—"get me wine!"

He turned to Suzanna. "And you, m'lady, do not scream if you know what is good for you. You would not want anyone else to learn of your secrets, now would you?"

Suzanna's chin lifted defiantly. "I do not know what you are talking about," she brazened.

Rhett's left brow rose. "Do you not, m'lady? Then let me refresh your memory. You are *Mrs.* Goodbody, the widow of Vicar Goodbody. Miss Goodbody is not your cousin, she is your daughter. But not by the good vicar. Miss Goodbody's father was old Lord Dunsby, which makes her half sister to the current Lord Dunsby.

"Now"—he paused for effect—"have I forgotten anything? We could speculate upon your true age, m'lady, but I think you would prefer not."

Suzanna exhaled the breath she had been holding and gamely accepted her fate. "Get the wine, Gaffe," she said.

Fourteen

For 'tis some virtue, virtue to commend.
—Congreve

Virtue awoke the next day bent on finding ways to entice Mr. Knightley. After morning prayers she took inventory of her assets. The list was woefully deficient. She could no longer count the art of redemption to her credit—the failure to redeem Suzanna still weighed heavily on her mind—which left only her considerable skill at housewifery to recommend her. If only she knew more of Mr. Knightley's likes and dislikes . . .

A thought struck her: Mr. Knightley loved the Manor. If she took it upon herself to see that it was cleaned and properly run, some of that love might rub off on her. She would consult with Fox immediately about hiring a few strong girls from the village to help.

She hurried from her chamber and down the main staircase, taking note as she went of the dirt that needed removing and the number of hands it would take to do the job. It seemed a daunting task, but she would do her best.

As she swept past the open door of the breakfast room, the aroma of scorched coffee and burnt bread wafted on the air. A voice called out, "Miss Goodbody?"

Virtue stopped in her tracks and peered around the

doorjamb. Lord Dunsby sat at the breakfast table, an empty cup and a plate of burnt crumbs pushed off to one side.

"You are an early riser, Miss Goodbody. Come and join me."

Virtue entered the room, telling herself that this encounter with his lordship was yet another instance of God's handiwork. She had wanted to find out more of Mr. Knightley's likes and dislikes, and what better source than his friend and bridesman, Lord Dunsby?

His lordship rose and held a chair for her. When she was seated, he poured a cup of coffee and placed it before her. "Liquid swill, if you ask me," he commented, "but at least it's hot." He resumed his seat and smiled across to her. "Where were you off to so early and in such a hurry?"

Unused to such kind attention from a gentleman—or anyone else—yet feeling oddly at ease in his lordship's presence, Virtue took a sip of her coffee. Grimacing, she set the cup down on its saucer. "I was on my way to the butler's pantry to seek out Fox. I had hoped to make arrangements to begin a thorough cleaning of the Manor."

"Bit late on that," Henry guffawed. "Roman hired a full staff from London, including a Scottish housekeeper and a top-notch cook. They arrive today with Perkins, Roman's valet."

Virtue was crestfallen. Housewifery was her *only* ability. Without thinking, she blurted out, "But then, what am *I* to do?"

"Do?" Henry questioned. He frowned, then brightened. "Roman is off seeing to the estate and will not be back until late. I am at loose ends. We could spend the day together."

* * *

Suzanna had not slept a wink the entire night, so distraught was she over Rhett's blackmailing scheme. If he revealed what he knew, all her plans for the future would collapse.

Fortunately, she had had enough money on her person to ensure the scoundrel's silence for the first week; the diamond necklace should suffice for a second, but after that she would have nothing. As she paced her chamber, searching for a solution, a knock sounded on the door.

She called, "Enter," and a frazzled-looking Fox appeared. He bowed. "Beg pardon for disturbing you at this early hour, madame, but the Earl insists that you come to him at once. The medication you mixed for him has made him feel so much better that he is demanding stronger doses to be administered several times a day."

To Suzanna, it was a sudden light at the end of a dark tunnel. An augmented schedule of medication meant she would have more time to search the Earl's bedchamber for the papers incriminating Sir William in nefarious doings. If she could find them, she could use them to blackmail her spineless lover for the amount Rhett demanded, and a bit more besides.

"That is good news indeed." She paused. "Is something wrong, Fox?"

He shook his head. "It is the Earl, madame. He is very restless this morning. Several times, in his sleep, he called out for a woman named Kitty."

Suzanna's eyes narrowed. In '06, the then Honorable Sir Arthur Wellesley, K.B., had married Lord Longford's daughter, Lady Catherine "Kitty" Pakenham. That must be the "Kitty" the Earl referred to. Was the Earl on the verge of lapsing into the Duke of Wellington's persona?

"I shall see to the Earl at once, Fox," she said crisply. "Please make certain that we are not disturbed."

"Very good, madame."

After Fox left, Suzanna filled a large bottle with "medicine" and hurried to the Earl's chamber.

She found him sitting up in bed, his new nightshirt crumpled and tea stained. He frowned at her. "Who are you, madame, and what do you want?"

Suzanna curtsied. "I am Miss Combs, your lordship, Miss *Kitty* Combs. I have come to give you the medication you requested."

She went to a side table and filled a large tumbler to the brim with the amber liquid. She was gradually eliminating the foxglove tea and increasing the brandy.

Carefully balancing the tumbler, she walked slowly to the Earl's bedside. He watched her every move, his eyes fever-bright. "Kitty?" he questioned softly.

Still staring at her face, he accepted the tumbler and took a large gulp. He regarded the liquid remaining as if it were molten gold. "Tell me, Kitty, what does this nectar of the gods contain?"

Suzanna smiled modestly and took a seat at his bedside. "It is my own concoction, your lordship, made from honey, boiled bark and herbs that I pick from Cook's kitchen garden. Simple ingredients, I assure you. It is the quantity and commingling of each that renders the finished brew so efficacious."

As the Earl finished off the contents of the tumbler, Suzanna rose and took his empty glass, making sure their fingers brushed in the process. The Earl sighed and settled down in bed, drawing the coverlet up to his chin. Already he could feel the medicinal effects of the pleasant-tasting potion. He felt warm and sleepy yet strangely . . . revitalized.

"You are an angel, my darling Kitty," he whispered to Suzanna. His eyelids fluttered closed.

Suzanna busied herself with straightening the bed-covers until a series of gentle snores emanated from the Earl. With one eye on her patient, she went quickly to the large oak desk in the corner and eased open a deep drawer. It was stuffed to the brim with papers. She rifled through them, her hands as steady as a pickpocket's.

There was nothing of importance to be found among them. Paid bills for the most part: a tailor's bill that was dated twenty years before. Good Lord, if the man saved everything from the past, she would need the devil's own luck to find—

Her hand encountered a leather sack at the bottom of the drawer. It was filled with coins. Quickly, she loosened the drawstring at the mouth of the sack. As it gaped open, a glimmer of gold greeted her. The bag was stuffed with guineas!

What a stroke of luck! She could use the money to meet the weekly disbursement to Rhett. Her eyes narrowed with anger. Not that she intended to remain under that blackguard's thumb for long. She would find a way to rid herself of him, *and* his threats.

Suddenly, the Earl groaned.

Startled, Suzanna quietly shut the drawer and hurried to his bedside. He appeared caught in the midst of a bad dream. He thrashed about on the bed, tossing his head from side to side. Groaning incessantly, he threw off his coverlet. After a bit, he quieted.

Suzanna had begun to back away toward the desk when the Earl spoke, his voice crisp and resonant in the stillness of the room. "I tell you, gentlemen, we must advance on the enemy no matter what the odds. I shall lead the men myself. Where is my aide-de-camp? I have need of my baton!"

As Suzanna stared, his lordship's manhood stirred mightily beneath his nightshirt. Her eyes widened in awe at the magnificent display. Quickly, she removed the lace tucker from the neckline of her low-cut bodice, leaned over and shook the Earl by the shoulder.

"Are you all right, my love? It is I, your Kitty, here to assist you."

The Earl opened his eyes to a bountiful display of womanly charms. He licked his dry lips. "I must lead my men into battle."

It was said, Suzanna noted, without too much enthusiasm.

"Of course you must, my love," she soothed him, "but first, let your Kitty comfort you."

Under "Kitty's" skillful comforting, the Earl lapsed completely. Not once, but twice.

The sun was warm; a pleasant breeze blew. How wonderful it was, Virtue thought, to enjoy a day without a list of must-do chores to complete.

She and Henry strolled comfortably side by side down a twisting path that led to a dilapidated folly at the edge of a large pond. Henry was in a loquacious mood, waxing eloquently over the perfection of his bride-to-be.

"Marie will arrive tomorrow by late afternoon, Miss Goodbody. I want you to be the first to meet her. You will find that her goodness and generosity equals, if not exceeds, her charm and beauty."

Although envy was a sin, Virtue envied Marie de Chalfant. *If only,* she thought, *Mr. Knightley would think and speak of me with such love and admiration.*

When Henry finally wound down on the subject of his Marie, she asked timidly, "I hope you do not think me forward, Lord Dunsby, but would you speak to me of Mr. Knightley? You see, I know so little of him. . . ."

Henry beamed a fond smile at her. "Not forward at all, my dear. Only fitting that a bride should want to know about her husband-to-be." There was an awkward pause. "You have been told about his . . . unfortunate birth?"

When Virtue nodded, the visibly relieved Henry grunted. "Good then, I can tell you the rest."

Mesmerized, Virtue listened as Henry related the story of Mr. Knightley's life. Though a by-blow, he had spent his first eight years as an Earl's son, catered to and spoiled by an indulgent father and devoted servants.

Mr. Knightley's destiny had changed drastically, however, when his father died suddenly and the present Earl came into the title.

Virtue tried to imagine her self-assured dark prince as a little boy, grieving over his father's death, being banished to the stables by his cruel uncle.

"For four years," Henry continued, "Roman was beaten and half-starved and made to work long hours. Finally, he could take no more. He ran away and joined the Gypsies. His mother had since died, but her people were happy to have him."

Henry chuckled indulgently. "It was during the years he spent with the Gypsy caravan that Roman perfected his uncanny skill with the devil's books."

Virtue quailed in fright. "The devil's books?" she gasped.

Henry reddened. "Beg your pardon, Miss Goodbody. I didn't mean to alarm you. I should have said 'cards.' Whilst in the army, Roman made a fortune playing cards, not that he was a Greek—a card sharper—or anything. He played fair and square. Invested his winnings in the 'Change when he returned to England. I tell you, he's a genius when it comes to speculation. He made himself a tidy fortune."

Puffed with pride over his friend's accomplishments, Henry bragged, "Roman don't need his uncle's money, it's the Manor he wants. He has plans for Bentwood, let me tell you."

He gave a profound nod. "All men feel strongly about their heritage, and Roman's no exception—even though he was born on the wrong side of the blankets."

Henry's cheeks went from red to scarlet. "Beg your pardon again, Miss Goodbody. I shouldn't be saying things like that to a lady, but hang it all, if I don't feel like I've known you all my life."

Virtue reached out and took his arm. "I feel the same way about you, Lord Dunsby, which is very unusual for me. I am plagued with shyness."

Henry patted her hand. "It's all right to be shy. Kind of nice, in fact."

They rested for a while on a fallen stone, pensive, engrossed in their own reflections. Virtue compared her childhood to that of Mr. Knightley's. Although her early years had not been as injurious as his, they did share many similarities. Was it not strange, she thought, how their respective hands divulged their solitary hardships?

Strange, too, that in spite of all the privations in Mr. Knightley's life, he had remained a gentle man. He had even saved her from Sir William's wrath.

At the thought, Virtue's love for Mr. Knightley swelled to an almost unbearable level. His irregular birth, the fact that he had served as a common soldier and had made his fortune with cards, now meant nothing to her. She was in love.

Presently, Henry mused aloud, "Roman saved my life once, you know. Took a hatchet in his— Well, he took a hatchet meant for my head. I would do anything for Roman. Anything at all."

He turned and smiled at Virtue. "And I would do anything for you, too, Miss Goodbody. You have only to ask."

The afternoon sun was sinking low in the sky when Roman rode his black stallion up the Manor's curving drive. He was angered and appalled at the conditions under which the tenant farmers were forced to live. Their dwellings had leaking roofs and broken windows; their wives and children were ill fed and sick from neglect. Not a penny had been spent on their welfare for years.

Damn his uncle for the tight-fisted ogre that he was! Swearing on his honor that the tenants would be his first priority, Roman rounded the last bend in the drive.

Fox had assembled the new staff on the broad steps of the Manor to greet their master. Like the parting of the Red Sea, two lines of servants stood in facing rows, all shined shoes, brushed trousers and crisp white aprons.

As Roman swung from the saddle, Fox came down the steps to meet him. "May I present the staff, sir?"

Roman handed the reins to a waiting groom. "Very good, Fox." Slapping his riding crop against his thigh, he followed the butler through a gauntlet of curtsies and bows.

Fox rattled off the servants' names and positions as they passed. The burly new housekeeper, a Mrs. Mac-Gregor by name, greatly resembled a sergeant of Roman's acquaintance. He would hate to meet either one of them in a dark alley.

Once in the entrance hall, Roman surrendered his hat and gloves to a waiting footman and started up the staircase. Already there were signs that the massive renovation of the Manor he had ordered was under way. Carpets had been removed for cleaning, the dome of the rotunda boasted a skeleton of scaffolding, and the air was redolent with the essence of beeswax.

Satisfied, Roman hastened his steps. With a decent cook installed in the kitchen, there was a better than good chance of getting a tasty meal for a change. And Perkins—if he knew what was good for him—would have a hot bath waiting, as well as a brandy and a change of clothes.

The long hallway was deep in shadows. Roman's boots made a hollow sound on the dirt-encrusted flooring. Suddenly, the hair on the back of his neck rose. A vigilant sixth sense told him that something or someone was in back of him. Cautiously, he slowed his pace. And then, quickly, he leaped to one side and whirled around. A knife appeared in his right hand, poised to strike.

There came a sudden laugh, and a tall gaunt figure stepped from the cover of a shadowed alcove. A deep voice called out. "Well done, Sergeant Major Knightley. I see the interlude between battles has not dulled your senses."

Roman stared, not believing his eyes. It was the Earl, yet it was not the Earl. There was an easy confidence about the man who stood before him, an air of command that was uncannily reminiscent of the Duke of Wellington.

The correct response to army authority was deeply entrenched in Roman's being. Without conscious thought, he snapped to attention.

"At ease, Sergeant Major. I shall see you at dinner, and tomorrow I will want a full report on your assessment of the surrounding territory. We have routed the Frenchies for now, but as commander, I must continue to be cautious."

With a friendly nod, the Earl turned and marched to his bedchamber.

Fifteen

Change in a thrice
The lilies and languors of virtue
For the raptures and roses of vice.
                              —Swinburne

As Roman stared after the Earl's retreating figure, Suzanna stepped from the shadows just a short distance from where Roman stood.

"Mr. Knightley," she said. "We must talk. There is a small sitting room next to the Earl's bedchamber. Sir William awaits us there. If you will follow me?"

Without waiting for an answer, she turned and nonchalantly strolled off, her pale skirts swaying like a beckoning lantern in the dimness.

Feeling as if he had wandered into someone else's bad dream, Roman obediently followed.

Suzanna knocked softly on the door to the Earl's sitting room. Without waiting for an acknowledgment, she entered, gesturing for Roman to do the same.

The small sitting room was as bleak as the rest of the Manor. Sir William, the chamber's only occupant, sat slumped upon a shabby silk sofa. Glaring at Roman, he used the sofa's arm for leverage and got unsteadily to his feet. He swayed slightly.

"About time you showed up, Knightley. You should

have been here, tending to your duties instead of racketing about the countryside. Miss Combs has had to bear the brunt of your mad uncle's delusions for the entire day."

His slurred speech and cock-of-the-walk attitude attested to the obvious. Sir William was pathetically drunk.

Roman brushed past him, not affording him a second glance. "I am sure, Sir William, that Miss Combs has found comfort from your *temperate* presence. Pray resume your seat—before you fall."

With a muttered oath, Sir William flopped down, leaned back and closed his eyes. Suzanna took a seat next to Sir William and, in an oddly maternal fashion, commenced patting his arm.

As Roman lowered his lanky frame between the arms of a ratty-looking wing chair, he surreptitiously studied Miss Combs. There was something about her that he did not trust. She seemed oddly composed for a woman who had spent the day being subjected to a madman's delusions.

Since Sir William had nodded off, Roman addressed his questions to her. Stretching out his long legs, he inquired crisply, "Tell me, Miss Combs, the events that led up to the Earl's lapse."

Suzanna stared off into space, one slender hand caressing her throat. She smiled dreamily. "The Earl summoned me to his chamber in the early morning. The medication I had been giving him for several days had proven so effective that he wished for more."

A small alarm sounded in the back of Roman's mind. "And what exactly is in this wondrous remedy, Miss Combs?" he asked.

Suzanna had anticipated the question. With uncanny foresight, she had had Gaffe boil up a quantity of bark with an infusion of bitter herbs, then strain the disgusting mess into a large bottle. Gracefully waving her hand, she indicated the small table next to Roman's chair. "I brought a bottle with me. It is there. You may taste it if you like. It will do you no harm."

She watched warily as Roman uncorked the bottle and took a sniff. She hoped he would leave it at that, as she had no idea if the brew were poisonous or not.

Roman grimaced in disgust. The evil-looking liquid smelled like a dank cave. He replaced the cork, set the bottle down and resumed his questioning. "It was after the Earl drank the potion, then, that his transformation took place?"

Relieved that he had not tasted it, Suzanna shook her golden head. "Actually, it was before. Fox was the first to notice. He said the Earl was very restless, frequently calling out the name 'Kitty' in his sleep.

"I also noted the Earl's restlessness when I went to tend him," she added. "After I gave him his medication, he slept, drifting into what I took to be a bad dream. He was very agitated, talked of 'leading his men into battle.' It was then I realized the Earl was lapsing into the Duke of Wellington's persona. When he awoke, he was convinced that I was his wife, the former Kitty Pakenham, the woman the Duke loved and eventually married."

"I found it curious that my uncle referred to me as *Sergeant Major* Knightley and was under the impression that I had been out on reconnaissance," Roman mused more or less to himself.

"I fear I am responsible for distorting the truth to fit the situation, Mr. Knightley," Suzanna confessed coyly. "The Earl was determined to leave his bed and lead his men into battle. To quiet him, I told him that the French had been routed, and that you were on reconnaissance to see that all remained calm."

"Levelheaded thinking, Miss Combs. You would make a good commander."

Suzanna blushed prettily. "The Duke of Wellington is an exemplary figure, and the Earl has assumed all of his fine qualities. As such, I feel it is an honor to protect and . . . comfort his lordship when he is in the throes of his fantasies."

"It is very good of you to nurse my uncle, Miss Combs. But what of your . . . sensibilities? You were alone with his lordship for an entire day. In his present state, I trust that he behaved as a gentleman?"

In Suzanna's book, any man who took his weight on his elbows was a gentleman. She thought of the hours she and the Duke had spent together in blissful embrace. Smiling sweetly, she replied, "The Duke was in every way a perfect gentleman."

"Damn it, Perkins," Roman growled, "you are strangling me with my own neckcloth."

Perkins sniffed and cast a contemptuous glance around his master's bedchamber. "Beg pardon, sir, but if I may say, sir, the accommodations are not what I am used to."

Henry chuckled from the depths of a moth-eaten sofa where he was enjoying a snifter of the Manor's fine brandy. "You can't blame your creased cravat on Perkins, Roman. You ain't stayed still for a moment. You're jumping about like a flea on a Frenchman."

"What in hell do you expect?" Roman growled back, slipping his arms into the black worsted jacket held up by the put-upon Perkins. "We are about to enter into a bizarre charade. My uncle thinks he is the Duke of Wellington, and to keep him in this longed-for state of mind, we must all pretend to be something we are not."

Henry held his brandy glass up to the candlelight to warm its contents. "Marie arrives tomorrow," he mused, *à propos* of nothing. "Can't wait for her to meet Miss Goodbody."

Staring into the amber liquid, he observed, "Your intended is a taking little thing, Roman. Had a very pleasant walk with her this morning."

"It was good of you to spend your morning with Miss Goodbody, Henry," Roman declared stiffly as he suffered through a last-minute inspection by Perkins. "I appreciate the effort."

In not-so-mock dudgeon, Henry retorted, "Wasn't any *effort* on my part. I *enjoyed* Miss Goodbody's company."

"That is because *you* do not have to marry her," Roman snapped.

He immediately regretted his words. He had not given Miss Goodbody a thought all day, yet in a month's time they would share a bed, create children together. . . .

Ashamed of himself, he gulped down the last of his brandy and clapped Henry on the shoulder. "Forgive my bad humor, old friend. I think it is time I take myself to the drawing room."

Henry rose to his feet, but Roman waved him back down. "Stay and finish your brandy. Join me later." He added wryly, "As 'Sergeant Major,' it is *my* duty, not yours, to ensure that the accommodations are in order for the 'Duke's' pleasure."

Suzanna felt as transformed as the Earl. The "Duke" was a strong and enthusiastic lover. She had never been so fulfilled, so happy.

Sir William was neither fulfilled nor happy. The more he thought of Suzanna spending so much time alone with the Earl, the more jealous he became. "I do not like it," he hissed at her. "The Earl believes you are his lawful wife. What if he—as the Duke—demands his conjugal rights?"

Under Gaffe's ever-watchful eye, Suzanna caressed Sir William's withered cheek. "You need not worry on that score, my darling. Unlike you, the Earl is a sick old man, well past his prime. I can assure you that not the slightest instance of intimacy took place between us whilst I was in his chamber."

Sir William had sobered up from his drinking bout of the afternoon, but his head continued to throb painfully. Suzanna *was* adroit at avoiding intimate situations, he thought fuzzily. It had been days since they had made love.

She was also adroit at following Sir William's circumscribed mental processes. She sighed tragically. "This role-playing is so arduous for me, my darling. Although I fear for my own sanity, the thought of what I can accomplish for you gives me the strength to go on."

Sir William perked up. "Have you searched yet for the papers?"

Suzanna, having found the guineas, had decided she would have no need to blackmail Sir William and was in no hurry to search for anything. She wanted to spend her time making love to the Duke, and she wanted Sir William out of the way. To accomplish her objectives she had concocted a clever plan.

She sighed heavily. "I search every free moment I have, my love, but as yet have found nothing. I am worried. The Earl has asked me repeatedly who you are, and what you are doing at the Manor. To explain your presence, I told him that you are a secret agent working for the English."

Bleary-eyed, Sir William stared at his beloved. "A secret agent?"

"Yes, my dear. You must represent yourself to the Earl as such. Tell him that he has documents you are charged with taking directly to the King. You should have the papers you so desperately desire in a matter of days."

A lump formed in Sir William's throat. His eyes misted over with tears. "You are an angel, my darling. You think of everything. Tonight, after dinner, come to my chamber. It has been so long."

Suzanna sighed as if the weight of the world were on her slender shoulders. "I fear I cannot. The Duke will take dinner *en famille* tonight. And afterward, he wishes me to . . . read him to sleep."

"I do not like it," Sir William began again.

Suzanna quickly rose, took Sir William's arm and led him to the door. After she had suffered through his frantic embrace, she whispered, "Remember, my darling, everything I do, I do for you."

The drawing room had undergone a significant change. The chamber had been aired, the furniture polished; and an excess of candles, wax not tallow, provided more than adequate light.

Virtue noticed little of the improvements. The moment she entered the room, her eyes fastened on Mr. Knightley and refused to budge.

Unaware of her entrance, he stood with one arm propped against the mantelpiece, staring down at the crackling fire.

At the sight of him, Virtue's heart pounded in her

breast, her mouth went dry. He was so handsome. His sun-warmed skin showed flawless against the crisp white linen of his impeccably tied neckcloth. She longed to go to him, to stand by his side as was her right.

Suddenly conscious of her presence, Roman looked up. Flustered, Virtue immediately lowered her head.

Dear God, he thought, she reacts to my glance like a dying plant. He sighed heavily. At least she wasn't wearing that ludicrous black bonnet. Forcing a smile to his face, he sauntered toward her.

"Good evening, Miss Goodbody. I understand you had a pleasant walk this morning with Lord Dunsby."

Head still bowed, Virtue bit her lip and nodded. "Yes, it was most pleasant."

"You have heard that the Earl has lapsed, have you not?"

Again Virtue nodded. "I have prayed for the Earl—for the Duke, that is—in his . . . in *their* time of affliction." She trembled slightly. "It is most confusing."

"Indeed it is."

There followed a painful excess of silence. Roman frantically sought subjects suitable to discuss with a dying plant, but found none. If only Miss Goodbody would look at him.

Annoyed, and without thinking, he took her pointed little chin in the palm of his hand and nudged it upward. She quailed at his touch; her head lifted reluctantly.

He saw a flash of gray from beneath dark lashes. Was it the gray of mist or sullen skies? he wondered.

He continued his scrutiny. Her skin was fine and white, like a spill of cream. Her lips, though pale, were full and had a tender look to them. Of its own volition, his finger lightly brushed across their ripeness. A sudden rush of pink flooded her cheeks.

Had his touch done that? As Roman stared in wonder, an odd thing happened to his heart. It began to ache with longing—longing for things that might have been—that *should* have been, for things he was not quite sure existed.

Slowly he released her chin. His hand dropped to his side. He was about to say, "Forgive me," when a spate of voices could be heard coming from the hallway.

The door swung open and Fox entered. His gait was sprightly. For once he could make a presentation without fear of interruption from the Earl. In resonant tones, he announced, "May I present His Grace, the Duke of Wellington, and Her Grace, the Duchess of Wellington."

The Earl and Suzanna made their entrance. She wore a gown of pale pink silk with a froth of blond lace trimming the low-cut neckline. She looked flushed and strangely happy.

Virtue stared in amazement at the Earl. As the Duke, his was a prepossessing presence. He was tall and gaunt and tired-looking, but his lined face now reflected the Duke's kind disposition rather than the Earl's nasty nature.

His dark worsted jacket, though of a cut popular twenty years before, was brushed and pressed to perfection.

With Suzanna on his arm, the Duke advanced into the room. He smiled at Virtue. "And who is this young lady? And why the somber gown?"

"It is my cousin, Miss Virtue Goodbody, Your Grace," Suzanna supplied. "She and Sergeant Major Knightley are to be married as soon as she is out of mourning for her father."

"Marriage is a good thing," the Duke pronounced,

looking adoringly at Suzanna. "I do not know what I would do without my dearest wife to guide me."

As Suzanna managed to look demure, the Duke turned his attention to Roman. In a stage whisper, he counseled, "Sergeant Major Knightley, a bit of advice. When you are a married man, buy your wife some pretty gowns and geegaws. Never mind the expense. Ladies like that sort of thing."

"I shall do that, Your Grace."

From the doorway, Fox once more intoned, "Lord Dunsby and Sir William Rushmore."

Henry and Sir William, both dressed to the nines, bowed and entered the room.

As they approached the Duke, he cocked his head to one side. "Lord Dunsby? You must be related to Miss Goodbody. I swear you two are as alike as two peas in a pod. Brother and sister, what?"

Suzanna's startled expression went unnoticed as Henry sputtered, "No, Your Grace. Not that I wouldn't be proud to have Miss Goodbody for my sister, or anything else for that matter."

"Ahhh," said the Duke. "You are sweet on her too, are you?" He rolled his eyes at Roman. "Look to your flanks, Knightley. I think Lord Dunsby would like to encroach on your territory."

In the midst of the embarrassed lull that followed, Sir William stepped forward. Suzanna turned and whispered something in the Duke's ear.

The Duke's demeanor grew grave. "Sir William, we must talk. Tomorrow I shall be in my tent going over battle plans for most of the morning. See my aide-de-camp for a time convenient to us both."

Sir William bowed, his face like Black Friday. "Very good, Your Grace."

In a loud aside to Roman, the Duke cautioned. "Keep close watch on Sir William. I do not like the look of the man. He is not to be trusted. His eyes are too close together."

Business concluded, the Duke rubbed his hands together. "Now then," he said, "let us go in to dinner."

Sixteen

What is a weed? A plant whose virtues have not been discovered.

—Emerson

Early the following morning, Gaffe took her workbag and sought out Virtue's company. She found her in her bedchamber, completing her toilette.

Settling comfortably into a wing chair, Gaffe picked up her knitting needles. "Now, tell me everything about last evening, Virtue dear. I have been bothered beyond all, wondering how it went."

With brows elevated in surprise, Virtue turned from the looking glass. "Did not Cousin Suzanna enlighten you?"

Gaffe pursed her lips. "She was summoned just past dawn to tend to the Duke. She barely had time to say a word."

Virtue turned back to the glass. She smiled at her reflection. "I do not like to boast, Gaffe, but I think my attempt at redeeming Cousin Suzanna is at last bearing fruit. Who would have thought her capable of such self-less allegiance? I am certain that it is her devotion—and her herbal remedies—that are responsible for the Earl's lapse."

Gaffe bent her head over her knitting to hide her look

of concern. Virtue was so naive and innocent. The truth of her birth, and of "cousin" Suzanna's connection to it, must be kept from her at all costs.

Virtue sighed with pleasure. "Oh, Gaffe, it was such a festive evening. The food was superb, and the Earl—as the Duke—was so kind and pleasant. We will all benefit from his improved temperament."

Some more than others, Gaffe thought, thinking again of Suzanna. She turned her knitting and began to purl a row. "What of Mr. Knightley? she asked. "How did he behave?"

With bittersweet recall, Virtue relived the feel of Mr. Knightley's fingers brushing against her lips. During those brief moments, time had stood still; her senses had soared with longing.

She frowned, remembering how quickly her euphoria had faded. Save for that instance of interest, it had been apparent that Mr. Knightley had forgotten her completely. He had treated her with polite indifference for the rest of the evening.

"Virtue?" Gaffe prompted. "I asked about Mr. Knightley's behavior."

"Oh, yes, Mr. Knightley. I sensed a warming in his manner toward the Duke as the evening wore on. But then, who could not like and admire such an honorable man?"

"And Sir William? How did he react to the Earl's unaccustomed good humor?"

"Sir William was not feeling quite the thing," Virtue replied carefully. "He excused himself during dinner and was helped—that is, he retired—to his chamber."

"Drunk as a lord," Gaffe translated under her breath. She was not surprised. Sir William was not the first of Suzanna's lovers to drink himself senseless.

Virtue rose from the dressing table, shook down her

skirts and reached for her bonnet. "I almost forgot. The most amusing thing happened early on in the evening. The Duke remarked that he was sure Lord Dunsby and I were related. Brother and sister, he thought. Is that not amusing, Gaffe?"

Gaffe's eyes crossed over her knitting. Out of the mouths of babes and Bedlamites, she thought. Recovering enough to speak, she inquired sharply, "Where are you off to so early? Not walking with Lord Dunsby again?"

Virtue laughed softly. "Not *with* Lord Dunsby, but *for* Lord Dunsby. Yesterday, during our walk, we came upon a field of wildflowers. I offered to make nosegays to brighten Miss de Chalfant's chamber. She arrives at the Manor this afternoon. She will stay for three weeks before proceeding to London to purchase her brideclothes."

Swinging the dreadful black bonnet by its limp strings, Virtue coaxed, "It is a beautiful morning, Gaffe. Would you care to come with me?"

Gaffe managed a wan smile. "No, my dear. You run along."

With worried eyes, she watched Virtue take her leave. Rest and exercise had placed a touch of color in the girl's cheeks, and good food had added a spring in her walk. Or was that Lord Dunsby's doing?

Fox awaited Roman outside the Earl's bedchamber. "His Grace is ready to receive you, Sergeant Major."

"Then there has been no change in the Earl's condition since last evening?"

"None, sir," Fox stated happily. "Miss Combs gave his lordship his medication very early this morning. After a long and restful sleep, the Earl awoke still convinced he is the Duke of Wellington."

Fox hesitated. "If I may say, sir, aside from the fact that his lordship refers to me as his 'batboy,' he is—as the Duke—a pleasure to serve. So kind and accommodating."

Roman grinned. "Do not worry, Fox. I shall do nothing to change matters. I, too, find the 'Duke' more pleasant to deal with than the Earl."

Nodding in relief, Fox knocked upon the door of the Earl's chamber. A strong voice called out, "Enter."

Roman did as he was bid, his eyes widening as he stepped over the threshold. A large space in the center of the room had been rigged up as a tent. Canvas had been placed over the four-poster and extended for ten feet in all directions.

Beneath the canvas canopy, the Earl, fully dressed, including his boots, sat cross-legged at the head of the bed.

He looked up from a sheath of papers he was shuffling through. "Ahhh, Sergeant Major. Do not stand on ceremony. Join me." He indicated the foot of the bed.

Roman obligingly climbed aboard. The only way to sit comfortably was cross-legged. The Earl waited until Roman had folded his legs under him, then demanded, "Your report, Sergeant Major?"

"I have good news, sir. There is no sign of the French. They have fled to a man."

"Good news indeed, Sergeant Major. You feel then that we can relax our guard?"

"Within reason, sir."

Roman hesitated. "However, there *is* a matter of concern which I would like to bring to Your Grace's attention."

"Out with it, man. As field marshal, I must know all the facts."

Roman knew from experience that Wellington had always struggled hard to improve the conditions under which his soldiers lived and worked. He had shown the same compassion for the innocent civilians whose lives had been shattered by circumstances they could neither control nor understand. Would the Earl be of like concern? Roman decided to try him out.

"It is the peasant farmers, sir. They are casualties of the war as much as our brave soldiers. Their homes were partially destroyed by artillery; there is little food."

The Earl's brow knit into a ferocious frown. "It is always like this in wartime, Sergeant Major. The innocent civilians suffer. We must offer our help."

"If I may make a suggestion, sir. With the lull in hostilities, I will have time to remedy the situation. May I have your permission to pursue the mission?"

"Of course, Sergeant Major. Spare no expense to right the wrongs of battle."

Unfolding his legs, Roman got to his feet. "If there is nothing more, Your Grace, I shall begin immediately. Permission to be excused, sir?"

"Permission granted, Sergeant Major. But, before you go . . . I was thinking. The men have fought long and hard. We should do something to boost their morale." The Earl stared off into space. "Some singing and music in the evenings, perhaps attendance at some of the local assemblies. I shall ask the Duchess for her thoughts on the matter."

"Yes, sir."

Roman saluted, did an about-face and marched from the room. Bloody hell, he thought, as he strode down the hallway. An entrance into local society at this time would be a disaster. Could he possibly introduce the *present* Earl of Larchmont and Miss Combs as the Duke and Duchess of Wellington and still retain any credence as the *next* Earl of Larchmont? He thought not.

There was another reason Roman was loath to mingle

with the locals, one that he was chagrined to admit, even to himself. He was ashamed of Miss Goodbody's appearance. Why must she be so plain?

He took a deep breath and sighed. His steps slowed as he recalled the feel of her pointed little chin resting in the palm of his hand. In spite of her plainness, damned if there was not something about the gray-eyed mouse that tugged at his heartstrings.

He had just started down the main staircase when yet another problem reared its ugly head, one that stopped him in midstep. Freemantle Hall was the nearest neighbor to the Manor, which meant the Freemantles and their guests would be in attendance at all the local assemblies.

Lady Freemantle was a notorious gossip, almost on a par with Lady Dimwitty. Roman's blood suddenly froze in his veins. Were not the two well acquainted?

Dear God! What if Lady Dimwitty came to the country and decided to carry on her vendetta against him? The thought of her meeting with Miss Goodbody brought a wave of despair crashing over him.

Bloody hell! he thought again. What was he thinking? The Earl forgot things as quickly as he thought of them. There was little chance that anything would come of his sudden yearning for amusement.

Roman quickened his pace. He had starving tenants to feed and house, neglected fields to cultivate, and a run-down manor house to refurbish. He must keep his mind centered on these most pressing issues.

Sir William clutched the portfolio of incriminating papers to his chest. "It worked exactly as you had planned, my darling. The Earl was actually anxious to oblige me." He leered at Suzanna. "How can I ever thank you?"

Sir William had the look of a lust-crazed monkey, Suzanna thought callously. At his insistence, she had agreed to join him in his chamber for a victory toast. She had brought a bottle of his favorite wine with her—and a vial of laudanum concealed in her hand.

Managing to hide her disgust, she smiled saucily. "As much as I look forward to your demonstration of gratitude, my love, I think we must first think of tomorrow."

Sir William's heart picked up its sluggish pace. By talk of "tomorrow" was his adorable and clever little minx signaling that she wanted marriage as much as he did?

Suzanna's eyes were guileless as she questioned gently, "You *are* aware that the Duke expects you to leave for London at dawn?"

Sir William gasped in dismay. "I never actually intended to go to London, or even leave the Manor. I planned to stay in my chamber, have my meals brought to me. In two weeks' time, I would reappear and tell the Earl that all had gone well with the King."

Suzanna shook her head. "That will not do, my darling. The Earl plans to see you off himself." She sighed tragically. "Surely you have seen how the Earl, as the Duke, is much more about the Manor. He notices every detail. I fear your charade would be found out."

Sir William's face crumpled, he looked close to tears.

"I had hoped we could be more together during my weeks of isolation," he moaned. "I cannot count the number of days that have passed since—"

Suzanna hurried to him and caressed his balding head. "Please hush, my darling, or you will make me cry. We still have what is left of today. Let us make good use of it."

She enthroned herself upon his bony knees and gave

him a heated kiss. As he fumbled with the lacings on her gown, she leaned past him to a side table and refilled his glass.

With a dexterity honed by much practice, she flipped the cork from the vial and carefully tilted it. Giving the laudanum-tainted wine a quick stir with her finger, she ran her wet finger across Sir William's thin lips, begging breathlessly, "Drink your wine, my gallant steed, then transport me to our love bower."

Sir William did as he was bid. He gulped down the wine, and carried Suzanna to his bed. Huffing from equal parts exertion and anticipated ecstasy, he lunged upon her.

Within moments he was snoring lustily in her ear.

As Henry had stated earlier, Lady Dimwitty *did* have other fish to fry, however, she was still interested in the one that got away. The announcement of Roman's engagement and upcoming marriage in the London papers had once more whetted her appetite.

It was now common knowledge that Knightley had to marry to please his uncle, and that his bride-to-be was a Miss Virtue Goodbody, a distant cousin to Suzanna Combs.

Anything that Suzanna Combs was involved in was suspect in Lady Dimwitty's books. She smelled a rat and was determined to find out more. To that end she invited Lady Freemantle to take tea with her. Lady Dimwitty hated Lady Freemantle, and the feeling was returned in full measure.

Like feral cats, the two women eyed each other across the tea table. Lady Freemantle smiled. "My dear Lady Dimwitty, it is so invigorating to be in your company.

One can always depend on you to come up with an amusing *on-dit*.

"Although"—she wagged an accusing finger—"you were so naughty not to have told me, one of your bosom bows, about your interest in Mr. Knightley."

Lady Dimwitty took a sip of her tea. "You saw Gillray's caricature of Mr. Knightley?" she asked.

Lady Freemantle arched a brow. "Who has not, my dear? So amusing, to be sure."

She paused. "Knightley's affairs afford much speculation and amusement for the *ton*. Society *wondered* who the girl in the wretched black bonnet could possibly be, now Society *wonders* who is this mysterious Virtue Goodbody and how on earth can more be learned of her?"

"I am told the Earl chose Miss Goodbody for her virtue and piety, in hopes of purging the Gypsy taint from the Larchmont name," Lady Dimwitty commented. "I fear Mr. Knightley will have a flannel-clad, Bible-carrying wife in his marriage bed. It will not be long before he looks elsewhere." *And when he does,* she thought, *I intend to be right there under his nose.*

Lady Freemantle nodded and selected a cake from the silver tray. She took several nibbles and waited.

After a significant pause, Lady Dimwitty sighed and directed her glance to a window. "The Season is at an end. Will you retreat to your country home, Lady Freemantle?"

"Of course. Dear Horace must have his hunting." Lady Freemantle smiled, a shark's smile. "You do know, do you not, Lady Dimwitty, that the grounds of Freemantle Hall march next to those of Bentwood Manor? I plan to give a ball immediately upon my arrival. I shall invite the entire county. You may be sure that Mr. Knightley and Miss Goodbody will be among my honored guests. I shall be sure to write to you and tell you of her looks."

The gauntlet had been tossed. Lady Dimwitty minced no further words. She looked directly at the enemy and presented her blunt request. "I feel the need of country air, Lady Freemantle. I should like to spend a few weeks—to include the week of your ball—as your houseguest at Freemantle Hall."

Lady Freemantle relished having the upper hand. She paused for a long moment before simpering, "Ordinarily, I would be delighted to have you, Lady Dimwitty, but dear Horace will invite many of his hunting friends. The Hall does not boast as many bedchambers as I would like. I do not know if there will be room for you."

Lady Dimwitty set her cup down with a sharp click. "You lost several hundred pounds at gaming hell recently, Lady Freemantle. I would be happy to pay your debts in return for an invitation."

Well gratified with the bargain, Lady Freemantle nodded pleasantly. "Agreed," she said.

Rhett felt like a pig at a trough. He had money in his pocket, fancier quarters, no work to do and all the wine he could drink.

He lifted his feet to the fireplace fender and took a swig from the bottle. He had showed The Slut who was boss, all right.

He smiled drunkenly while contemplating the antics of his "betters." He had to admit that he admired The Slut's abilities. While keeping Sir William at bay, she had screwed herself into the Earl's good graces. She would get the lunatic Earl to marry her before The Stick's wedding to Knightley. Rhett was convinced of it.

Yes, sir, The Slut was a formidable opponent, but no match for him. At the thought, Rhett shivered. It was as if a cold wind had suddenly blown through the room.

Seventeen

Ne'er blush'd unless, in spreading Vice's snares,
She blunder'd on some virtue unawares.
> —Charles Churchill

The arrival of Marie de Chalfant at Bentwood Manor was as earth-moving for Virtue as the Earl's lapse continued to be for Suzanna.

The two young women met for the first time before dinner. Marie, Henry and Roman were already in the drawing room when Virtue made her entrance.

The three stood before the fireplace, deep in conversation. It was apparent that Marie was relating an amusing tidbit, as the gentlemen chuckled and beamed at her throughout the telling.

The reason for Henry's adoration of his intended was quite obvious. Marie looked like an angel. She was dressed all in white, her gown of fine translucent muslin with a deep panel of white-on-white embroidery at the hemline. A wreath of white silk roses encircled her topknot of dark curls, and dainty seed pearls adorned her throat and ears.

Virtue felt a pang of envy. Although not a classic beauty, Marie possessed a vivacious Gallic charm. "She can coax the birds out of the trees with her smile," Henry had once said, waxing proudly on his beloved. Petite and dark-haired, with flashing brown eyes, Marie was all that Henry desired, and all that Virtue desired to be.

Feeling like a dark cloud about to drift over a picnic, she started toward the group. The conversation ceased. Three pairs of eyes turned in her direction.

The look of pity in Mr. Knightley's intense blue stare as he watched her approach was more painful to Virtue than a blow. For a moment, she thought he would ignore her; then he came forward and offered his arm.

This renewed proof of his kindness worked powerfully upon her tender sensibilities. Her hand, less reddened than it had been, the nails longer and more shapely, rested upon his strong forearm. She felt a lessening of fear. She could entrust her life to this man who would be her husband.

Henry beamed at Virtue. "Ahhh, Miss Goodbody. Do let me introduce you to my fiancée, Miss de Chalfant."

Marie, as Henry had boasted, was a generous and kind young woman, in addition to being a charmer. Forewarned by Henry of Virtue's plain appearance, she was prepared to meet, and to make comfortable, her shy young hostess dressed—as Henry had put it—in crow feathers.

Thinking that Henry had not exaggerated Miss Goodbody's lack of fashion in the least, Marie executed a graceful curtsy. In flawless, but delicately accented English, she said, "Miss Goodbody. I am delighted to meet you. I want to thank you for the lovely nosegays you made for my chamber. I adore flowers, and you arranged them so charmingly."

Conscious of her drab black gown and clumsy boots, Virtue returned the curtsy. "You are most welcome, Miss de Chalfant. It was my pleasure to make you feel welcome."

Marie threw a saucy glance at Henry. "I feel *most* welcome, Miss Goodbody, never fear."

Under Marie's skillful guidance, the conversation flowed smoothly. By the time the four had dealt with the discomforts of travel and whims of the summer weather, the others appeared at the drawing room's entrance.

Henry had prepared Marie for *all* the peculiarities that existed in the household. Therefore, upon the presentation of the "Duke and Duchess of Wellington" by a puffed-up Fox, she was able to greet the pair in a natural and most respectful way.

Sir William, who had had several hairs of the dog during the afternoon, eyed Marie suspiciously. "De Chalfant? Frenchie name, what?"

Marie raised her chin. "But loyal to the king, I assure you, sir," she replied stoutly. "I lost many members of my family to the Terror."

"Poor child," the Duke cooed, already under Marie's spell. "You are most welcome at the Manor. Is she not, my love?"

"Indeed she is," Suzanna said. Marie was too young and too pretty for Suzanna to actually *want* her at the Manor, but the French girl's lively looks would put an end to a nagging worry brought on by Gaffe's suspicions. If Virtue *were* developing a tendre for Lord Dunsby, she did not stand a chance against the likes of Marie de Chalfant.

Relieved, Suzanna smiled at Marie. "Shall we go in to dinner, my dear?"

With a "Duke" in residence, a change in the hierarchy was necessary. Uncontested, the Duke claimed the head of the table and seated Suzanna at the foot.

Roman was placed on Suzanna's right and Henry on her left. Marie occupied the place of honor at the Duke's right with Virtue directly across from her. Sir William as odd man out, sat between Virtue and Roman.

Throughout dinner, Virtue carefully observed Marie's every gesture, her every flirtatious glance. She also noted how the gentlemen, with the exception of Sir William, responded to Marie's charms with gentle teasing and champagne toasts.

Mr. Knightley's preoccupation, so apparent last evening, seemed to have vanished into thin air. He looked relaxed, and was responding to Marie's pert remarks with good-humored wit.

If only she could look, and act and speak like Miss de Chalfant, Virtue thought longingly, she could entice Mr. Knightley into loving her. She could learn so much from Miss de Chalfant. Dare she ask for her help? Certainly, if guidelines for enticement existed, this lovely French girl would know of them.

If guidelines did exist, Marie could have written them. In matters of the heart, she had no equal. Being French and naturally perceptive helped immensely.

There was nothing she enjoyed more than an amorous intrigue. The moment she observed Virtue and Roman together, she sensed one in the making. Miss Goodbody was obviously in love with Mr. Knightley. Her furtive glances, her rising color when her eyes rested on him, were solid indications. Mr. Knightley, however—how like a man—was unaware of her love.

To a Frenchwoman, unrequited love was akin to a mortal sin. Marie decided she would help Miss Goodbody gain her objective if she could. But not tonight.

Tonight, when the household was asleep, her darling Henry would join her in her chamber. Marie sipped her champagne and smiled.

Observing Marie's smile, Roman recognized it for

what it was. While he did not envy Henry his good fortune, he wanted some of it for himself.

His eyes automatically turned to Miss Goodbody. Again he was reminded of a dying plant. She would perform her marital "duties" out of obligation, not desire. Had she always been so spiritless, he wondered, or had someone in her early life thrashed the spirit out of her?

After the cloth had been removed and apples and walnuts demolished, the gentlemen decided to forgo their port and directly join the ladies in the drawing room.

The Duke had forgotten his request that there be music and singing after dinner. He had had quite a bit of wine with the meal and was longing for the "comfort" that only his Kitty could provide.

Marie, with her acute perception, sized up the sexual predilections of the group at once. She ticked off the list: She had sensed at once that the mad Earl and Miss Combs were sleeping together, and that Sir William would *like* to be sleeping with Miss Combs, but obviously was spending his nights, as well as his days, with a bottle. Since she and Henry were sleeping together, that left only Miss Goodbody and Mr. Knightley who *should* be sleeping together, but were not. Mr. Knightley looked bored, and Miss Goodbody looked morose. *Ahhh, the English,* Marie thought, *God save them.*

She finished her tea and patting over a delicate yawn rose from the settee. With a provocative glance at Henry, she addressed her host. "I beg to be excused, Your Grace. It has been a most enjoyable evening, but a very tiring day. I find I am in need of my bed."

Virtue sat at her dressing table. The evening had come to an abrupt end with Marie's departure, as the rest of the group—some in unseemly haste—sought the sanctuary of their bedchambers.

Resting her chin on the palm of her hand, she stared at her reflection in the looking glass. It was an action driven not by vanity but by self-assessment. Having been fully absorbed with her immortal soul since reaching the age of reason, she had had little concern for her outward appearance. Except for cleanliness. Cleanliness was her lone cosmetic. She had felt she needed no more. As the Bible said: "What God hath cleansed, that call not thou common."

Now she wondered if a *bit* of artifice might be permissible? Would it be flying in the face of God to pinch color into her pale cheeks, to loosen her hair? She wanted Mr. Knightley to notice her and come to love her. Was it not God's will that a husband should love and desire his wife?

It suddenly struck Virtue that it had been days since she had sought refuge in her world of daydreams. The reason must be that her daydreams were so diverse from her reality. Mr. Knightley was not in the least like her dream hero. Prince Orlando was fair haired and slight of build, with slender, elegant hands. Common soldiering and Gypsy caravans were far from his world.

Yet it was Mr. Knightley she loved.

Without another moment's hesitation, she rose from the dressing table and tightened her wrapper around her slender waist. If she wanted Mr. Knightley to love her, she must seek expert counsel at once.

Moments later, she knocked softly on the door to Miss de Chalfant's chamber. A soft, inviting voice whispered, *"Entrez!"*

Slowly, Virtue cracked open the door and peeked in. Marie, a vision in white, was lying on the sofa, a silken slipper dangling provocatively from one dainty foot. The room was aglow with candlelight. A bottle of red wine and a grouping of crystal glasses reflected the dancing flames of the crackling fire. There was only one discordant note. From the dressing room came the sounds of raucous snoring.

When Marie spotted Virtue, her eyes widened. "Why it is you, Miss Goodbody. What a surprise! I was expecting Lord Dunsby, but do come in."

Shocked, Virtue advanced into the room like a cautious cat. Miss de Chalfant wore only her nightgown, and she was about to receive Lord Dunsby in her bedchamber. Could it be some sort of odd French custom?

Unaware that she had scandalized the prim Miss Goodbody, Marie rose from the sofa, strolled to a side table and poured two goblets of wine. With a toss of her head, she indicated the dressing room. "Please overlook the noise. It issues from Madame Claqueur, my abigail. She takes a bit of wine in the evening to help her sleep."

From the volume of the snores, Virtue concluded that Madame Claqueur had imbibed more than just a bit. She glanced at her hostess. Good heavens! Miss de Chalfant's nightgown was of such diaphanous muslin that in the candlelight every line and curve of her naked body was visible.

With a guileless smile, Marie offered Virtue a glass of wine.

Virtue drew herself up in an attitude of censure. "I do not drink spirits."

Marie gave a Gallic shrug. "Perhaps it is time that you started."

Meekly, Virtue accepted the glass. She would hold it to be companionable. It was not as if she were going to drink from it.

Marie pulled on a flimsy wrapper and gestured to a pair of wing chairs. "Let us sit and be comfortable, and you can tell me why you are here."

Virtue took a seat and stared into the fire. For the life of her, she could not think of a word to say to justify her presence. She took a small sip of wine. The idea of trying to entice Mr. Knightley suddenly seemed sinful and wicked.

After a lengthy silence, Marie took pity on Virtue. She chuckled softly. "Then *I* will tell *you* why you are here. You are in love with your Mr. Knightley, and you wish for me to tell you how to make yourself more attractive to him, *n'est-ce pas?*"

Virtue stared at Marie in amazement. "How did you know?"

Marie shrugged. "I am French. And, as a Frenchwoman, I can help you. There will be much to do in the three weeks I remain at the Manor. You must be transformed from *within* as well as from without. You must develop a presence, your own style."

"But I want to look and be just like you," Virtue blurted out.

Marie smiled graciously. "I thank you for the compliment, Miss Goodbody, but you must be yourself, only better. Stand up please."

Virtue got to her feet.

"Turn around. Slowly, please."

Virtue rotated, her eyes wide.

"Hmmm," said Marie. "Very good. You may sit down now."

She took a sip of wine, her expression reflective; then she decreed, "You have all the physical assets needed to attract a gentlemen, but they must be subtly brought out. Between Madame Claqueur and me, we will transform you into a beautiful butterfly. Your Mr. Knightley will beg for your attention."

After a lifetime of being told how plain she was, these were heady words indeed. Virtue took a gulp of wine and set the glass down with a bang. "Do you really think so?"

Marie winced. Fine crystal was another of her passions. She never traveled without her own complete set. She said firmly, "I would not have said so if I did not think so. You must trust me, Miss Goodbody. If you truly wish to entice Mr. Knightley, you must do exactly what I say, even if you do not subscribe to what I tell you. If you agree to my terms, we will begin your lessons tomorrow."

Virtue eagerly acquiesced. "I wake at dawn."

Marie winced again. "That, then, will be your first lesson. A lady does not rise at dawn. At ten, you will ring for your maid and demand your chocolate and rolls."

"I have never done so."

"Tomorrow, you will. Finish your wine and have another glass. Wine helps one to sleep long and deep. Only hear what it does for Madame Claqueur."

It had been drummed into Virtue's youthful head that an excess of spirits led to sin and corruption, but as she stared at the contents of her glass, Roman's lean, sun-bronzed face with its piercing blue eyes danced before her eyes.

Her resolve weakened. The wine *did* have a most pleasant taste. Surely a bit more would not hurt. Closing her eyes, she finished off the glass and held it out for more.

As Marie was pouring the wine, a soft knock sounded on the door.

Her face glowed. "It is Henry. Come in, *chéri,*" she called.

Virtue jumped to her feet as Lord Dunsby entered. He wore soft slippers and a blue silk banyan. When he saw Virtue, his gray eyes bulged, and his cheeks turned red with embarrassment. "Ahhh, I was just passing by. Saw the light. Thought something might be wrong."

Marie chided, "Nonsense, Henry. Miss Goodbody knows that I was expecting you." She shook her head. "You English. You are so amusing.

"Sit down *chéri,* and I shall pour you a glass of wine. Miss Goodbody and I have embarked on a plan to transform her into a butterfly. We will need your help for its execution."

Studiously avoiding Virtue's eye, Henry took a seat.

"Miss Goodbody is in love with Mr. Knightley," Marie announced.

Henry felt he had to say something. He addressed his feet. "Good thing, what?" he blustered. "Seeing how she's going to marry him and all."

Marie eyed her intended with a stern countenance. "It is not a good thing, *chéri.* There exists an unbalance."

Henry gulped. If Marie was going to talk "female" stuff to him in front of Miss Goodbody, he'd sink through the floor.

He took a bracing gulp of wine and ventured, "Imbalance?"

"*Oui.* Mr. Knightley does not, *as yet,* love Miss Goodbody."

The emphasis on "as yet" chilled Henry to the very marrow of his bones. He was well acquainted with Marie's penchant for amorous intrigues. What did she want of *him?*

She answered his unspoken question. "When you are

in the company of Mr. Knightley, you are to praise Miss Goodbody. At every opportunity, you are to bring her name into the conversation. Do you understand?"

Relieved to be let off so easily, Henry nodded eagerly. "I'll do it, don't you fear."

His hopes as to the extent of his participation were cruelly dashed when Marie next informed him, "There will be other things needed of you, *chéri.* I will let you know what they are as I think of them."

Eighteen

Knowledge gained and virtue lost . . .
— Housman

Dressed in rustic riding clothes, Roman sat savoring his third cup of coffee. The windows of the breakfast room were open. The twittering of early birds filled the air, and the scent of newly scythed grass wafted on the light breeze.

He took a deep breath. His head was clear and his mind alert. For the first time in months, he was not suffering the effects of overimbibing.

His immediate thoughts were occupied with his plans for the morning. In an hour's time, he would meet with Ted Haskins in the village. Haskins was an honest man and jack-of-all-trades. He would be in charge of renovating the tenant cottages, while Roman attended to the farmlands.

It would be many seasons before he could trust the property to an estate steward. The fields were worn out, some needed to lie fallow for a season or two, while others could be enriched immediately by fertilizing and crop rotation. There were also several innovative planting methods that Roman wanted to implement next spring.

He now had the blunt and the "Duke's" blessing to restore Bentwood Manor to the productive, self-sufficient haven it had been under his father's guidance. Rescuing the tenant farmers from their miserable existence was the first step. The land could not be productive if those who labored on it were not well fed and well housed.

Oddly enough, Roman was content with his role of gentleman farmer and cautiously optimistic. His first days at the Manor—with the exception of his initial meeting with Miss Goodbody—had gone better than he could have possibly dreamed.

There was only one fly in the proverbial ointment. He knew that his plans for restoring the estate rested on the Earl continuing to think of himself as the Duke of Wellington. Miss Combs played her part well, and Roman knew she played for high stakes. She could have only one motive in mind for catering to the Earl: She wanted to be his countess.

Roman was a man of the world. He had surmised early on that as the "Duchess," Miss Combs was giving the "Duke" more than medication to keep him in his present mellow mood, but for the nonce, he was prepared to overlook her ambitions and even encourage them. Mutual needs made strange bedfellows.

The thought of strange bedfellows brought Miss Goodbody to mind. Roman got to his feet and pulled on his leather riding gloves, idly wondering how his intended would spend the day. He sighed. No doubt as she always did: in prayer.

Prayer was the last thing on Virtue's mind when she met with Marie in her bedchamber the following morning. She had been shocked, yet titillated by the obvious assignation between Miss de Chalfant and Lord Dunsby.

Although country born and bred, Virtue knew little of

what went on between a man and wife when they were alone in their bedchamber. From observation, she knew that almost immediately after the wedding night, the bride commenced to swell.

Although, that in itself was not a hard and fast rule. Several of the village girls had swelled before their weddings, and the condition had led to great consternation and occasional fisticuffs amongst the concerned family members.

Lord Dunsby had remained with Miss de Chalfant after she had taken her leave last evening. Since it was obvious that was not the first time the two had been alone together in a bedchamber, there was a good chance Miss de Chalfant would begin to show the first signs of swelling. Virtue was determined to see for herself.

Marie sat at her dressing table. Her maid was putting the finishing touches to a simple but becoming hairdo.

Marie looked up and smiled. "Miss Goodbody. Do come in."

She dismissed the maid and gestured for Virtue to take a chair by the open window. Presently, she joined her. She settled her sprigged muslin skirts and crossed her feet, shod in dainty, laced kid slippers, at the ankle.

"Did the wine help you to sleep well, Miss Goodbody?"

"Very well," Virtue admitted. So well, in fact, she thought, that she could scarcely remember getting undressed and into bed.

"That is good."

There was a small silence. Virtue twisted her hands in her lap. With skimming glances, she examined Miss de Chalfant's front for signs of swelling. There were none. She was as slender as she had been last night. She looked, in fact, better than she had last night. She had a glow about her, as if a small flame smoldered within.

Marie was aware now of how shocked Virtue had been last evening. Henry had enlightened her as to the curious mores the English held about sex before marriage. The English were an odd lot, she thought. Still the subject would have to be dealt with. If she and Miss Goodbody were to be mentor and pupil, they would have to be honest with each other.

"Why do you examine me in such a way, Miss Goodbody?"

Virtue's face flamed, but she decided to be brave. "Forgive me. I was looking for signs of swelling."

Marie's eyes widened. "Swelling?"

Virtue nodded miserably. "When a man and a woman are alone in a bedchamber for several nights, the woman commences to swell. You know, with child."

Marie rolled her eyes to the heavens. "The woman does not *have* to swell, Miss Goodbody," she said carefully. "There are ways of preventing this from happening. Have you ever heard of a 'French letter'?"

Virtue thought hard. "I do not think so. Since I can read French, I would certainly know if I had ever received one."

Marie sighed. This was going to be more difficult than she had imagined. "Ahhh, Miss Goodbody, you misunderstand. A 'French letter' is a preventive. It is something a man wears on his . . . front."

Virtue's smooth brow knit in contemplation. "Like a fob?" she asked.

Marie sighed again. "Yesterday afternoon, Henry and I took a walk in the formal gardens. There is a statue tucked away in an overgrown area that might provide enlightenment for you. It is a very pleasant morning. Let us take a walk."

Marie carried a dainty parasol to protect her face from the sun. Virtue in her coal-scuttle bonnet needed none. The two strolled through the bee-laden, overgrown gardens. Although neglected, vestiges of the gardens' past glories were still evident.

Marie led Virtue off toward a secluded maze. Tucked in a leafy corner was a statue, a replica of Donatello's Renaissance-style *David*. Time and the elements had eroded his face, but the important parts were intact.

Marie closed her parasol and pointed with its tip. "You see, there is where the French letter is placed."

Virtue stared. "But would it not fall off?"

"Women are not the only ones capable of 'swelling' in certain areas," Marie stated candidly.

A sudden memory from Virtue's childhood flashed before her eyes. It was of a stallion being led to a mare. Suddenly, the pieces fell into place. "Yes," she whispered, "I think I understand now."

Well pleased with her pupil, Marie nodded. "Good. Now you are ready to begin your lessons in enticement."

Freemantle Hall could comfortably house thirty guests. Weak-chinned gentlemen and their insipid wives came in fancy carriages to spend a month or more of pleasure—most of it illicit—at the expense of the Freemantles.

One sunny morning, Lady Freemantle and Lady Dimwitty sat at opposite sides of a writing table in the Hall's pleasant morning room. A stack of steadily mounting cards of invitation formed a barrier between them.

"I do think that is the last one on our list, Lady Dimwitty," Lady Freemantle observed as she applied sealing wax to vellum. "How clever of you to suggest I give a masquerade to receive my neighbors." She arched her painted-on brows in mock concern. "Although, there is something about being masked that seems to encourage licentiousness."

Lady Dimwitty tittered obligingly, though both she and her hostess knew from experience that masks were not needed for licentiousness. Lady Freemantle's guests had played musical beds for the past week, leading to delight for some and disappointment for others.

She shuffled through the stack of invitations on her side of the table. "I have addressed a card to the Earl and his household, and separate cards to Mr. Knightley and Miss Goodbody. As the future Earl and Countess, I felt they were entitled to special consideration."

"How very solicitous you are, Lady Dimwitty."

Lady Freemantle smirked. "I must admit, I can scarcely wait to make the acquaintance of the mysterious Miss Goodbody."

Lady Dimwitty said nothing. She was more interested in renewing her acquaintanceship with Mr. Knightley. He was all she could think of. She was obsessed with thoughts of possessing him, if only for one night.

Two weeks had passed since the anatomy lesson in the garden. The days sped by in a whirl for Virtue. In the morning Marie conducted exercises in the proper way for a future countess to conduct herself. There were lessons in conversation, flirting, manners, and the correct use of a fan.

In the afternoons, Virtue learned to dance, both the country dances and the controversial waltz. While Marie played the pianoforte, Henry whirled Virtue around the little-used music room until they both were breathless.

For dancing, Virtue wore a pair of Marie's slippers with fabric scraps stuffed in the toes. Without her heavy boots, she felt free and as light as thistledown.

She still wore her shabby black gowns, but a new wardrobe would soon be in the making. Marie had generously donated a half-dozen of her little-worn gowns to Virtue, and Madame Claqueur, a skilled seamstress with the French flair for fashion, would be in charge of the alterations.

Henry had not had much success with the duties assigned to him by Marie. Although he tried at every turn to speak of Virtue's assets, he often grumbled, "Roman's so tied up with making life better for his tenants that I swear, he don't hear half of what I say."

The rich food, the rest and exercise had gradually put color in Virtue's cheeks and a sparkle in her eye, and the pleasant companionship of people her own age worked magic on her shyness. She bloomed under Marie and Henry's unfailing kindness and approval.

The three were in the music room, having a restorative cup of tea after a particularly strenuous stint of dancing.

"I am very proud of my *protégée*," Marie proclaimed, beaming at Virtue. "I only wish we had an occasion for you to show off your skills."

Virtue bit into a sweet biscuit and chewed thoughtfully. "I must admit, I am glad we do not. I would be afraid to mix with Society, even on the local level."

"Afraid?" Henry harrumphed. "That's the last thing you have to be. Anyone so much as looks cross-eyed at my little sister, and I'll draw his cork."

To Marie and Virtue's quizzing look, Henry sputtered sheepishly, "Confound it, that's the way I've come to think of you, Virtue. I love Roman like a brother, but he should get to know you and not let a black sack color his—" Henry blushed painfully. "What I mean is, a man's got to look beneath the covering. Oh, confound it, that ain't what I mean."

Virtue reached over and patted Henry's arm. "I know what you mean, Henry dear, and I would be so proud and happy to have you as my brother."

Marie, who was very sentimental, dabbed at her eyes with a lawn handkerchief. "Please, say no more, or I shall cry."

Although the subtle changes in Virtue's looks and manner grew more apparent with each passing day, Roman was too busy with the affairs of the estate, and Suzanna too busy with her affair with the "Duke," to notice. Gaffe was the only one who saw that Virtue was beginning to bloom. And she suspected that Lord Dunsby was the reason.

The invitation from Freemantle Hall was greeted with great glee and anticipation by the "Duke," and with great gloom and apprehension by the other occupants of Bentwood Manor.

Roman was aghast. After reading the invitations, the Duke had immediately sent a footman to Freemantle Hall with acceptances. The fat was in the fire.

The Freemantles had a houseful of their London acquaintances staying at the Hall. Could Lady Dimwitty be one of the invited?

Dear God—Roman groaned—how could he ever live down the shame? The Earl as the Duke would make a laughingstock of the Larchmont title, and Miss Good-body, with her black gown and Bible, would make a laughingstock out of its heir apparent.

He sought out Suzanna at once to discuss the potential pitfalls of the situation. Over the weeks, the two had formed a symbiotic relationship based on individual wants and mutual concerns. They no longer felt the need to mince words.

Fox directed Roman to the Earl's sitting room where Suzanna was purportedly having a cup of tea while the Duke slept.

Suzanna was not having tea, but wine, and a very large glass of it, while she paced back and forth across the chamber.

Virtue was also present. She sat quietly in a corner by a window, embroidering the Ducal coat of arms on a pair of slippers destined for the Earl.

Suzanna was obviously very worried. She quit her pacing and turned. Without waiting for an exchange of greetings, she addressed Roman the moment he entered the chamber. "I greatly fear, Mr. Knightley, that if the Earl puts aside the Duke's persona and assumes yet another identity for Lady Freemantle's masquerade, even for one night, it could bring his current lapse to a crashing end."

With a sigh, Roman threw himself into a wing chair and propped one booted foot upon the fireplace fender. "I agree, Miss Combs. It is imperative for the well-being of the tenants and the restoration of the estates that the Earl continue thinking he is the Duke of Wellington."

He paused meaningfully. "Since we *both* have a great deal at stake in the situation, it behooves us to come up with a solution."

Suzanna resumed her pacing. Her mouth was set in a firm line. She would not have the Earl become an object of mockery! If necessary, on the night of the ball she would give him a strong dose of laudanum and see that he was kept at home under Fox's care.

This concern for others was a new emotion for Suzanna. She was not sure that she liked it, but she had no control over it.

Virtue looked up from her needlework. "I believe I have a solution. The Earl can attend Lady Freemantle's ball *as* the Duke of Wellington. It would not be thought odd at a masquerade, and his lapse would not be placed in jeopardy."

She carefully set a stitch. "While the ploy is not a permanent solution, it will resolve the immediate problem."

Suzanna gaped, and Roman swung around in his chair. After staring intently at Virtue for a long moment, he chuckled and glanced at Suzanna. "Out of the mouths of babes. Why did *we* not think of that perfectly simple and very workable solution? Well done, Miss Goodbody."

Virtue glowed with the praise, and her cheeks colored becomingly. Roman did not turn away, but continued to study her. There was something different about the gray-eyed mouse, he thought, besides the fact that it was the first time he had heard her offer an opinion.

It was a physical change, he decided. He couldn't quite put his finger on it, but Miss Goodbody looked . . . better.

After the first shock of hearing Virtue actually speak when not directly spoken to had subsided, Suzanna felt an unaccustomed glow of pride. The nut did not fall far from the tree. "Cousin" Virtue had a head on her shoulders, and an almost natural bent for intrigue.

Roman got to his feet, his eyes straying again to Virtue. Although he hated himself for doing it, he imagined himself introducing her—even the improved edition—to Lady Freemantle's guests, all select members of the *ton*.

What would they think of Miss Goodbody's black dress, her shabby boots? If Lady Dimwitty were there, she would recognize Miss Goodbody as the girl from the Goose and Gander. He would never live it down.

Virtue stitched serenely on, not glancing in his direction, seemingly unaware of his perusal. Then, suddenly, she set aside her sewing and rose gracefully.

"I have promised Gaffe to wind wool for her, Cousin Suzanna. If you will excuse me."

As she made her way past Roman, she paused. Her head rose, and she looked him straight in the eye. "You will no doubt be pleased to know, Mr. Knightley, that I have decided to effect a change in my attire for the ball. I shall add a white fichu to my black gown and masquerade as a puritan." She lowered her eyes, dropped a small curtsy and left the room.

Roman stared after her. Was he imagining things, or had there been an odd, laughing light in Miss Goodbody's large gray eyes? Had she, perchance, been teasing him?

Nineteen

*Dreams are like dormant seeds that suddenly sprout
and spread, and breathe with a life of their own.*
                                              —Anonymous

"It was the perfect riposte," Marie raved. "Tell me,
how did your Mr. Knightley look when you left him?"

With a devilish shiver, Virtue thought back to her beloved's face. "He looked perplexed, but . . . interested."

"Very good! His reaction could not be better. You were
inspired, *ma petite.*"

Virtue shook her head. "All credit must go to you,
Marie. You are the teacher, and I am but your inexpert
pupil." She added wistfully, "I wish you could be here
for the ball. Aside from wanting and enjoying your company, I also need your support."

Marie surveyed Virtue with mock chagrin. "Do you
forget? Madame Claqueur will remain behind to dress
you for the ball. She is all that you will need."

Virtue sighed. "It is not that I am ungrateful for Madame, but"—she sighed again—"could you not postpone
your trip by just one day?"

Marie shook her dark curls. "Alas, I cannot. My maid
and I must leave for London the day before the ball and
no later. My *tante* Marie, for whom I was named, meets
me there, and we will shop together for my brideclothes."

She tilted her head to one side and smiled. "Do not worry your head, *ma petite*. You have an innate talent for enticement. Your Mr. Knightley will soon be beseeching you for crumbs of your attention."

She grew suddenly serious. "I have but one worry, Virtue. You are too kind and generous. You must remember that once Mr. Knightley falls in love with you, you must back away and make him suffer. You must ignore him and flirt with the other gentlemen at the ball. You must make him jealous. This is most important."

Virtue nodded guiltily. She now thought of Marie as a sister, yet there was a small rebellion brewing against this one edict. If Mr. Knightley came to love her, she would not, she *could* not, do anything that would cause him pain.

Sensing Virtue's hestitation, Marie sighed. "When the time comes, *ma petite,* remember my words."

She turned toward the dressing room and raised her voice slightly. "Madame Claqueur, we are ready now for you to take Miss Goodbody's measurements."

Madame whirled out of the dressing room like a figure on a cuckoo clock. She was a small morose woman with hooded eyes, a lined face and suspiciously coal black hair.

She curtsied. "I shall help you to remove your gown, mademoiselle."

Blushing, Virtue suffered Madame's attentions. Soon, she stood in only her shift and petticoat. Madame shuddered. "Those boots and coarse stockings. They must also be removed."

Virtue sat down at the dressing table and removed the offending articles. "That is better," Madame conceded. "Please stand, Mademoiselle."

Marie also rose. With narrowed eyes she and Madame circled Virtue as if she were a prize ewe at auction.

Marie gasped. "Virtue, you have a bosom. Where on earth have you been keeping it?"

Virtue's pale skin took on more color. "I have gained weight. I have increased everywhere."

"How very fortunate," Marie enthused. She stepped back. "Well, Madame, what are your thoughts?"

In heavily accented French, Madame ticked off Virtue's qualities. "Mademoiselle has perfect skin and a perfect body. Her feet are excellent, but her hands need attending to. The color of her hair is most unusual. The guillotine cut would take advantage of its natural curl and show off Mademoiselle's elegant neck and shoulders."

"The guillotine cut?" Virtue questioned, registering alarm.

"It is a cut that was at one time very prevalent in my country," Marie replied dryly. "But Madame is right. It will suit you admirably."

Again consulting Madame, Marie inquired, "Which of my gowns will you make over for the masquerade?"

It had been decided after much discussion that Virtue would attend the masquerade as a lady of ancient Rome.

Madame cocked her head to one side. "The lavender sarcenet silk. The color would be excellent on Mademoiselle, and the fabric, being less tightly woven than other silks, will produce a more elegant draped effect. I shall remove the gold-key trimming on your white tunic to use as decoration on Mademoiselle's costume."

Lavender silk, Virtue marveled. It was the color she had worn in her daydreams. Were they at last taking substance?

* * *

Henry took his assignment from Marie to heart. Every chance he got, he extolled the many virtues of Virtue to Roman. So far, his ravings had not evoked much interest.

"You're wool-gathering again, Roman," he complained. "All you think about is your tenants. Not saying that's a bad thing, mind you, but talking to you is like talking to a wall."

Roman laughed. "I am sorry, Henry. Talk to me now, and I swear you will have my undivided attention."

Somewhat mollified, Henry grunted, "I was talking about Virtue."

Roman looked at him blankly. "Virtue?"

"Miss Goodbody."

Amused, Roman questioned with mock ire, "*You* are on a first-name basis with *my* intended?"

Henry glared at him. "Someone has to be. You don't pay her a whit of attention." He shrugged defensively. "Marie and Virtue got started calling each other by their first names, and I just fell into it."

There was a small silence; then Henry huffed, "I can tell you some things about your intended I'll bet you don't know. Did you know she taught herself to read Latin and French? Got a mind like a steel trap, she does. Catches on quick. Nice manners, too."

He thought hard for a moment. "And while she don't come right out and say it, she's had a miserable life. Her father was a sanctimonious old sod, sounds like, who didn't spare the rod.

"Yes, sir, mark my words, Virtue will make a great countess when the time comes—and once she gets out of those black sacks."

Roman looked thoughtful. "No, Henry," he said, "I did not know those things about my intended. Thank you for enlightening me."

He stared off into space. Miss Goodbody had been on his mind more and more of late. Her subtle teasing, if that was what it had been, had intrigued him.

He found himself suddenly wondering what she would look like with her hair loosened from its confining noose. Would it curl beguilingly about her face, perhaps soften that pointed little chin of hers?

The next few mornings dawned sun-scented and very warm. Virtue was at loose ends. At the vicarage, she had had a daily routine of chores that had filled her time from dawn until dusk. Today, her lesson with Marie was her only commitment—a pleasant one at that—but it would not begin until eleven.

Feeling vaguely guilty and out of sorts, Virtue took herself to the morning room with the thought of writing a letter to Mrs. Ramsay. It had been weeks since she had written.

The French doors stood open to the terrace. An inviting breeze blew through the room, bringing with it the rich smells of freshly turned earth and ripening fruit. The scent was like a beckoning hand inviting Virtue to follow.

And follow she did. She stepped out upon the terrace, shading her eyes from the sun. Some distance beyond the formal gardens lay the path that she and Henry had walked. It would be pleasant to retrace their steps and sit beside the water. Not bothering to go back for her bonnet, she set off.

It was a longer walk than she had remembered. She daubed at her bedewed forehead and fanned her neck with her handkerchief.

As she neared the pond, she heard splashing noises.

An animal of some sort enjoying a bath? she wondered. Just the sounds of it were refreshing.

She crept closer through the underbrush. Hidden behind a stand of leafy saplings, she parted the foliage and peered in the direction of the pond.

A pile of clothes and a pair of boots lay upon the shore. A movement in the water drew her eye. It was Mr. Knightley swimming in what appeared to be a state of complete undress.

Bronzed arms lifted high and cut through the water, jeweled drops danced upon broad shoulders, lean buttocks snaked just below the surface, muscular legs scissor-kicked in slow motion.

Virtue swallowed hard, the sound of it like thunder in her ears. She knew it was wrong to spy on Mr. Knightley in such a state, but she could not move.

He was in the middle of the pond now, treading water. His hair was sleek and studded with rainbow-colored droplets. Slowly he turned and stroked toward the shore. When his feet touched bottom, he stood. He was in Virtue's direct line of vision.

She knew what she was doing was unconscionable! Taking a trembling breath, she pulled the foliage farther apart to get a clearer look. The water streamed from Mr. Knightley's broad shoulders as he made his way to shore, parting the rushes as he went.

Visions of Donatello's *David* danced before Virtue's eyes. Mr. Knightley was in waist-high water and moving more quickly. She could now see his lean hips, his . . . Oh, my heavens! She gasped, her eyes widened. This was not Donatello's *David*—this was Goliath!

Without thinking, she let go of the foliage. The supple branches snapped back with a whistling noise. Terrified that Mr. Knightley had heard, she pelted up the path and back to the Manor.

In the safety of her room, she threw herself upon the bed and stared at the frayed canopy above her head. She was in a state of shock from what she had observed. Marie had said that coupling with the man you loved was very pleasurable. In view of the evidence, how could this be so?

Suddenly, she was bombarded with erotic visions: Donatello's *David;* Mr. Knightley walking naked from the pond; the mare being led to the stallion. . . .

Virginal fears assailed her. While she now knew the male parts involved that led to female swelling, the how of it continued to elude her.

A field soldier's survival depended on his being constantly alert for the unusual: a noise, a movement, a color not indigenous to the natural surroundings.

Coming out of the pond, Roman had caught a glimpse of black retreating swiftly through the bright green of the summer grasses. Miss Goodbody was the only person in the household who wore black and who would be at the pond at that time of day, yet he could not believe the prim Miss Goodbody had been spying on him. She had probably chanced upon him in the altogether and run for her life.

He had more to worry about than offending Miss Goodbody's sensibilities. Henry had seen Lady Dimwitty's coach in the village. Her attendance at the Freemantle's ball was beyond doubt.

He knew Lady Dimwitty would recognize Miss Goodbody as the girl at the Goose and Gander. He could almost hear that penetrating voice of hers telling all and sundry, "That is not a costume Mr. Knightley's intended is wearing. That is her usual attire."

Then she would retell the story, perhaps even circulate Gillray's caricature to those who had not seen it—if there was anyone present who had not seen it.

Within twenty minutes of his arrival at Freemantle Hall with Miss Goodbody, he would be the laughingstock of the county.

Sir William's departure from the Manor had been welcomed with great relief by all who had come in contact with him, from the "Duke" down to the lowliest of the servants.

Marie's departure two days later had the exact opposite effect. Everyone in the household was sorry to see her go, Henry and Virtue in particular.

It was early morning. The three were in Marie's bedchamber. Her trunks were already loaded, and her carriage waited at the entrance.

Marie had said her private farewell to Henry last night in the middle of her four-poster. Her farewell to him in front of Virtue and Madame was more circumspect. She stood on tiptoe, kissed him on both cheeks, French-style, then straighted his cravat.

"I shall return in two weeks, *chéri,* in time for our dear little sister's wedding to Mr. Knightley. I leave her in your hands. Remember now, whatever you do for her, you do for me, *n'est-ce pas?*"

Still in a state of sated bliss, Henry sighed and nodded.

Marie turned to Madame and embraced her. "You know what I expect from you, my dear Madame?"

Madame nodded, her eyes wet with tears. "I shall not fail you, my dear little Marie. With you not in attendance,

Mademoiselle will be the most beautiful woman at the ball."

Her loyalty was rewarded with another embrace; then Marie hastened to where Virtue stood apart from the others, looking like a lost lamb.

Virtue felt like a lost lamb. Her bravado of the past days had quickly evaporated now that Marie's departure was imminent.

Marie grasped her by the shoulders. "Do not fret. You have learned all that I can teach you about the art of enticement. You now have the skills to make Mr. Knightley love you. Remember my one caution to you, and all will be well."

"What one caution is that?" Henry asked with a bewildered look on his face.

Marie gave him a saucy smile. "There are some things men need not know, *chéri*. One last embrace and I must be off."

Warily, Suzanna eyed Mr. Knightley, her thoughts jaundiced with suspicion. He had asked her to meet with him in the Earl's sitting room. What was on his mind? she wondered.

Roman had thought of a potential pitfall for the Earl's first foray into the local Society, and he would need Miss Combs's cooperation in order to avoid it.

He and Suzanna shared a sofa. He sat at one end, she at the other, with a respectable expanse of cushion between them. He smiled at her. "May I speak frankly, Miss Combs?"

She returned the smile. "Since we are soon to be related, Mr. Knightley, I feel it would be appropriate for you to do so."

"Thank you." He paused. "While I do not mean to offend you, I am sure you are aware that masquerade balls are notorious for their air of licentiousness."

Suzanna nodded. She knew that from some very enjoyable firsthand experiences. For convention's sake, however, she frowned. "I know of what you speak, Mr. Knightley, and I fear Lady Freemantle's ball will be no exception. One hears things when one is out in Society. Lord and Lady Freemantle are well known for their scandalous entertainments."

Roman sighed like a bad actor. "If Lady Freemantle's ball turns into bacchanal, and her guests' behavior more akin with that of the denizens of Shadwell than members of Society, it could upset our carefully laid plans to preserve the Earl's dignity."

Suzanna was suddenly all ears. She leaned forward in her chair. "What do you mean, Mr. Knightley?"

"As you know, I was privileged to serve under the Duke of Wellington's command. He is well known for his abhorrence of dissolute lifestyles. I fear if the Earl—as the Duke—is exposed to such behavior at the ball, he would make a stand against it, and perhaps expose himself to much ridicule."

It was something Suzanna had not thought of. The consequences of it chilled her bones. "What do you propose we do, Mr. Knightley?"

The "we" was not lost on Roman. "I suggest you and the Earl leave the ball *before* it becomes an embarrassment to the Duke's sensibilities. He is devoted to you, Miss Combs. If you were to plead the headache and ask to be taken home . . . and insist Miss Goodbody accompany you . . ."

He paused and regarded the toes of his boots. "I suggest that Miss Goodbody leave with you because she is unused to the ways of Society, and I would not want her to be scandalized. There is also a question of propriety. The Duke will travel to the ball in his Berline. Lord Dunsby and I will take my curricle. It would not do for me to take Miss Goodbody home in an open carriage."

Suzanna gave Roman a shrewd look. She knew he was thinking of his own "sensibilities" as much as anyone else's. The less time he would have to spend with the drab Miss Goodbody on his arm, the better he would like it.

Although she agreed with him about Virtue, she was not going to let him get away with looking noble when he had a personal objective in mind.

She rose and glanced down at him. "I shall do as you suggest, Mr. Knightley. Your plan is a sound one and advantageous to *us* both.

"Now, if you will excuse me. It is time for the Earl's medication."

Roman stood and bowed.

He continued standing long after Suzanna had left the room. He stared at the closed door. He felt like a cad. He had used his legitimate fears for the Duke to lessen the time he would have to be seen with Miss Goodbody. And Miss Combs had seen right through him.

Damn it all, he *was* a cad.

Twenty

Virtue knows to a farthing what it has lost by not having been vice.

—Horace Walpole

Virtue lounged in a lilac-scented bath, her cropped hair curling in wispy ringlets about her smooth forehead. She felt fragile and light-headed, yet strangely self-assured.

The direction of her life had always been strictly controlled, and although she was being *forced* to marry Mr. Knightley, she now basked in a newfound conviction that it was the right path for her to take. She loved her dark prince, and tonight, she would be his princess. They would waltz together in a festive ballroom and drink champagne. He would kiss her and tell her that he loved her.

She smiled. In her dreams Mr. Knightley had led her to their marriage bed. He had wanted to fill the cradle. Now, in spite of her girlish doubts and confusion, she *longed* to fill the cradle.

"It is time for you to dress, Mademoiselle," Madame called out as she rounded the bathing screen. She held out a large soft towel.

Flushed with yearning, and unconscious of her nakedness for the first time in her young life, Virtue rose from her bath and permitted Madame to wrap the towel around her shoulders. The flannel smelled of soap and sunshine.

Madame patted her dry. "Monsieur Knightley will be a happy bridegroom, *non?*"

"I hope to make him so," Virtue murmured without thinking.

She was rewarded by a giggle from the usually dour Madame.

Wearing the towel like a toga, Virtue went to the four-poster bed on which her underclothes were laid out. They were a froth of fine white muslin, trimmed with minute tucking, blue ribbons and ruchings of narrow lace.

Madame held up the shift. Virtue stepped under it and released the towel. The shift settled upon her slim body like a drift of snow. As she reached for a pair of stays, Madame chided, *"Non, Mademoiselle.* You are already slender enough in the waist. You do not need the corsets—they will only distort the line of your gown."

A muslin slip and white silk stockings were donned next. As Virtue slipped on a pair of gold-laced Roman sandals, Madame brought forth the lavender silk. The simple gown was a tribute to Madame's eye for fashion and her meticulous sewing skills.

It went over Virtue's head in a whisper and lay upon her bare shoulders like a lover's caress. The deep-necked bodice, simply cut with just a suggestion of tiny sleeves, was bound beneath the bosom by silk-covered cording. The skirt, trimmed with a gold-key border, fell in elegant folds to the tops of Virtue's sandals.

"Please now, Mademoiselle, the gloves."

The over-the-elbow evening gloves of French kid were tugged on, and while Madame smoothed away the last wrinkle, Virtue took up her white satin mask and peeked through the eye slits.

"You remember how to use the mask on a cane correctly, Mademoiselle?" Madame questioned.

Virtue nodded. "I believe the proper use of a caned mask was covered in the lesson on flirting with the eyes."

"You are correct, Mademoiselle. Very good!"

Madame then placed a circlet of silk ivy leaves entwined with tiny white roses on Virtue's curls, and a delicate necklace of beaten gold around her slender throat. She gestured for her to take a seat at the dressing table.

Both of the chamber's looking glasses had been draped with cloth until, as Madame put it, "The picture is complete."

She squinted her eyes at Virtue. "You have a perfect complexion, Mademoiselle. It needs but a bit of brightening."

She opened the Chinese box of colors and pored over the selections, finally applying a pale pink blush to Virtue's cheeks and a dusting of fine rice powder to her face and shoulders.

"Now, a touch of alcanet for the lips." When the tint had been added to her satisfaction, Madame stood back to assess her work.

"Hmmm. Mademoiselle's lashes are very long and dark on their own. A blessing, I assure you." Tilting her head to one side, she reached for a packet of burnt cloves. "Some darkening for the brows, however."

Satisfied at last with her work of art, Madame whipped the cloth from the looking glass. *"Voilà!* Behold yourself, Mademoiselle. You will be the most beautiful woman at the ball."

Virtue stared at the face of a stranger. Her pale, golden hair curled in silken spirals around her elfin face. Her gray eyes were huge ashen pools, her cheeks a blush of rose.

"There is more to be seen, Mademoiselle."

Taking Virtue by the hand, Madame led her to the cheval glass in the corner. She removed the cloth covering and positioned Virtue in front of the full-length mirror.

Virtue looked at her silken image in amazement. She was reed slim, but rounded in a way she had not been before. Her daydreams had become a reality.

"I shall wait up for you, Mademoiselle. Remember all your lessons."

Virtue nodded. In a daze, she collected her mask and a cloak of white silk from Madame and walked to the door.

It was an odd grouping gathered in the Manor's vast entrance hall. Two wing chairs had been placed at the foot of the double staircase for the comfort of the Duke and his Duchess while they awaited the appearance of the last member of their party.

The Duke wore a navy worsted, single-breasted jacket with a Prussian collar buttoned to the waist. His tight-fitting navy pantaloons had side slits, closed with loops and buttons, from the calf down to the ankle. Under one arm was tucked a silk chapeau-bras.

Suzanna wore a stunning gown of amber silk, richly embroidered at the neck and sleeves, and with a heavy gold fringe at the hem. For the occasion, she had donned a dark brown wig, as "Kitty" was actually a brunette.

The affectation was not distracting for the Duke, for Suzanna had thoughtfully worn the wig when last she had "comforted" him.

No chair had been provided for Henry, but he could have used one. He was desolate without Marie and had been drowning his sorrow most of the day. He was not yet in his cups, but fully intended to be pot-valiant before the night was over.

A Barbary Coast pirate completed the grouping. Roman wore skintight, black pantaloons tucked into soft leather boots, and a voluminous white linen shirt open to the waist. The shirt was belted in black leather, providing a roost for a curved sword in an ornately tooled scabbard. His dark hair was covered with a knotted red scarf, a gold ring was fastened in his left ear and a black leather eye patch served as his mask. All in all, he felt like an ass.

He paced up and down at the foot of the staircase, damning himself for not following Henry's direction. Henry, in a pettish mood because of Marie's absence, had refused to wear a costume, condemning the practice as a piece of foolishness. His only concession to the masquerade was an uninspired black silk domino and mask, which he would don in the curricle before arrival at Freemantle Hall.

As Henry swayed gently, the pirate continued to pace. What in hell could be keeping Miss Goodbody? Roman wondered grimly. How long could it possibly take to drape a white scarf over a black gown?

"Anxious for *your* Miss Goodbody to appear?" the Duke questioned with a twinkle in his eye.

Roman forced a smile to his face. He was not only anxious, he felt physically sick. He had been more at ease before going into battle. Better to face a field of Frenchmen than the derisive eye of Lady Dimwitty.

Although still ashamed of himself over his shabby treatment of Virtue, Roman had succeeded in rationalizing his conduct and was back to feeling noble.

This evening could prove to be sentiently devastating

to Miss Goodbody, and he, as a gentleman, vowed to support her for the short time she would spend at the ball. She was an innocent, unused to the ways of Society and unable to defend herself. He would shield her from the cutting comments of their "betters" while absorbing the venom himself.

Suzanna was as nervous as Roman. She was in love for the first time in her life—in love with the "Duke." Her fears were for him, that he would say something inappropriate and reveal his madness to those who would not understand. The thought of her beloved becoming an object of mockery was almost more than she could stand.

She glanced impatiently at the staircase. She had not seen Virtue for the entire day. What could be keeping her?

She experienced a sudden sting of conscience. Actually, she had been so taken up with the Duke, she had not really *seen* Virtue for the past three weeks. Was she, at this moment, cringing in her chamber, too afraid to come down?

Suzanna was about to excuse herself and go check when Virtue's soft questioning voice and Madame's accented answer were heard coming from the upstairs hallway. All heads turned upward.

There was a collective intake of breath as a vision in lavender suddenly appeared at the top of the landing. It paused for a moment, then began a slow descent down the stairs.

Like an angel floating to earth, Virtue did not acknowledge her stunned audience. With her caned mask covering the upper half of her face, she looked straight ahead, her chin elevated, a small smile playing about her lips.

Roman's one uncovered eye widened in wonder. Was

it a living woman who moved toward him or some sort of celestial fantasy?

Damn the eye patch! He tilted his head to the side to better focus on the approaching goddess. His eye narrowed. He had seen those full lips before, he had held that pointed little chin in the palm of his hand. ... .

Good Lord, could such loveliness have been embodied in the prim Miss Goodbody all this time without his being aware of it?

When the vision was in the middle of the staircase, he took a step forward and called up, "Miss Goodbody, is that you?"

Virtue continued her descent, but did deign to turn her gaze downward in Roman's direction. Her darkened brows rose above the satin mask. "Miss Goodbody?" she questioned, an amused lilt to her voice. "I know of none by that name. I am Lady Selena, a citizen of ancient Rome."

"But you were supposed to be a puritan," Roman blurted out.

Her soft laugh, more beguiling than mocking, drifted down to him. She continued her descent. A few steps from the bottom of the staircase, she paused and slowly lowered her mask. With her huge gray eyes smoldering like a snuffed flame, she leaned forward and whispered for Roman's ears alone, "You forget, Sir Pirate, a lady can change her mind."

Roman felt as if he had been hit by a bolt of lightning. Miss Goodbody had somehow assumed the undeniable essence of womanhood, becoming the eternal Eve. In her gray-eyed gaze, not bold but provocative, he read an age-old challenge: "Pursue me if you dare!"

He definitely dared. Completely forgetting that Miss

Goodbody and he were engaged and *had* to marry, he began, at that moment, his courtship of her.

He offered his hand. "Miss Selena, I believe I have the honor of being your escort for the evening."

Virtue extended hers. "Sir Pirate."

He bowed low and kissed her fingertips.

Through her kid gloves, she could feel the warmth of his lips. Unnerved, she stared at him. His unpatched eye stared back, intently, as if absorbing her image. A current of longing seemed to flow between them.

Then he offered her his arm. She placed her elegantly gloved hand lightly upon his wrist and allowed him to escort her to where the Duke and Suzanna sat waiting in dumbfounded silence.

She dipped into a graceful bow before them. "Your Graces. Forgive me for keeping you waiting. I am Lady Selena, and I have come all the way from ancient Rome to be with you tonight."

Slowly, the stunned Duke rose to his feet. "By Jove, Miss Selena—Miss Goodbody," he trumpeted, "you are a beauty." He turned to the still-seated Suzanna. "With the exception of you, my dearest Kitty, your cousin will put every other lady at the ball to shame."

Speechless, Suzanna could only sit and stare. Something extraordinary was happening to her. Tears clouded her vision. Instead of being jealous of Virtue, she wanted to claim her as a daughter. She wanted to rise up and shout, "Virtue Goodbody is not my cousin, she is my daughter. And is she not beautiful?"

Virtue turned to Henry and curtsied. Then she went to him, stood on tiptoe and kissed him, French-style, on both cheeks. She gave him an adoring smile. "Would you, dear Henry, do me the honor of being my partner for the first dance at the ball tonight?"

It was at that moment that Gaffe came up from the servants' kitchen and entered the hall. At first she did not recognize Virtue. When she did, she gasped. In horror, she watched as Lord Dunsby blushed a beet red under Virtue's caress. She heard him stammer, "The honor will be all mine."

Gaffe's blood turned to ice in her veins. Was she the only one who saw the handwriting on the wall? Lord Dunsby was in love with Virtue and she with him!

She began at once sidling over to Suzanna to inform her of the disaster in the making, but before she could reach her side, Fox huffed in from the portico.

"The carriages have been brought up from the stables, Your Grace."

"Good man, Fox!" the Duke roared. He turned to the others. "Shall we go?"

The ladies' cloaks were settled upon their bare shoulders, the Duke placed his chapeau-bras firmly on his head, and the party streamed through the front door and down the steps to the waiting carriages.

Gaffe had lost her chance.

It was a beautiful moonlit evening, the air warm as a lover's sigh. The Duke had insisted that Suzanna and Virtue accompany him in his Berline to protect them from the elements, mild though the night might be, while Roman, who disliked a closed carriage, had opted for a curricle for Henry and himself. It was a decision he now regretted.

As the ladies were handed into the carriage, Henry, who was ham-handed to the extreme, looked over the Duke's Berline with the eye of a seasoned four-in-hander.

"I say, Your Grace. I would like to try my skill at driving your rig one of these days."

The Duke clapped Henry on the shoulder. "Anytime you wish to drive the Berline, Lord Dunsby, you have only to inform my coachman, and he will have it made ready for you."

"Good of you, Your Grace." Henry beamed. "Good of you."

When the Duke's carriage started down the drive, Henry climbed into the curricle beside Roman. "What do you think of my driving the Duke's Berline?" he asked. "We could have a race, don't you know. The Berline against your curricle."

Roman glanced at Henry. His old friend was in an odd, feisty mood tonight. He sprang the horses. "Do you remember what happened that time you bribed the coachman to give over the reins?"

Henry hung on to the side rail and frowned. "None of the passengers got hurt," he mumbled defensively. "Just a little shaken up."

Roman shook his head, a sign of disdain that was not lost on Henry.

Henry glowered. He thought of Roman as a brother, but confound it all, sometimes he was so demmed condescending.

They followed the Duke's carriage in silence.

Roman no longer had anything to fear from Lady Dimwitty and her ilk. "Lady Selena" would be the toast of the ball.

His brow furrowed. Then why did he feel so . . . *diminished?* Was it because it had been Henry who had first noticed Miss Goodbody's innate beauty and goodness, or was it because she had asked Henry to have the first dance with her? Or was it both?

Twenty-one

There is no road or ready way to virtue.
—Sir Thomas Browne

The Larchmont carriage pulled up to the entrance of Freemantle Hall with Roman's curricle directly behind it. Two footmen liveried in blue velvet rushed forward to open the carriage door, while a waiting groom took the reins from Roman. After he and Henry had alighted, the horses were led away.

The Duke got out of the Berline, then turned and assisted the ladies to descend. Virtue stepped down, staring wide-eyed at the splendor before her. She could not believe her eyes. Lady Freemantle had spared no expense. The formal gardens were a maze of lights that twinkled in the darkness like well-behaved fireflies. Tiny lamps marked the manicured walkways and illuminated the profusion of velvety flowers and lush shrubbery.

In a daze, she accepted Roman's arm, and they followed the Duke and Suzanna up the broad stone steps and into the vast entrance hall. Henry, now clad in his black domino and mask, trailed at their heels.

The entrance hall was two storied with a marbled floor. Huge displays of hothouse flowers banked the walls while smaller baskets of wildflowers had been strung along the railing of the impressive staircase.

After a gentle nudge from Suzanna, Virtue followed her to a small salon that had been set aside for use as a retiring chamber for the ladies.

Suzanna was over her initial shock at the change in Virtue, but she felt strangely shy before this beautiful stranger. "You look very lovely, Cousin Virtue," was her only crisp comment. "How did you accomplish the change?"

Virtue surrendered her silk cloak to a waiting maid, then turned to Suzanna. "Marie gave me lessons in the ways of Society, and Madame Claqueur made up a proper wardrobe for me. So you see, Cousin Suzanna, I will no longer be an embarrassment to you."

The words, softly spoken and without a hint of censure, wounded Suzanna to the quick. She wanted to cry out, *I* am your mother. *I* should have taught you the ways of Society, *I* should have seen to your wardrobe. But, being so inexperienced with contrition, she did not know how to go about it.

Instead, she adjusted an errant curl on Virtue's forehead and responded coolly, "It is an improvement.

"Now, shall we join the gentlemen?"

The intimate gesture almost moved Virtue to tears. It was the first time Cousin Suzanna had ever touched her. Was another of her dreams about to come true?

When the two returned to the entrance hall, a low, rolling murmur of admiration traveled through the queue waiting upon the curving staircase. Gentlemen raised their quizzing glasses, and ladies turned jealous eyes in their direction.

Suzanna preened. She knew it was Virtue's unusual beauty that drew the most admiring stares, and oddly enough, it bothered her not a whit.

While the Duke and Suzanna chatted with an Indian

princess and a chimney sweep, Virtue leaned over the marble banister. "Oh, look. How clever. One of Lady Freemantle's guests has dressed himself as a tree."

Roman glanced down to where a squealing, effeminate-looking gentleman wearing skintight brown tights raced across the tiled floor below. His upper body was encased in layers of green silk leaves complete with stuffed birds, and he was being relentlessly pursued by another young reveler dressed as a shaggy dog.

"A pair of backgammon players, if you ask me," Henry muttered.

Unaware that "backgammon players" was slang for gentlemen who preferred members of their own sex, Virtue marveled, "How did you guess that, Henry? Do they carry their playing boards with them?"

Roman shot a dark look at Henry, who missed it entirely.

Slowly they inched their way to the head of the staircase, where an austere butler stood waiting at the entrance of the ballroom to announce the guests. Just to the right stood the Freemantles.

Lady Freemantle, who had an equine cast to her features, was attired as Queen Elizabeth. Her face was painted white with two bright dots of color on each cheek. For historic accuracy, she had had her maid shave her front hair to mimic the Queen's high forehead, giving her ladyship the look of a painted plow horse.

Lord Freemantle masqueraded as Queen Elizabeth's consort, Robert Dudley, the tall, athletic master of the Queen's horses. The comparison was unfortunate. Lord Freemantle was a stubby man with legs so bowed it was often jested that he had been born riding a sow.

Each guest was announced as the character he or she had assumed. While many could easily be guessed, only at the midnight unmasking would identities be formally disclosed. It was shortly before the unmasking that Suzanna planned to plead the headache.

The Duke whispered to the butler, who turned to the assembly and bellowed, "Their Graces, the Duke and Duchess of Wellington."

The Duke and Suzanna stepped forward. There was a moment of silence; then a scattering of applause greeted them. Lady Freemantle was heard to gush, "How very clever. I would swear the Duke and Duchess of Wellington stand before me."

The "Duke" bowed and answered, "You would not be mistaken, Madame."

Lady Freemantle neighed in delight, and Lord Freemantle, who was already drunk, bellowed, "Good show!"

The ploy had worked! Virtue's heart pounded with excitement. It was their turn next. As the three stepped forward, Roman whispered their assumed identities to the butler who called out, "A gentleman in a domino, a pirate of the Barbary Coast, and a lady of ancient Rome."

Lady Freemantle gawked. Her eyes raked the pirate and the lady from head to toe. There was no mistaking Knightley. Few men in London had such broad shoulders, and the leather eye patch did little to disguise his handsome face.

But the unusual beauty with him . . . could it be the mysterious Miss Goodbody? If it was not, it meant Knightley was already playing fast and loose on his intended, but if it was so—Lady Freemantle gloated—what a shock awaited Lady Dimwitty.

With an effort, she collected herself. After the proper greetings had been exchanged, she indicated the crowded ballroom. "Do go and enjoy yourselves. My guests' costumes are all so very clever."

She gave Roman an arch look. "Be sure to introduce your lovely partner to the Queen of Hearts." Her eyes glittered with malicious glee. "I am sure that she and your 'Roman' lady will find much in common to talk about."

Roman bowed, damning his horse-faced hostess to perdition. The Queen of Hearts could only be Lady Dimwitty.

They moved forward into the ballroom. Virtue was awestruck. The vast ballroom was decorated with potted palms and exotic blooms. The orchestra was playing a sprightly country dance, and servants circulated with trays of sparkling champagne. Overhead, twin crystal chandeliers blazed with candles. It was like a fairyland.

The Duke had already taken his Duchess to the floor and was proving himself very lively for a gentleman of his years. Roman scanned the dance floor, looking for Lady Dimwitty, but she was nowhere in sight.

Unfortunately, Roman looked in the wrong place. Lady Dimwitty had watched the three make their entrance from one of the flower-bedecked boxes that lined both sides of the ballroom. She had been drinking heavily. Her nostrils flared and hatred gleamed through the slitted eye openings of her red satin mask. She recognized Roman immediately, but who was this pale-haired beauty who had so obviously besotted the Gypsy's bastard? Her lips curled with contempt as she watched him use his strong arms and lean body to protect his partner from the crowds.

A milk-and-water miss, she thought jealously. Roman needed more of a woman than that in his bed. She would see that he had one.

She elbowed her way through the crowd and sauntered up to where they stood.

"Incoming fire from the right," Henry muttered.

Virtue recognized Lady Dimwitty at once. She wore a white muslin gown trimmed with a profusion of red ribbons and tiny red silk hearts. The gown's low-cut neckline made the most of a pair of generous breasts. As Lady Dimwitty drew closer, it could be clearly seen through the almost transparent muslin that her nipples had been rouged to the shapes of hearts.

Ignoring Roman, Lady Dimwitty subjected Virtue to an insolent appraisal. "Do not tell me, let me guess." She sneered. "You are a Roman courtesan. My, my, what a naughty costume."

Virtue felt Roman tense beside her. "Watch what you say, Madame," he said softly. "You are speaking to my intended, Miss Goodbody."

Restraining him with a touch upon his arm, Virtue turned to Lady Dimwitty and observed coolly, "Since I know nothing of courtesans, I shall have to rely on you, the Queen of Tarts, for your knowledge and experience."

Lady Dimwitty gasped. "I am the Queen of *Hearts*, not *Tarts*," she snapped.

Virtue's brows rose. "Oh? If I mispoke, do forgive me."

Dismissing Lady Dimwitty as if she no longer existed, she turned to Henry. "I wish to dance, Lord Dunsby."

Henry bowed. "My wish is your command, my lady."

As Henry led Virtue away, Lord Freemantle scurried up to Lady Dimwitty. Although he bowed low, his eyes remained fastened on her rouged breasts. "You have promised this dance to me, my Queen of Hearts." She gave him a poisonous smile, but took his arm and walked off with him.

Roman stood by himself on the sidelines. What a fool he was! What colossal brass he possessed! He had vowed to protect Miss Goodbody, this slim slip of a girl, from Society. She needed no protection; she was intelligent and witty and beautiful. What a countess she would make!

He watched her move sylphlike though the complicated dance, her steps as light as thistledown on the wind. Her lavender gown shone silver, her elfin curls pale gold.

He heard a woman dressed as a Gypsy remark to a knight in armor. "Who are those two, the gentleman in the domino and the lady in lavender? Isn't she a beauty, and don't they make a perfect pair? Even the color of their hair is similar, that same odd shade of gold."

Noting that the dance was about to come to an end, Roman snagged two glasses of champagne from a passing tray. When Virtue returned, flushed from dancing, he presented one to her, keeping the other for himself.

She accepted the champagne with a smile and took a sip. "Thank you, Sir Pirate. It is most refreshing."

"Where's mine?" Henry demanded.

Roman looked properly contrite. "Beg pardon, old man, I must have forgot."

Henry caught Roman's drift. "Of course you did," he muttered. "I'll find my own."

As Roman and Virtue watched Henry's domino move away through the crowds, she observed, "That was not kind, Sir Pirate."

"Pirates are not noted for their kindness; they are noted for their cunning."

The orchestra began playing a waltz. Roman took Virtue's glass and deposited it and his own on a tray table. He removed his eye patch and tossed it among the empty glasses. He bowed low. *"This* dance is mine, my lady."

He led her to the floor. They stood for a moment, face-to-face, the music swelling around them. Virtue gazed up at her dark prince. His blue eyes were knowing, yet kind; his smile half-teasing, yet containing an intensity of feeling that was somehow beyond her.

He took her hand; their fingers entwined.

She felt an encircling, a firm possession of her waist. Suddenly she was frightened. He was so tall, his chest so expansive. . . .

Then, unexpectedly, like the emergence of a painted-over image on canvas, she recalled how he had looked that day at the pond—his powerful naked body coming toward her, water sluicing from his bronzed skin.

Blood pulsed to her cheeks.

He sensed her confusion. His head dipped down. She could feel his warm breath stir the tendrils at her temples.

"What is wrong?" he asked.

She answered with a white lie, her throat taut with tension. "I have never danced at a ball before."

The hand at her waist tightened. His voice was suggestive. "There is a first time for everything, Lady Selena."

Skillfully, without another word, he whirled her out among the dancers. An odd sensation invaded Virtue's body. She felt as if she had entered a pleasure palace where only she and her dark prince existed. Her senses sharpened. The rustle of silken skirts, the heady scent of summer flowers, the pulse of the music itself, all merged and intermingled to create a magical sound she had never heard before. Abandoning herself to the magic, she leaned back in Mr. Knightley's strong arms as they whirled and whirled around the ballroom. The crystal chandeliers spun above her head, the candlelight melding and glowing like a celestial wheel. Dreams became reality; reality became dreams. She waltzed on and on in the arms of her beloved, unaware that the other dancers had stopped to stare at them, unaware even when the music had stopped.

Roman drew her to him, staying her steps, steadying her against his lean body. He laughed down at her, as if they shared a secret. She glanced around, saw then that they were alone in the middle of the ballroom, ringed with admiring and jealous faces.

Among the admirers was the Duchess of Wellington. Suzanna knew well the signs. Knightley had fallen head over heels in love with Virtue. She smiled to herself. Too bad their evening would come to an early end, but then, it served Knightley right for being so "noble."

Among the jealous faces was Lady Dimwitty's. She watched, hidden from view behind a potted palm. She was furious with the pale-haired bitch, and vowed she would make her pay.

Roman took a deep breath. Virtue swayed against him. "A bit of fresh air, my lady?" Without waiting for an answer, he guided her over to the side of the room toward the French doors.

Lady Dimwitty watched the two disappear onto the terrace. Then, with single-minded determination, she pushed and jostled her way through the crowd to follow them.

Twenty-two

Be to her virtues very kind;
Be to her faults a little blind.
　　　　　　　　—Matthew Prior

Roman led Virtue from the terrace, down a set of shallow steps and out beyond the lighted pathways. The velvety night closed about them like a cloak.

"Are you not afraid we will become lost, Sir Pirate?" Virtue whispered after they had gone a short distance into the moonlit darkness.

Mr. Knightley's throaty chuckle floated on the warm night air. "I am more afraid we will be found."

They came upon a stone bench set in a dark leafy alcove. The air was scented and very warm. A soft, suggestive breeze blew Virtue's shimmering skirts against her limbs.

Roman turned to face her. His voice was husky. "There is something I have been longing to do since I first laid eyes on you this evening."

She took a tentative breath. "And what is that, Sir Pirate?"

His lips curved in a faint smile. He pushed his sword aside and took her into his arms. "This," he said.

For a long moment, he held her to him, not doing anything more. Just holding her.

From the shadows, Lady Dimwitty watched jealously. Then, silently, she withdrew. She hurried back along the path to find a footman. She had a plan.

Virtue sighed and leaned her head on Mr. Knightley's chest. She breathed in the warmth of his skin, the faint pungency of his cologne. She could hear the thumpety-thump of his heart, or was it her own? *If only this moment would not end,* she thought. She wanted to stand in Mr. Knightley's arms for eternity, reveling in his quiet possession of her.

But Mr. Knightley had more in mind. With the knuckle of one hand, he nudged her chin upward until their eyes met. He lowered his head slightly and smiled down at her.

"You have the most beguiling little chin. Did you know that?"

She shook her head.

"Well, you do," he confirmed. "And your lips? They were made for kisses—*my* kisses."

Then he kissed her. Tenderly at first, his lips just touching, just skimming over hers. Emboldened by his gentleness, Virtue sighed against his undemanding mouth. Her hands flattened against his chest, crept beneath his pirate's shirt, caressed his smooth skin and hard muscle. When the tip of Mr. Knightley's tongue flicked the inside of her lips, they parted, quite naturally.

She stood passively as his tongue explored the soft recesses of her mouth; then a strange new excitement began to build within her, racing through her slender frame like a runaway fire. Her hands left the warmth of his shirt. With her fingertips she traced his face, his eyelids, his jawline, then touched where their lips were joined.

Roman groaned. His arms tightened around her, the

heat of his body searing her breasts' tips. She made a mewling sound like a hungry kitten and pushed against him.

He deepened the kiss. His hands moved down her back and waist, making a claim upon her body, then moved lower still, pulling her to him. . . .

"Miss Goodbody?" a voice cried out. "I am looking for a Miss Goodbody."

Roman raised his head and muttered a soft oath. As he drew away from Virtue, she swayed against him. He held her to him, his arms supporting her, and led her to the bench. When she was seated, he leaned over her. "Are you all right?" he whispered.

She took a deep breath and nodded.

Only then did he respond to the inquiry. "Over here," he called.

A footman appeared, holding a lantern aloft. "Beg pardon, sir, but I have a note for Miss Goodbody. I was told to wait and escort the young lady to her cousin."

Damn, Roman thought. Miss Combs was about to plead the headache and whisk the Duke and Virtue back to the Manor. But how had she known where they could be found, and why had she sent the note so early? Could it be the Duke was already showing signs of wear?

Having collected herself, Virtue accepted the note from the footman and unfolded it. "Cousin Suzanna wishes my presence in the ladies' retiring chamber. She does not say why, but I suspect it is a torn flounce. I told her when I sewed that heavy fringe to her silk gown, I did not think it would hold." She rose from the bench.

Mr. Knightley's hand immediately cradled her elbow. "I shall accompany you."

"That is not necessary, Mr. Knightley. The footman will escort me," Virtue rejoined, her eyes not meeting his. She added shyly, "But do walk with me to the terrace. After I have attended to my cousin's gown, I will rejoin you there."

Knowing that this was not to be, Roman sighed to himself. "As you wish," he said.

On her way to the retiring room, Virtue and the footman came upon Suzanna in the ballroom. "Cousin Virtue, I was looking for you."

Virtue was about to respond that she had just got her note, when Suzanna grabbed her by the wrist and towed her off to the side of the room.

"Listen carefully," she whispered. "We must leave at once. The Duke had decided to court-martial Lord Freemantle for insubordination. As I speak, he is seeking officers for the board of inquiry among the guests. At first it was considered an amusing lark, but now, the Duke is being regarded askance."

"What can we do?"

"We must leave immediately. I shall plead the headache and ask the Duke to take me home. You must accompany us."

"But Mr. Knightley awaits me."

"You cannot go home in an open carriage. It is not done." She paused. Her expression softened. Gently, she turned Virtue to her and looked her directly in the eye.

"You are in love with your Mr. Knightley." It was a statement not an inquiry.

Virtue nodded, Suzanna's tender interest affecting her in a way that made her want to cry. "With all my heart," she answered.

The tender interest ended as quickly as it had begun. Suzanna looked away, saying crisply, "I have observed

Mr. Knightley closely. Since he is in love with you, one interrupted evening will not be the end of it. I shall go to the Duke; you go to your Mr. Knightley and tell him that you must leave at once to attend me." She added wryly, "He will understand."

Roman strolled about on the terrace, looking up at the moon and contemplating the wages of sin. In a few minutes, he could expect another note from Miss Combs, telling him of her indisposition and that she and the Duke—and Miss Goodbody—would depart for Bentwood Manor immediately.

This magical evening had come to an abrupt end—he chuckled wryly—and he had brought it upon himself.

What a fool he was! Until tonight, his approach to women had been cavalier, a take-me-or-leave-me attitude. Always he had been taken, never left. He had sauntered into the lives of many women with an easy air, and had sauntered out with his heart untouched.

Tonight he had been humbled by Miss Goodbody's love and passion, overwhelmed with a feeling of gratitude that the heavens had so smiled upon him.

He was in love, pure and simple. He felt relaxed, at ease with life. Tonight was over, but there would be other nights, many, many nights to come. He sat down on a bench and stared out upon the gardens, imagining what his future would be like with Miss Goodbody.

It was winter. A chill wind rattled the mullioned windowpanes of Bentwood Manor, and soft snowflakes drifted together to huddle in heaps against the deep stone sills. But inside the Manor it was snug and warm. He sat before a crackling fireplace with Mrs. Knightley on his knee. A dark-haired baby was cradled in her arms. . . .

Suddenly a pair of soft hands covered his eyes. His heart sang. For one impossible moment he thought it was Miss Goodbody. Then Lady Dimwitty's drunken voice whispered in his ear. "Good evening, Sir Pirate. I saw you here by yourself and wanted to apologize for my naughty behavior."

Roman pushed her hands away and glared at her over his shoulder. "Naughty? You made me the laughingstock of London, and tonight you insulted my intended."

She came around the bench and stood in front of him, her eyes downcast, her hands clasped in mock contrition. "I know, but I *am* sorry, and I long to make it up to you."

Her eyes rose saucily; a salacious smile curved her lips. "Having met your Miss Goodbody, I would wager that you will receive no more than a chaste kiss or two until your wedding night. I can promise much more than that. Meet me at the inn on the outskirts of the village."

Roman felt only disgust for Lady Dimwitty and for himself. He had been an ass to have ever found this woman attractive.

He said tightly. "Do not demean yourself any further, Lady Dimwitty. Say no more, and get out of my sight. Miss Goodbody had the right of it. You are the Queen of Tarts."

Lady Dimwitty's temper flared. "How dare you!" she snarled. "No man has ever spoken to me thus."

From the corner of her eye, Lady Dimwitty saw Virtue suddenly appear at the French doors. She would fix them both.

She threw herself onto Roman's lap with such force that he fell backward, head over heels, grabbing onto Lady Dimwitty's *derrière* in a vain effort to retain his leverage.

She snaked her arms around his neck; her mouth ruthlessly claimed his.

Virtue came to an abrupt standstill. She stared out onto the terrace. She could not believe her eyes. Mr. Knightley was on his back, his long legs propped up on a bench. Lady Dimwitty was draped over him, her shapely limbs exposed. Their lips were locked in a greedy kiss.

From where Virtue stood, the embrace looked consensual and downright damning to Roman. His hands clutched Lady Dimwitty's *derrière* as if for dear life, and he appeared to be pulling her closer still.

Virtue could bear to see no more. With a stifled cry, she turned and fled.

The Duke was most solicitous of his Duchess. During the carriage ride home, he held Suzanna in his arms as she snuggled against him. "You must go right to bed the moment we arrive home, my dearest Kitty. I shall see that you are not disturbed."

Suzanna sighed happily. "I am feeling much better, Your Grace. By the time we arrive at the Manor, I shall be well enough to give you your medication and to stay awhile to . . . comfort you."

The Duke's loins twitched in readiness. He called up to his coachman. "Proceed a little faster, John."

With a happy smile on his face, he glanced over at Virtue. "You, too, must be anxious for your bed, Miss Goodbody. I saw you dancing with the Sergeant Major *and* Lord Dunsby. Can't make up your mind, what?"

Virtue smiled wanly, but did not answer. Her mind was in a whirl, trying to make sense of the shocking scene she had witnessed on the terrace. If Mr. Knightley was in love with her—cousin Suzanna had said that he was, and certainly *she* had had enough experience to know—then why did he consort with Lady Dimwitty the moment her back was turned?

Virtue was not too innocent to know that men often turned to loose women—the type who were stoned in the Bible—when lust overcame them.

Lust, she reflected, a word once found only in the Bible, was more familiar to her now. A faint heat traveled up her throat and lightly stained her cheeks. In that dark and leafy alcove she had experienced the beginnings of lust. In Mr. Knightley's arms, she had come alive and eager for an elusive pleasure, one that her body had never known but desperately wanted.

Had it been the same for Mr. Knightley? Had their lovemaking so inflamed his passions that he had had to douse them immediately with the likes of Lady Dimwitty?

Virtue was not quite sure what the "dousing" entailed, however, this new perspective on the humiliating incident did much to soothe her outrage. In view of such overwhelming lust, Mr. Knightley *could* be forgiven, yet . . . Virtue's newfound confidence demanded revenge. He must be made to suffer. But how?

She sighed and pushed back against the squabs. If only Marie were here. She would know what to do.

Suddenly, as if Marie were in the carriage next to her, Virtue heard her words of counsel, "Remember, once Mr. Knightley falls in love with you, you must back away and make him suffer. You must ignore him and flirt and dance with the other gentlemen at the ball. You must make him jealous. This is most important."

Of course, that was it! Virtue thought. That was where she had gone wrong. She had not followed the rules. She had danced only with Mr. Knightley—and with Henry, of course, but Henry did not count.

Or did he?

Virtue was in many ways her mother's daughter. Suddenly, a plan to make Mr. Knightley jealous delivered itself to her intact.

It was so very simple, she marveled. Why had she not thought of it immediately?

After good nights had been exchanged, the Duke and Suzanna retired to the Duke's chambers. Virtue watched the two, arm in arm, stroll down the hallway. She was now quite certain of what Suzanna's ministrations to the Duke included, but, oddly enough, it did not offend her. She merely wanted a like situation for herself and Mr. Knightley. And she would get it. Virtue smiled as she stepped into her bedchamber.

She was greeted by the raucous snores of Madame Claqueur. Madame had waited up for her as promised, but was, unfortunately, incommunicado due to too much wine.

Virtue tiptoed past the sleeping woman to the writing table by the window. Although Madame was necessary to her plan, she would not be needed until later. Better that she sleep while Virtue paved the way.

Seating herself at the writing table, she slipped the white silk cloak from her shoulders and draped it over the back of a chair. Drawing a sheet of paper to her, she took up a sharpened quill and commenced to write.

When the note was finished, she read over her words. Satisfied, she sanded the sheet and sat back to ponder her next step. First she must change her "Lady Selena" gown for something more suitable for traveling. Then she would keep vigil at the window, awaiting the arrival of both Lord Dunsby, the gentleman she planned to elope with, and Mr. Knightley, the gentleman she planned to marry.

Twenty-three

Let them recognize virtue and rot for having lost it.
—Persius

Virtue quietly entered Henry's bedchamber. He was
lying fully dressed on the coverlet, facedown, sound
asleep and snoring. She tiptoed over to his side and shook
him by the shoulder.

"Henry, wake up. I want you to elope with me."

Henry grunted. He turned his head on the pillow. One
reddened eye surveyed Virtue with groggy disbelief.
"You want me to do *what* with you?" he asked.

"I want you to elope with me," Virtue repeated.

Henry moaned and reburied his face in the pillow. "It
must be a bad dream," he muttered. "Please, God, let it
be a bad dream."

Virtue shook him more forcibly. "You are not dreaming, Henry. Please wake up. I need you to elope with
me."

Henry shook his head. "Can't do that. I love Marie."

Virtue sighed. Men were so dense. "Love has nothing
to do with our elopement," she explained patiently. "I
am doing it to make Mr. Knightley jealous." She paused
and played her trump card. "You did pledge to help me,
did you not, Henry?"

Hoisted on his own petard, Henry sighed into the

goose-down. Bracing himself on his elbows, he slowly pushed himself up to a lizardlike position. Confound it, he thought fuzzily, he *had* pledged to help his little sister.

He turned his head—the room swam before his eyes—and gave Virtue a reproachful look. "Marie will be mad at me if I elope with you."

"No, she will not, Henry. For propriety's sake, Madame Claqueur will accompany us. Besides, Marie would be the first to tell you to elope with me. Where do you think I got the idea to make Mr. Knightley jealous, if not from Marie?"

It registered in some part of Henry's befuddled brain that a pretend elopement *was* something Marie would suggest. He waited a few moments, hoping that Virtue might get tired and go away. When it was obvious that she meant to stick like a burr, he laboriously rolled over and swung his legs off the bed.

His booted feet hit the floor with a resounding thud. "Oh, God!" he moaned, cradling his aching head in his hands. "Ain't there another way?"

"No, Henry," Virtue said firmly, "I fear there is not. Just do exactly as I say, and all will be well."

She gave him an encouraging pat on the shoulder. He winced. "Confound it, my skin hurts as much as my head."

"You must be brave, Henry dear. First, you must go to the stables and have the Duke's Berline made ready for travel."

Madame Claqueur proved less difficult to rouse than Lord Dunsby. A small shake and she came awake immediately. She hiccuped once, then narrowed her eyes and focused in on Virtue. In a trembling voice, she asked, "Is the rabble at the gate, Mademoiselle?"

"No, Madame, calm yourself. I need you to accompany me. Lord Dunsby and I are planning to elope."

Madame crossed herself. "For shame, Mademoiselle . . ."

"It is not what you think, Madame. It is a pretend elopement. As Mademoiselle Marie often advised me, the time would come when I must make Mr. Knightley jealous." Virtue paused dramatically. "That time has come."

"Ahhh," said Madame, rolling her eyes, "and you use Lord Dunsby for the purpose. *Now* I understand." She rose and smoothed down her skirts "I shall pack a small bag of essentials for each of us, Mademoiselle."

Staggering slightly, Madame went to the clothespress and threw open the doors. Virtue watched her pull two wicker traveling baskets down from a top shelf and begin filling them with nothing but shoes.

Good heavens, Virtue thought, Madame Claqueur was as foxed as Henry. She gave a Gallic, Marie-like shrug. Ahhh well, the night air would do them both a world of good.

How easy it had been! Henry marveled. He had walked into the stables, all blustery and lordlike, and demanded the Berline be made ready. The bleary-eyed coachman, who did not dare go against the "Duke's" earlier dictum that Henry could drive the carriage whenever he wished, had obliged without a murmur.

The Berline was pulled by four horses, all thoroughbreds. Henry prudently kept them to a walk, proceeding down the Manor's long drive as quietly as possible. He was suffused with Dutch courage, his brandy-steeped brain now accepting the elopement as a very clever scheme in which he would play a significant part. That he was about to venture out onto the Brighton Road in an unwieldy carriage he had never driven before, and without grooms or an outside man, worried him not at all.

By Jove—he preened, enjoying his lofty perch atop the box—*Roman wouldn't be so dashed condescending if he could see him now.*

A small wavering light appeared at the side of the drive directly ahead of him. He brought the horses to a cautious stop. Virtue stepped out of the shadows, holding a lantern in one hand and Madame Claqueur in the other.

She was relieved to see her accomplice. Stealing out of the Manor to their rendezvous had been most difficult for her. Madame had insisted on taking a bottle of wine with her, for "medicinal" purposes, and seemed bent on seeing how quickly she could drink it.

"Did you have any problem at the stables, Henry?" Virtue whispered, as she hoisted Madame and her bottle, and the two bags containing the shoes into the carriage.

"Not a one," he assured her.

The carriage dipped slightly under the weight of the two women; then Virtue rapped upon the window frame and called up, "Proceed with caution, Henry dear."

His lordship frowned at the implied censure. Of course he would temper his speed while on the back roads. Once on the Brighton Road, however, *that* would be another matter. Henry chuckled to himself, imagining how he and Roman would laugh about this lark in the days to come.

Inside the carriage Virtue was also quite comfortable with her decision. Causing a gentleman to suffer was in many ways a form of redemption, she reasoned. Her actions would bring Roman—the sinner—back to the fold.

She smiled and made herself more comfortable. Like Lady Estelle she waited for her prince to come.

Roman awoke just before dawn. He felt at peace with the world. Last night had been the most wonderful one that he could remember. Even the debacle with Lady Dimwitty could not dim its splendor. He had found his true love at last: Miss Goodbody.

Locking his hands behind his head, he stretched out his long legs and stared up at the ceiling. Who would have guessed that the passionate Lady Selena lurked beneath the prim and proper person of his intended? Innocence and ardor made a heady embrace.

He began to plan his day around his newfound love. He would dress and get to the business of the estate. Then, later in the morning, he and Miss Goodbody could walk together—he grinned—perhaps picnic by the pond.

Suiting action to thought, Roman sat up and swung his legs over the side of the bed. He stretched and yawned, enjoying the unusual sensation of having a clear head.

He had held his wine consumption to a minimum last night. It was a good thing he had. Henry had had enough for both of them. Would he remember being dragged up the stairs and deposited none too gently upon his bed? Probably not.

Out of the corner of his eye Roman suddenly noticed a white square of paper lying upon the carpeting close to the door.

What in hell was that?

He ambled over to it and scooped it up. It was a note, very simple and to the point.

Dear Mr. Knightley.

I witnessed you and Lady Dimwitty embrace on the terrace last evening. Your actions have led me to the conclusion that you do not love me. In view of this, I have decided to seek happiness over duty. I have eloped with Lord Dunsby. We go to Gretna Green.

Sincerely,
Miss Goodbody

Roman stared at the words. His chest tightened. He could scarcely breathe. *His* Miss Goodbody had eloped with his best friend? Could it be so?

His mouth straightened into a thin, uncompromising line. There was only one thing a man of honor could do in a situation like this. And, as painful as it would be, he must do it. He had no choice. He took a deep breath and roared, "Perkins!"

In the time it took Perkins to stumble from the dressing room, Roman had pulled on his pirate's trousers and shirt.

Perkins gawked. "Sir?"

Roman reached for his stockings and boots. "I want my stallion saddled and at the front entrance at once."

"Very good, sir."

As Perkins scurried off, Roman went to his gun box and removed one pistol from its velvet-lined enclosure. Tucking it into the waistband of his trousers, he took up the note and strode from the room.

He marched down the hall to Suzanna's chamber and

pounded on the door. "Miss Combs, it is Roman Knightley. I must speak to you at once."

Suzanna had just returned from the Duke's room. She and Gaffe exchanged startled glances; then Gaffe rushed to open the door.

Roman stormed in.

"What is wrong?" Suzanna inquired in a trembling voice.

"This, Madame." Roman thrust the note at her. "Miss Goodbody has eloped with Lord Dunsby! I am going after them."

Suzanna snatched at the note and read it hastily. Feeling faint, she dropped upon the sofa. Virtue and Lord Dunsby? Her fingers closed convulsively upon the note. At that moment, a wave of maternal love suddenly rose within her, cresting with a heart-stopping roar. She realized that she loved Virtue more than she loved herself, and while she had breath in her body, she would see that no harm came to her.

Unaware of Suzanna's change of heart, Gaffe pointed an accusing finger at her. "I knew it. I told you Virtue and Lord Dunsby were in love, but you would not listen!"

Roman was already out the door, but he heard Gaffe's last damning words. So, he thought grimly, the flirtation had been going on under his nose, and he had failed to see it.

Boots drumming, he sped down the stairs, across the entrance hall and through the oaken doors to the portico. His black stallion awaited him, snorting and pawing the ground, anxious to be off.

As was Roman. Leaping into the saddle, he nudged his steed to action.

* * *

It was just as well Roman did not hear the rest of the conversation between Gaffe and Suzanna.

Gaffe was beside herself with fear. "What will you do, pet?" she wailed. "If Mr. Knightley overtakes the runaways, he will kill Lord Dunsby. If he does not, Virtue will marry her half brother."

Suzanna had weighed her options and made her decision. It was time to act as a loving mother in Virtue's behalf, but first—

Clearheaded and determined, she rose from the sofa. "Gaffe, ring for Rhett. Do not stand and stare at me. We have to move fast."

She went to her dressing table. "Do you remember the incident with Lord Turnberry?" She flung the words over her shoulders.

Dumbly, Gaffe nodded.

"Good. On my signal do the same as you did then, but this time, make sure the chamber pot is empty."

Before Gaffe's wide-eyed gaze, Suzanna then dusted her face with rice powder and ripped the bodice of her silk gown until her breasts spilled forth.

When Rhett appeared, both women were ready.

Clutching closed her ripped bodice, Suzanna addressed him. "Something dreadful has happened. Sit down, we must talk."

Intrigued, Rhett sat down on a slipper chair. It was the last thing he remembered.

Gaffe sneaked up behind him and beaned him with a chamber pot. Groaning, he fell sideways to the floor.

"Nicely done, Gaffe," Suzanna approved. "Now ring for Fox. Tell him to have a curricle brought to the front entrance at the soonest."

Gaffe hurried to do as she was told. She was smiling. It was like old times.

Suzanna was already out the door. She ran down the hall to the Duke's chambers and entered without knocking.

The Duke was in his nightshirt, sitting up on the bed. At the sight of Suzanna, he leaped down and hurried to her. "My darling, what has happened?"

Suzanna released her hold on her ripped bodice and threw herself, half-naked, into his arms. "The butler did it!" she sobbed. "He attacked me. Gaffe subdued him, but the blackguard remains in my chamber."

The Duke took in Suzanna's ripped gown and pale face. "By Jove," he roared, "no rascal attacks my wife and gets away with it. Fox, bring me my horsewhip, at once."

Rhett got groggily to his feet. What in hell had hit him? He staggered to the door and out into the hallway. As he paused to brace himself against the wall, he spotted the Duke in his nightshirt coming toward him, horsewhip in hand. Christ on a crutch, Rhett thought, The Slut had outwitted him.

Before the Duke could get within cutting distance of him, Rhett took off at top speed toward the staircase. Like a hound after a fox, the Duke stayed at his heels.

Suzanna fastened a cloak over her ruined bodice and followed the two men down the stairs. A curricle hitched to a pair of frisky bays waited at the entrance. She climbed into it and snapped the reins. The horses took off at a trot.

The Duke, barefoot but showing great endurance, was running ahead of her. He kept after the fleeing Rhett, inflicting painful punishment on him for his transgressions.

She pulled alongside the Duke and slowed down. He spotted her. Was she off on some secret maneuver? he wondered. If so, she would need him along to protect her. Giving Rhett one last cut, the Duke flung himself sideways. With an agility granted only to madmen and drunks—luckily, the Duke was a bit of both—he captured the side of the curricle and leaped, without mishap, into the rear rumble seat.

Suzanna urged the horses on to greater speed. There was not a moment to lose.

Twenty-four

A virtuous woman is a crown to her husband.
—Proverbs

Less than an hour into the elopement, Henry was already experiencing dire misgivings. He sat hunched over on the carriage box cursing his stupidity. It was misting lightly, and the traffic on the Brighton Road was increasing with the dawning light. To make matters worse, he had sobered up considerably.

Confound it! He had been a fool to agree to elope with Virtue. Roman would not laugh this "lark" off; he might very well put a bullet through him.

Within the lumbering carriage Virtue's thoughts followed similar lines. Her feelings of excitement and romance had faded. All she felt now were the clammy discomfort of dew-dampened slippers and a growing sense of panic.

Mr. Knightley was trained as a soldier. He might very well dispatch Henry first and ask questions afterward. She should never have involved dear Henry in such a disreputable scheme.

Suddenly, she made a decision. She would put a stop to the elopement before further damage was done. Leaning past Madame Claqueur, who was asleep and snoring, Virtue stuck her head out the window. It was not yet light, and the carriage was moving at a great rate. She shouted up to the box, "Henry, I fear we have made a terrible mistake. We must turn back to the Manor at once."

The words were like a shot of French brandy to Henry. The Berline was built with two underperches in parallel, which made for a better turning circle. The road was relatively clear. He would attempt a half-circle turn.

Before undertaking the maneuver, however, some atavistic tendency urged him to open the toolbox by his side. Keeping his eye on the road, he groped around until his hand came upon a knife. Closing the box, he extracted the knife from its sheath and thrust its point into the seat beside him. Just in case.

Roman galloped along the Brighton Road. Far ahead of him, he spotted his objective. The Berline was traveling at a fast pace, too fast for the hazy light, but Henry seemed in control. . . .

Now what in hell was he up to? The Berline was slowing down. Was Henry going to stop? Good Lord! He would not attempt a half-circle turn in such conditions, would he?

Before Roman's horrified eyes, Henry pulled sharply to the side. Too sharply. The coach's wheels swerved off the road and into a deep rut.

They are going to crash! Roman thought wildly.

With a muttered oath, Henry faced the approaching danger. His soldier's training immediately asserted itself. Without thinking, he put the knife between his teeth, rose to his feet and with a mighty leap launched himself forward. By some miracle, he landed on the broad back of one of the horses. Hanging on for dear life, he frantically hacked away at the traces.

When Virtue felt the carriage swing off the road, she grabbed hold of the inert Madame and pulled her down to the floor. The two women were thrown from side to side. There came a tooth-rattling jolt, a prolonged grating sound; then the carriage came to a shuddering stop tilted on its side against an embankment.

There was a moment of infinite silence before Madame whispered. "Have we stormed the Bastille, Mademoiselle?"

"No, Madame. Our carriage has crashed. You stay here, I shall crawl out and see to Lord Dunsby. Help will soon arrive."

Fear gave Virtue strength. How had Henry fared? Was he dead or dying by the side of the road? Grasping the sides of the door opening, she heaved her bruised body out of the carriage and dropped lightly to the ground.

She looked around her. To her relief, she saw Henry running toward her. His clothes were covered with dirt and grass. "Virtue, are you or Madame hurt?"

Virtue threw herself into his arms, sobbing, "We are not, Henry, but you?" She gripped him tighter. "If my foolish jealousy has injured you, I will never forgive myself."

Henry patted her awkwardly on the back. "I'm fine, Virtue, nothing broken. When I cut the traces, there was no stopping the horses, so I had to jump. Got a bump or two is all. Don't cry now, there's nothing to worry about."

Henry had made many misstatements in his life. The words were no sooner out of his mouth when he realized that he had made yet another.

Over Virtue's shoulder, he spied Roman making his way toward them. Henry's face went ashen. "Roman's here," he whispered. "Get behind me, Virtue."

Virtue turned and stepped to one side. Fearfully, she watched Mr. Knightley's approach. His face showed no emotion, none whatsoever. In his right hand he held a pistol.

When he was almost upon them, Virtue threw herself in front of Henry, shielding him with her body. "If you intend to kill Lord Dunsby, Mr. Knightley, I swear to you, you will have to kill me first."

"Stand aside, Miss Goodbody," Roman said quietly. "I have not come to kill Lord Dunsby *or* you. I have come to wish you happy."

He extended the pistol, butt end first, to Henry. "It is a long way to Gretna Green. You might have need of this."

Virtue stared at Mr. Knightley in disbelief. This was not the way it was supposed to happen. He was supposed to be in a jealous rage.

Her chin quivered. With her heart close to breaking, she whispered, "Then you care for me so little?"

Roman eyed her steadily. "You have it wrong, Miss Goodbody. It is because I love you *so* much, that I willingly give you to Lord Dunsby, if that is where your happiness lies."

"You love me? Oh, Mr. Knightley, I love you, too. I made Henry elope with me to make you jealous."

At that most inopportune moment Suzanna and the Duke pulled up in the curricle. Suzanna leaped down, arms outstretched, and ran toward Virtue. "My dearest daughter, you are making a grave mistake. You cannot marry Lord Dunsby. He is your half brother."

"Mother!" Virtue cried, ignoring the rest of what Suzanna had said, "You called me 'daughter.' "

"Yes"—Suzanna sobbed as she gathered Virtue to her—"and I shall never deny you again. Lord Dunsby, Henry's father, was your father also. The vicar had nothing to do with it."

"By Jove!" Henry gasped, "Virtue actually is *my* little sister." The astounding news, on top of the other activities of the morning, brought him close to tears. Unabashedly, he enfolded both women in a bear hug.

The Duke had followed Suzanna. Joining in the group hug, he beamed down at Suzanna. "I did not know we had a daughter and a son, my darling Kitty. What a delightful surprise."

Roman stood forgotten on the sidelines. He cleared his throat. "If I may intrude on this family reunion? I wish to speak to Miss Goodbody in private."

The Duke gave him a frosty glare. "You wish to speak to *my* daughter in private?"

Suzanna stood on tiptoe and whispered in the Duke's ear. He was immediately all smiles. "Ahhh, yes, of course, Sergeant Major Knightley. You and my daughter are engaged to marry. You are soon to be one of the family. Slipped my mind for a moment."

He detached Virtue from the rest. "Here you are, young man. Take her off with you and find your private spot. Must not interfere with young lovers, now must we?"

Roman took a firm grip on Virtue's arm and led her to a nearby stand of trees. Once within its leafy protection, he held her at arm's length and stared down at her. "I ought to shake the life out of you," he said, "but I won't, because *I* am also to blame for this fiasco. While

I did not seek Lady Dimwitty's attentions that night at the ball—"

"You need not say another word, Mr. Knightley," Virtue cut in. "I know that *I* am to blame for your behavior with Lady Dimwitty. If I had not returned your kisses so wantonly, you would not have felt the . . . need to consort with a woman of her low moral standards."

Roman threw back his head and roared with laughter. When he got control of himself, he wiped the tears from his eyes and asked incredulously, "Do you honestly believe that, my darling?"

He had called her darling. Taking a page from Marie's lesson book, Roman's darling pressed the advantage. She fluttered her lashes and smiled up at her dark prince. "I have had so little contact with the opposite sex, Mr. Knightley, that I do not know what to believe."

"Then you obviously need more contact, Miss Goodbody, and I shall be happy to oblige." He took her into his arms and kissed her soundly.

A bit later, a breathless Virtue inquired, "Then you still want me as your wife now that you know the sordid details of *my* birth?"

Roman grinned down at her. "We by-blows have to stand together. Cousin, daughter, half sister—whatever you are to others—first and foremost, you are my intended, and I will never let you go. I love you wildly and passionately."

"And I love you, Roman, with all my heart."

Throwing her arms around his neck, Virtue kissed her prince with a fervor that left no doubt in his mind of her devotion.

It was he who broke the kiss. With obvious reluctance, he put her from him. "We must leave this for later, my darling Virtue. Our family awaits us."

* * *

Within the month, two weddings were celebrated at Bentwood Manor. The Earl and Suzanna were joined in holy matrimony, the Duke thinking that he and Kitty were renewing their vows, and a week later, Roman and Virtue were wed.

The Earl of Larchmont lived but a few years after his marriage to Suzanna, but they were the happiest of years for both of them.

The next Earl of Larchmont and his Countess lived many, many years, and were blessed with a host of good friends, the dearest of whom were Lord Dunsby, Virtue's beloved half brother and his wife, Marie.

Sir William never got over his disappointment at losing Suzanna to the Earl. To ease his pain, he consumed great quantities of wine and consorted with loose women. The cure was most effective. Sir William lived to be eighty, although he remembered little of the intervening years.

Rhett spent his days drinking in Gin Lane and muttering invectives against The Slut, The Maggot, and The Stick. His denizens in drink thought him a Bedlamite.

In due time, Virtue, having found that reality was much more pleasant than daydreams, presented Roman with four stalwart sons and four beautiful daughters. Suzanna proved a most attentive grandmama to each and every one of them.